SURVIVOR DIARIES

OVERBOARD!

SURVIVOR DIARIES

OVERBOARD!

BY TERRY LYNN JOHNSON

HOUGHTON MIFFLIN HARCOURT
Boston   New York

hmhco.com

The text was set in Adobe Caslon Pro.
Illustrations by Jani Orban

The Library of Congress has cataloged the paper over board edition as follows:
Names: Johnson, Terry Lynn, author.
Title: Overboard / by Terry Lynn Johnson ; with illustrations by Jani Orban. Description: Boston ; New York : Houghton Mifflin Harcourt, [2017]. | Series: Survivor diaries ; [book 1] | Summary: Eleven-year-old Travis and twelve-year-old Marina, separated from their families after being thrown into the Atlantic off the coast of Washington, battle hypothermia as they struggle to survive. Includes Coast Guard–approved cold-water survival tips.
Identifiers: LCCN 2016028377
Subjects: | CYAC: Survival—Fiction. | Lost children—Fiction. | Atlantic Ocean—Fiction. | BISAC: JUVENILE FICTION / Action & Adventure / Survival Stories. | JUVENILE FICTION / Nature & the Natural World / Environment. | JUVENILE FICTION / People & Places / United States / General. | JUVENILE FICTION / Animals / Marine Life.
Classification: LCC PZ7.J63835 Ove 2017 | DDC [Fic]—dc23
LC record available at https://lccn.loc.gov/2016028377

ISBN: 978-0-544-97010-6 paper over board
ISBN: 978-1-328-51905-4 paperback

Printed in the United States of America
DOC 10 9 8 7 6 5 4 3 2 1
4500710664

For my fellow officers in the marine unit, past and present. I've learned so much from all of you.

CHAPTER ONE

"Tell me how you survived the whale attack," the reporter said.

Not this again. I sank back into the couch cushions and rubbed my face.

"That's not the real story," I told him. I could hardly believe what had actually happened.

He leaned in. "Then tell me the real story. That's why I'm here. As I explained, I'm writing a series about survivors—kids like you—who made it home alive after a life-threatening experience. I want to hear about that afternoon while you were on vacation. You and Marina were the only ones who didn't make it to the life rafts."

He glanced over his shoulder toward the kitchen. The smell of peanut butter cookies drifted toward us.

"I want to hear the truth so young people who read these survivor diaries can learn from you. There aren't many eleven-year-olds who've had an experience like yours."

He placed his phone on the coffee table between us and pressed Record. "So, Travis, how did you survive?"

I stared at the bald man sitting in my living room. He was asking me to talk about the worst moments of my life.

I blew out a breath. "I didn't even know what was going on at first. Marina just yelled the warning and then the next thing you know I'm in the water. Everything was crazy loud. You know that bubbly kind of sound you hear underwater? Except not the peaceful kind like when you're swimming. It was even worse on the surface with the waves smacking me in the face and the wind howling and people scream-ing and . . ."

"No, no." He scratched at his tiny beard on his chin. "I want you to start at the beginning. The whole story. Take your time."

I took a sip from my lemonade. "It all started with the whales."

CHAPTER TWO

Four months earlier

The boat swayed beneath me. I spread my feet apart to balance and lifted my face into the wind. It smelled like seaweed and salt and some kind of animal poop and it was awesome.

"Put this on, Trav." Mom ambushed me with a red and black suit. She held it open for me to step into like I was five, and stuffed my arm into a sleeve.

"What? No, what is that?"

"An immersion suit. It's rough today, and it's going to be chilly on the water."

"Stacey's not wearing one," I said.

"Older. And wiser." My sister didn't look up from texting, but she smirked for my benefit.

I let Mom do up the zipper—no point in arguing. Ever since my gym accident, Mom had been hovering. It was my life.

"And I hid some animal crackers in the pocket in case you want a snack."

"Mom," Stacey said. "I think the last thing Chunky Monkey needs is a snack."

"Welcome aboard the *Selkie Two*," a man said through the speakers attached to the outside of the cabin.

The *wheelhouse* is what Dad had called it. I could see inside through the big windows to where people were sitting on benches.

"I'm your captain, Alfonso Hernandez. My daughter Marina and I are happy you've chosen to come with us this afternoon. July is a great time for whale watching in the Strait of Juan de Fuca."

The captain was talking into a microphone while steering the boat from the front of the cabin. A dark-haired girl next to him waved.

"For the next three hours, we hope to find you some harbor seals and sea lions. If we're lucky we'll see orcas, and maybe humpbacks. There's a ten-knot northwest wind, we'll have a bit of chop, but nothing our fine vessel can't handle. Let's hope the wildlife cooperates. We do guarantee jellyfish sightings."

Someone standing next to me at the railing chuckled.

"So let's get to the introduction, and then we'll be all set. We've got twenty-three on board today, including crew. This is a fifty-foot vessel equipped with all the latest safety features."

I watched the girl, Marina, through the giant windows. She walked through the cabin pointing at things as her dad talked about where everything was.

My focus drifted back to the water. White lines raced across the surface. Rolling waves curled at their tops. The waves slapped against the boat as we headed out, directly toward the mountains in the background. I couldn't believe we were finally here.

"Think we'll see a whale?" I asked Dad.

Out of everything we had planned on our vacation to Washington State, this was what I'd been looking forward to the most. I'd never seen a whale.

Dad's knuckles whitened as he gripped the rail. "Uh . . . er . . . maybe. I think I should go sit for a bit. You keep watch." He was pale already and we'd just started.

"Aren't those magic bands working?" I asked, pointing to what he wore on his wrists to stop seasickness.

"Come on, Travis," Mom said. "We'll all go inside."

"But I want to see the whales," I said. "Look, I've got my suit on."

"Leave him be, Mandy," said Dad, as he lurched toward the cabin.

"I'm going up," Stacey said, and she headed for the stairs to the platform on top of the cabin. "Better cell reception."

I started to follow but Mom pulled me back. "No, I don't want you to slip."

Once I got closer to the stairs, I could see Mom was right. They were steep, and that platform looked high. I was glad she'd said no, but I pretended to be disappointed.

Mom glanced back at me with worried eyes before she helped Dad into the cabin. I walked to the other side of the boat.

Freedom! The wind blew through my hair. With the suit on, I wasn't cold at all.

"Harbor porpoises!" a voice said beside me.

I turned and saw Marina pointing out into the water. Her wide-brimmed hat was attached with a chin strap. A blue-checkered bandanna flapped around her neck, making her look like an adventurer from a magazine.

"There's a pod of them following the current line! Do you see?"

I searched the water and saw nothing but waves.

"You can tell they're harbor porpoises because their dorsal fins are shaped like chocolate chips."

A small black fin popped out of the water and dipped back in again.

"There! I saw it," I said. "They swim so fast." I looked at her and grinned.

She wore a short red life jacket over her Windbreaker. The life jacket had things attached to it, including a small knife sheath.

"That's cool," I said, pointing to the knife.

"It's my marine knife. I always keep it on my guide vest. All mariners wear them in case we have to cut a line real quick."

"You're a guide? How old are you?"

"Twelve. But you don't have to be old to know stuff. I've been doing this my whole life."

I tried to think of a way to change the subject because I didn't want her to ask how old *I* was next and find out that I was younger than her. But she wasn't looking at me; she was gazing across the waves.

I followed her gaze and saw what she was looking at. More fins sticking out of the water, but these were long. Some of them looked as tall as Mom.

Marina waved to her dad through the window and pointed.

"J-pod," she yelled. "Starboard side." Then to me she added, "That's marine-speak for the right side of the vessel. The left side is called port."

I nodded as if I knew that because I didn't like the way she said it to me, as if I didn't.

The boat slowed down and it seemed as if all the people who had been inside were running out of the cabin and up the stairs to the viewing platform.

Black fins that looked like sharks' sliced

through the water directly toward us. They were all clumped together. "What did you call them?"

"They're orcas, also called killer whales. They live here in the Salish Sea. All the whales in a family that swim together are called a pod. This pod has Granny, the oldest killer whale. She's over a hundred years old!"

"But how can you tell which pod this is?"

"They all have a unique saddle patch on their dorsal fin."

I couldn't see the difference at all, except that some of the fins were longer than others. One of the orcas lifted its head out of the water and I glimpsed the white markings for a moment before it disappeared.

A gust of wind pushed me forward. The boat rocked harder with the waves and I gripped the railing to steady myself.

Almost everyone was up top taking pictures. I peered over to the other side of the boat, to the port side. The biggest whale I'd ever seen in

my life leaped out of the water, its body arched. Long fins on its side stuck out like airplane wings. It splashed back down with a loud slap.

"Humpbacks!" Marina squealed. "That was a juvenile breaching. A young one."

A line of mist suddenly shot out of the water, and I heard a sound like Grandpa blowing his nose real loud.

"The mom whale is coming beside it!" Marina hopped. "They're going to pass right in front of us!"

I caught a whiff of something like bad breath. Fishy. "That was a young one?"

"Yeah, adults are almost fifty feet. That's longer than a school bus!"

I couldn't believe our luck. I searched the cabin to see if Mom and Dad were watching, but I couldn't see them.

"I should go get my parents," I said.

"Where—?" But before she could finish, she gaped at something behind me, her eyes growing wide.

"DAD!" she screamed.

I didn't have time to look. The boat rocked violently out from under my feet, and then hurtled me into the air.

CHAPTER THREE

Darkness. Black and cold. I didn't know which way was up. How deep did I plunge? Weird hollow noises. Must get air!

Up, up, my suit pushed me up like a beach ball.

I broke the surface and gasped a loud sucking noise. Freezing water filled my lungs. I coughed and coughed.

Chaos.

Waves slammed my face. Wind screamed. The ocean spun around me. Cold water everywhere. Something shrieking. What was that noise?

"Mom!" I tried to yell, but my mouth filled with salty water. I gagged and wiped my eyes. Turning my head from the waves, I tried to look around. My breathing was fast and choppy. Something was in the water off to my right. What was that? A whale?

"The whale attacked the boat," someone behind me sobbed.

Waves crashed against the thing in the water. People screamed all around me.

"Help! I can't swim!"

"Hailey! Where's Hailey?"

"Dad!" I yelled, just as a wave broke over my head. I tried again, pushing myself higher in the water. "DAD!"

Where were they? Where was my sister?

Someone was climbing the thing in the water. I realized it was the bottom of the boat. It looked so wrong upside down. I flailed my arms, trying to swim closer.

"Get away from the boat," I heard someone yell. "It's going down."

"Help!" Someone close by yelled.

I turned and saw Marina barely bobbing on the surface. She was thrashing weakly with one arm, trying to twist her face away from going underwater. She moaned, holding her arm close to her body.

I spun back toward the boat, but heard Marina moan again. A wave broke over her face.

The panic cleared from my mind. I had to get her! I swam toward her and grabbed the back of her jacket.

She clung to me, screeching, "I can't move my arm."

The wind was blowing us farther away. There was something red in the water next to the boat. It grew on the surface like a balloon. People were helping each other climb in. A life raft.

"Come on," I said, trying to kick toward it. Cold waves washed over my face. The salt stung my eyes. I couldn't see. Suddenly, it seemed impossibly far to swim.

"Mom! Dad!" I yelled. "Stacey!"

"Hu-huddle with me," Marina said. "Get into the HELP position."

"What?" I yelled at her.

"Tuck your arms to your sides. Hug yourself. Bring your knees toward . . ." She coughed as a wave filled her mouth. ". . . chest. Keeps your heat in. Heat. Escape. Lessening. Position."

It was getting harder to hold her up. I kept kicking toward the life raft, but it was so far now. How did it get so far away?

"We have to kick toward the island," Marina said, nodding her head toward a small island behind us.

The wind and waves were pushing us in that direction, so it was easier to turn away from the waves that were breaking over my face. Something bumped me in the back. I screamed, thinking it was a whale.

Marina yelled, "Grab it!"

It was a long piece of plywood, just barely on the surface of the water. When we both grabbed it, it didn't sink far. It was such a relief to have something to hold on to.

Marina stretched across it as if it were a surfboard and started kicking toward the island. "Come on! Kick!"

I draped my body next to hers on the board, and we both kicked like motorboats. But it was tough to make the board go where we wanted. It was square and didn't move through the water well.

Waves crashed along the shoreline. Big splashes of water shot up from the rocks straight into the air. I kicked as hard as I've ever kicked in my life, but we were still too far away to swim to shore. The waves were going to sweep us past the tip of the island.

"Should we try to swim?" I yelled.

Marina shook her head. "Too much energy. And I think my wrist is broken."

My heart pounded in my head. I panted big gulps of air as we surfed on top of the waves. We sailed past the island and watched it go by. I didn't think I'd make the swim anyway.

"We lost too much body heat with all that kicking," Marina said. "Get as much of your skin out of the water as you can. The water sucks out your heat faster than the air."

We crawled farther up on the board, but it

started to sink with my weight. I slipped off a bit.

"Here, I'm wearing the suit, you stay on the board," I said. I craned my head as high as I could to look behind us. But I couldn't see over the waves. I'd lost sight of the boat and the life raft. I looked around at where we had drifted.

There was nothing but endless water. We were all alone out here.

CHAPTER FOUR

We weren't entirely alone. Long ships passed in the distance, too far away to see us.

"We have about an hour," Marina said. "Then we'll probably lose consciousness."

"What?" I didn't want to die. I started breathing faster again, searching around for my parents. For anyone.

"After you fall into cold water, a bunch of things happen. The big thing is, it makes you gasp. You can't help it. And if you're underwater, that's bad. The first minute is where you panic and hyperventilate. You breathe too fast and suck in water and drown."

We tucked in our chins as a wave pushed us from behind. I remembered panicking. But I saw Marina and it made me think about something else.

"But if you don't panic," she continued, "then you have about ten minutes to set up your life raft before you start to lose feeling in your fingers. Our arms are going to stop working properly."

Marina sounded like a robot. Wasn't she as scared as I was? I watched her face as she talked, and slid even closer to her on the board. Her calmness made me feel better.

She looked around. "Maybe we have more than an hour since we're out of the water, and wearing lots of layers." She glanced back at me. "And you'll last longer than me with that suit. Also, body fat insulates."

"I used to be good at gymnastics." I wanted

to explain I wasn't always like this. When I was on the team, I didn't have time to play Minecraft. But that was over a year ago. Now that's all I do.

"Dad must've released the life raft," Marina said, as if she didn't hear me. "Someone will spot that. He wouldn't have had time to radio a distress call, it happened so fast."

"What happened? What did you see?" I asked her. "Did the mom whale get angry and attack?"

I couldn't imagine a whale larger than the one that had jumped out of the water, but it would have to have been big to sink our big boat.

Marina looked at me then. "What? No, that's ridiculous. It was a rogue wave. The biggest monster I've ever seen. A wall of water hit us. And everyone was on the starboard side looking at the orcas. All the weight on the top deck and on one side . . ." She trailed off, looked like she was about to cry, then shook her head. "He's okay. He must have gotten in the life raft."

"My family too. They're all in the raft too, right?"

"I don't know. Probably." Marina looked above us. "Any minute we'll see the helicopter searching for us."

Every fourth or fifth wave was bigger than the others and broke behind our backs, then crashed on top of us. The board shot forward, then drifted, then shot forward again. We wobbled and splashed, trying to stay on top out of the water. Neither of us spoke, but I thought I could hear Marina sniffling.

My legs draped into the water and I kicked to keep us straight. I was glad now of the suit Mom had made me wear, though I could feel the cold water around my ankles. I rubbed my hand over my eyes. The salt water stung and caked my skin. It was all I could taste.

Marina held her right hand to her chest and clutched the board with her left.

"Does it hurt?" I asked.

Her expression slipped for a moment and she bit her lip. But she tossed her hair from her eyes and stared ahead. "When we make it to shore, we're going to need to build a fire right away. And a shelter."

She described how we were definitely going to make it to shore. And then how we'd make a shelter. How we would use it to get warm and how we'd need to build a signal fire for the rescuers to find us.

I nodded, but my thoughts raced along with my heart. Where were Mom and Dad? Did Stacey find them? Did they get in the raft? Were they looking for me right now? How would they find us out here? There was so much water. Nothing to see but curling, frothing waves in every direction. Splashing, crashing, endless.

The waves were like hills taller than me now. I threw my arm over Marina so she wouldn't be washed over. My fingers were cold and stiff. How long could we last out here?

"Twenty-five-knot wind," Marina mumbled. "Drifting about five knots with the current. Ebb tide." She was starting to sound weaker.

Was she going unconscious? I nudged her with my shoulder. "Keep talking to me. How come you know all this stuff?"

"Just Dad and me. Mom left when I was six. Dad was a commercial fisherman, but we could make a better living in the tourist industry. I take care of him. I learn about the whales. Going to be interpreter onboard tour boat. Teach people about marine life."

As I listened to her, my problems at home didn't seem so bad. At least my mom was around.

I lifted my head, got a hard wave in the face, wiped my eyes. I couldn't see the ships anymore. It looked like a cloud was tumbling over the mountains.

The wind howled behind us, screaming like a wild animal. It tried to tear us from the board. Waves smacked my back. But I started to become aware of another noise. It sounded like wet breathing.

It was right behind us.

I twisted but didn't see anything. What was that? I kicked to get away. The breathing returned, closer. I turned to look over one shoulder and then the other. And that's when I saw it.

A dark head with big eyes staring right at me.

CHAPTER FIVE

"Achh!" I splashed water at the thing. The head dove under.

"What?" Marina asked.

"There's something following us!" I yelled.

The head popped up again on my side of the board. It was so close I could see long nose slits. They opened wide, then closed. Its wet breathing sounded like a big, hissing snake.

"Harbor seal," Marina said. She smiled weakly and adjusted her grip so she could turn over and look at it.

"It's coming to watch over us. That makes

sense," she said. "Our boat's called the *Selkie*. That's a half seal, half person. It's a myth, like a unicorn. People in Scotland used to call them selkies."

The seal dove under.

Marina rolled back to her stomach. "Now we have our own protective selkie."

It didn't seem like it was protecting us.

It popped up again in front of us. The head was a sleek black with light gray specks and white whiskers. They were long and coarse, sticking straight out like the whiskers of a cat. Some poked up like eyebrows too.

I followed the whiskers down to meet the seal's gaze. Her big dark eyes were soft and sort of sad-looking. I felt like the seal was sorry this had happened to us. She was looking right into my eyes.

"She's not so bad." I hoped she would stay with us now. She made me feel better somehow. Like we weren't alone out here. I wished she could tow us to shore.

I looked around for the line of cliffs that marked the shore, but couldn't see it anymore. I couldn't see much of anything except a cloud. It had crept along the water and wrapped us up. It seemed like we were in our own world, and it had gotten a lot smaller.

"Fog. That's bad," Marina said. "Hard for Coast Guard to find us." Her lips had a blue tinge to them.

I flexed my fingers. They felt fat and awkward with cold. How long had we been out here bobbing on the waves? It felt like days.

"Got to get warm," Marina was saying.

She only had on the life vest over her coat, but I was wearing a thick, insulated suit with wide cuffs and a zipper up to the chin. "Do you want to wear this?" I said.

She shook her head. "Both of us drown. Keep it. Too hard to take off in water."

Her face was pale and she shivered violently. She wasn't looking good.

My heart started to pound again. How could I help her out here? When were the rescuers going to get here? Could they come in the fog? What was I supposed to do? Why was this happening to me?

The seal popped up next to me. She spun like a top and peeked at me, as if to check whether I was watching.

"Hi, seal. I'm watching. Stay with me."

She swam a little ahead, then came back to stare, then swam again out in front of me.

"You want me to chase you?" I kicked. My feet were so numb I could hardly feel them. "Wait up! I'm not as fast as you."

The seal swam ahead and I kicked to follow. She twisted, spun, and dove. She popped up next to me as if this were all a giant game. She made me smile. Gave me something to look at besides the dense fog and the endless waves. Made me forget to be scared.

The fog made the waves seem bigger. They

pounded me into the board, shoved us violently. Then I heard something ahead of us. Crashing like waves on a shore.

I kicked harder. Suddenly, tall trees appeared out of the fog like King Kong looming over us.

"Marina! There's the shore!"

"Rip current," she said quietly.

I kicked desperately toward it, but a strong current pushed us back. I used the last of my energy, pulling with one arm while gripping the board with the other. It looked like a river of foam between us and the shore. My arms and legs flailed madly. Still we were no closer. The current was too strong.

"Marina, help me kick!" My voice sounded faint behind the pounding in my ears.

There was no way I could get us in. My whole body vibrated with exhaustion. I gripped the board and leaned against Marina, taking in big gulps of air. We were going to drown twenty feet from shore.

Suddenly, Selkie popped up next to us again. I stopped fighting the current and drifted toward her. Her gaze drilled into me. She seemed to be telling me to find the strength to follow her again.

I let the current push me out, and then along the shoreline, following Selkie. I managed to kick a little as the waves battered us from the side. We crept farther along the shore, past the thick foam into a floating patch of kelp. Finally, the current stopped pushing us out. Selkie barked at me and then disappeared.

I struggled toward shore. We were going to make it!

Powerful waves picked us up and sucked us backward. I clutched the board and yelled. Then we were shoved forward, hurtling down the face of a wave. As we approached the shore, I stretched my feet toward bottom, but they didn't quite touch. Another wave sucked us back, then spit us closer. My feet dragged on gravel but I couldn't hold. We shot backward again and then forward, slamming hard onto the rocks. Marina cried out.

I clutched, scraped, clawed to get out of the water. It pulled, tried to yank us, but I fought it.

Marina struggled to get up. I grabbed her and pulled her with me. She still held the board as if she was frozen to it, or didn't want to give it up.

My legs shook so bad, I could hardly stand. In my desperation to get out of the water, I stumbled and fell. Waves and kelp pulled at my legs, my arms. The air felt warmer but the wind chilled my icy skin.

Had to stay onshore! No more cold ocean!

I dragged Marina and the board, tripping and flopping until we collapsed in a heap on top of a bunch of slimy, thick seaweed.

"We made it, Marina! We're saved."

I lifted my head and looked around for houses or cars or people. There were no houses or roads or docks. All I could see were rocks and trees.

"Help!" I screamed.

The only sound back was the roar of the surf.

CHAPTER SIX

"What should we do now? Where are we?" I asked.

No response. I turned. "Marina?"

She was curled in a ball where I'd left her. "Need warm" is all she said.

I helped her lean against a clump of bushes so she looked more comfortable. What had she said out on the water? We needed to start a fire and make a shelter. But how? "Marina, tell me again what to do."

She looked at me and shivered.

I scanned up and down the shoreline. Rock

walls on either side. We were lucky to have drifted to this spot; otherwise, we'd have been smashed against the cliff face. Waves crashed brutally onto the beach, flinging water high into the air. The rest of the water went on beyond the fog. How was there fog *and* wind?

There was a narrow strip of dirt and seaweed in a line about midway between the waves and a flat section of tall, swaying grasses. The forest loomed behind the grass.

I thought of all the times I wished my mom would leave me alone, stop babying me. All the times I wished my older sister hadn't been around. Now I wished so badly there were a grownup here. Anyone who would know what to do.

I looked at Marina again. I *did* know what to do. She had to get warm.

I yanked open the snaps on the front pockets of my suit. Nothing but an empty candy bar wrapper and a Ziploc bag with crumbs in it.

"Marina, do you have a lighter?"

"No." She trembled.

"Do you have anything we can use besides your knife?"

She gazed ahead, eyes unfocused. She had something in her pocket, but I couldn't clamp my thumb and fingers together hard enough to pull the zipper open. I realized I was shivering. My feet felt like blocks of ice. Both of us needed to get warm.

Coach used to make us do burpees to warm up. I dropped to the ground, my hands in the wet gravel as I did a pushup, then leaped up with my hands in the air. Again, down to the ground, push up, jump.

My heart started to pump; my breathing came faster. I hadn't done burpees since I quit the team. They were harder than I remembered. But it worked. I could feel and move my fingers. I yanked my zipper down and peeled off my suit. Kneeling next to Marina again, I pulled off the little vest she was wearing and helped her into my suit. It was wet, but still warm from my body heat.

She yelled when I tried to stuff her right arm into the sleeve. "M-my wrist!"

It looked swollen and sort of purple under the skin as she cradled it to her chest. When my friend Chad sprained his wrist breaking a fall on the mats, Coach wrapped it so it wouldn't move during the trip to the hospital.

Searching the ground next to us, I found two straight sticks and held them up next to her arm.

"Hold these," I said. "You don't have any tape, do you?"

Then I got an idea. I ripped the lace out of my right shoe and tied the sticks with that. Marina still had her bandanna around her neck. I reached under her hair. The knot was wet and hard to undo, but I got the bandanna free and laid it out in a triangle like Coach had done with a piece of cloth from the first-aid kit. I cradled Marina's arm in that and tied the bandanna around her neck so that her fingers pointed up next to her collarbone. "Does that feel better?"

"Fire," she mumbled.

I searched through the pocket of her vest. My hand pulled out a plastic bag with a lighter and a small box of matches in it.

"Yes!" I cheered, until I took a closer look at what I had thought was a lighter. It was just a black rectangular block the size and weight of a lighter.

What was this thing? Why couldn't this be a lighter? I hated matches. I could never work them.

The little box of matches was dry from being in the bag, but it stuck when I tried to slide it open. The box slipped from my fingers and most of the matches fell into the mud.

"No!" I lunged for the box and collected the few matches that weren't wet. More carefully, I pulled out one of the matches that were still in the box. "The box says they're waterproof, so it should work, right?"

I tried to rub the match head along the side of the box. The thin matchstick broke in my fingers. I threw it to the ground and tried another one. Again.

There weren't that many dry matches left. I crouched on the ground and carefully laid the match along my finger so it wouldn't break, but when I dragged it along the strike strip nothing happened. I had never understood the coordination it takes to make matches work.

"Argh!" I yelled in frustration.

I looked up in surprise when I felt a splash. I'd been so focused on the matches, I hadn't noticed what was going on around me. My attention now traveled along the line of seaweed and sticks. The ground above that line was a lighter color than the side closer to the ocean. Now I understood that this was how high the tide came up. And we weren't on the right side of the line.

Calm down. I had to concentrate. And I had to get ready to light the fire. I didn't have anything prepared to burn. I needed to stop panicking and think. What had Marina said about how much time we had before we'd get hypothermia? If I didn't get this fire started, we were both going to die.

I helped her crawl above the seaweed line to an area that was level with some boulders. Then I crouched behind the biggest boulder and scraped a bare patch in the dirt. I piled some twigs and driftwood that I found lying between the rocks and then I crouched over the pile and pulled out another match. I flicked it quick across the box and it made a snapping sound like when Dad lit matches. It worked!

The wind blew behind me and puffed it out.

I could feel myself starting to panic again. We needed to get warm right now. I tried again and again until I had one match left.

I focused on the match. Pressed my lips together, lined up the matchstick against my finger.

This was it.

This one would work. I had the hang of it now.

I flicked it across the matchbox. The match head flared up bright. And then died. I was left with nothing but a smoking match and darkness falling fast.

CHAPTER SEVEN

Marina pointed at the bag on the ground with shaking hands. "Mag. Magnes. Inside."

I pulled out the block I had thought was a lighter.

Marina made sawing motions. "S-shave. On tinder." She gestured weakly.

I peered closer and saw there were little cotton balls inside the baggie. What was she talking about? "This black stuff will light the balls on fire?"

Marina closed her eyes and sank into the coat.

"Marina. Don't leave me here alone. I need help!"

No response.

"Marina!" I leaned toward her. My heart pounded as I tried to hear hers. *Please let her stay alive.* I pressed my ear to her nose. I sighed when I felt and heard her breath.

Then I studied the block, turning it over in my hands. It looked like one side had been gouged away by a knife or something, and the other side had a black stripe down it like the matchbox. The cotton balls dropped onto my small pile of sticks when I shook out the bag. They were coated in some kind of goo.

I pulled Marina's knife from its sheath. When I saw it on the boat, I never would have guessed I'd be using it.

I scraped the knife down the side of the block and little pieces came off that looked like metal shavings. I pushed harder on the knife with the blade facing up, and dragged it along the block toward my foot. More pieces came off. Then I

flipped over the block and studied the stripe again.

How did this light a fire? I tapped it with the knife and was surprised when a little spark flared off it.

"Whoa!" I looked at the knife in my hand, then back at the block.

Holding the block up, I struck it with the knife again, harder. This time a shower of bright sparks came off. This was easier than thin, small matches; the knife wasn't going to snap in my fingers.

After a few tries, I figured out how to aim the sparks onto the shavings. They burst into flames, and then the cotton balls ignited.

I sat back, stunned. "I made a fire!"

I turned to Marina. "Hey, look! I made this!"

I dropped the block and put my hand in front of her nose again. Still breathing.

The flames were starting to die. I put more sticks on top and the flames caught. Pretty soon, the fire was crackling and popping and the heat bounced off the boulder toward us. I held my palms toward it and smiled. But my smile faded as I looked up. Darkness was falling fast.

"Are they going to find us at night, Marina?"

Relief crashed through me when she opened her eyes, but she said nothing. We looked at each other over the smoke of the fire. She looked scared. I remembered how scared I was in the ocean and how her calmness had helped me feel better.

"Don't worry," I said, forcing my voice to sound relaxed. "I'm going to make us a shelter. We're going to survive the night. And then the rescuers will come." I wasn't sure about any of it, but it looked like Marina needed to hear it.

I tried to picture what our tent looked like when we set it up in the yard. Back when Stacey used to do cool things like that with me.

"I need a long branch to use as a ridgepole," I told Marina. "I'll be right back."

Racing toward the forest, I searched the ground as I went. I brought all the things I gathered back to the fire and piled them next to Marina. As I worked, I kept talking.

"We have to make sure we don't set up next to an ant nest. I made that mistake before. Stacey had ants crawling up her legs and biting her inside her pajamas! You should have heard her screaming! It was hilarious. But let's not do that tonight."

There was another boulder near the fire that was as high as my chest. We were above the tide line here, and the ground was dry. I propped one end of the long bare branch I'd found against the top of the boulder with the other end on the ground. Then I leaned the board we had brought to shore with us against the branch so it looked like one side of a tent.

I had to stop to add more wood to the fire. "I don't like the dark," I told Marina. "Not since I had to sit in a dark room for two whole days. No TV, no computer, no games. It sucked."

I didn't tell her the other thing I was even more afraid of than the dark.

For the other side of the shelter, I used pieces of driftwood, and then filled in the spaces between the driftwood with dried seaweed and smaller branches. Once it was done, it looked like a lumpy lean-to, with the opening facing the fire and the ocean. I bent and crawled in. There was enough room to turn and lie down with my feet at the narrow end and my head just inside. Though it looked dry, the ground was uneven and damp.

It was almost too dark to see. Mosquitoes whined in my ears. I brushed them away and raced back to the forest to collect armfuls of leaves. I brought them to the shelter and threw them inside. Then I pulled branches off trees, the kinds with lots of needles on them. Needles and cobwebs and mosquitoes stuck to my neck and face. I swatted at the bugs and ran back toward the light of the campfire.

"This is our mattress," I told Marina as I arranged the branches on top of the leaves. I could see with the light of the fire. The mosquitoes weren't as bad around the smoke.

"Come on." I pulled Marina up and helped her slide in feet first. With the fire in front of us and the walls up, the heat from the fire filled the little shelter. After collecting more firewood, I crawled in next to Marina.

Once I stopped moving, I heard the quiet the waves had left in their wake. Instead of crashing, now they barely made a noise like frying eggs as they hissed up and down the

gravel. An owl hooted somewhere behind us
and I tensed.

"Marina, are you awake yet?"

She mumbled.

I needed someone to talk to so that bad
thoughts wouldn't come. The noises were scary
out here, not at all like our backyard with the
porch light on and the sound of the neighbors'
TV and of cars driving by.

Suddenly, I heard a loud spray burst out of the ocean.

"What?" I yelped.

Then I recognized the blowing noise I'd heard on the whale tour boat, and my racing heart calmed. I threw more wood on the fire, and watched the sparks rise into the black toward the stars.

I lay back down. "Tomorrow, rescuers are going to find us—right, Marina?"

No answer.

The sounds of the humpbacks breathing kept me company.

CHAPTER EIGHT

I woke to the sound of barking.

"What—?" Marina said. Her voice was hoarse. She'd been puking in the night, but I must've fallen back asleep.

I stumbled out of the shelter. It was still too dark to figure out what the weird shadows were on the beach. When my eyes adjusted I saw that the tide had slid up to the rocks.

Bark-bark-bark.

"Hello?" I yelled, hoping there were rescuers with dogs. I started toward the shore but stopped short when I saw what the noise was coming from.

"You found me," I said. "And you brought your friends."

"Huh?" Marina said from the shelter, louder.

Two dark, hulking outlines wriggled into the water with a splash. I gazed out at the sleek heads bobbing in the ocean. I was sure I recognized that mottled one with gray specks. She let out a loud bark when she saw me and dove under.

"Seals," I told her. "Selkie is checking up on us."

My tongue felt glued to the roof of my mouth. A throbbing pain pulsed at my temples and my throat ached.

Marina rolled over slowly to peer out of the shelter. "Where are the rescuers? They need to find us. I can't stay here."

My suit was draped over her like a blanket after she'd taken it off during the night. Her lips were cracked and peeling, and her hair was matted to one side of her head. She looked like she was about to cry.

We both desperately needed water. I looked at all the water in the ocean next to us. All the wet noises from the seals splashing around were making me crazy. But I knew from those salty waves crashing into my face that we couldn't drink any of it.

"We must be out of the search grid," Marina wailed. "Remember that island we missed? What if they don't find us? My arm hurts. I'm so thirsty. If we don't find water, we're going to die."

I stared at her. What had happened to the robot girl from yesterday? Her freak-out was making me freak out. I could feel my pulse speeding up. I needed breakfast. I needed to know where my parents were. I needed to go home.

I saw the blackened fire pit. It reminded me

of that feeling I had last night when I lit the fire. I had felt in control. We needed to get warm, and I had done it. If I figured out that problem, I could tackle this one, too.

"We need to stop and think," I said. "Where would we find water?"

Marina was too busy peeking under the bandanna at her wrist. It was as if I were the older one now. "I'll go find a stream," I said.

But after searching the thick forest behind the shelter, all I found were spider webs, an old tire, and a long white balloon, the kind they use to drape over the sides of boats to keep them from banging into things.

I also found a plastic water bottle, but it was empty. I licked my dry lips. The pounding in my head got worse.

When I stepped out of the forest, I noticed that all the grasses were bent over and wet with dew. I licked one, and the moisture felt so good in my mouth. I looked at the empty bottle in my hand and then at the grasses covered in water. If only there was a way to get the dew into the bottle.

I shrugged out of my sweater and tore off my shirtsleeve. Then I used the sleeve as a rag to mop up the dew. I squeezed the rag over the bottle and it began to fill. It took a while, but I managed to collect almost a quarter of a bottle. I brought it carefully back to the shelter. Marina was still huddled under my suit. When she turned and saw me, her eyes went big. "Oh!"

I was proud of the way she looked at me then. Not like I was someone who didn't know port from starboard.

"How's your arm?" I asked, handing her the open bottle.

She took a drink, measured how much was left, then took another small sip. "I'm really sick. It's making me scared." She wiped her mouth and ducked her head.

"I get scared too," I said. "I'm the most scared person of anyone I know."

"About what?" She handed me the rest of the water.

I thought of my parents and sister, of my gut worry over whether they got into the life raft, but couldn't talk about any of that.

"I was on the gymnastics team." I started gathering more sticks for a fire. "My friend Chad and I dared each other to do a giant swing on the high bar. You're not supposed to go on the bar without Coach to spot you, but we snuck in. I landed on my head and got a concussion. For two days I had to sit in a dark room to heal my brain. Since then, my mom treats me like I'm about to fall on my head again any minute."

"So you're afraid of gymnastics? Is that why you're not on the team anymore?"

I stopped scraping the black block with the knife. I'd never told anyone why. "What is this?" I held the block out to her.

"This is magnesium. The scrapings burn quick and hot. You can light fires if you don't have matches."

"Yeah," I said, striking the knife against the block.

I sighed. "I guess I didn't realize how high the horizontal bar was. I couldn't do any of it after the accident. Not the rings, not the vault, not even the horse. Floor wasn't my best event, so I quit. I can hardly climb stairs now. If I go too high, I start to shake and feel all fluttery."

Marina paused, eyeballing me. Finally she gestured at the fire. "We need green branches." She looked calmer now, not so freaked. I was relieved to see her eyes focus. It must've helped her to hear about other people being scared.

"Green?" I asked.

"Live branches to put on the fire. It makes smoke. We have to be ready to signal when the helicopters come." She licked her lips. "And we need more water."

My stomach growled so loud, we both looked around. Our eyes met and she gave me a shaky smile. "Food, too, I guess."

"My pocket." I pointed to the immersion suit on the ground next to her. "Animal crackers," I said as she pulled out the Ziploc bag.

"You thought of everything," she said.

We both dipped our fingers into the crumbs and licked them off. It didn't make me any less hungry. Then I looked at the bag I'd left on the ground yesterday. It had a few drops of condensation in it. It reminded me of something Stacey had done in eighth grade.

"Hey, we can use this to make a solar still."

"A what?"

"My sister had to do a school project for environmental science. Something to do with clean energy. I was surprised she was so smart, but then she told me she had read about it online."

I laid out the plastic bags we had. One large one from Marina's pocket and two small ones from mine. "If we fill these bags with plants, something green, and leave them in the sun,

they sweat inside. We can make our own water to drink!"

Marina grinned. "That *is* smart!"

I found clean stones and put one in a corner of each bag with the leaves and then carefully laid them out in the sun. The water would collect at the lowest point, where the stones were, and I could add water to the bottle again.

During the day we waited, ready with the fire. But there were no rescue helicopters overhead. No boats coming to get us. We saw big ships passing through the mouth of the strait, but they were far away.

"How are they going to find us if they don't come close enough to see our smoke?" I asked.

Marina craned her head to look up. She'd been drinking most of the water we got out of the solar stills, but she was still sick. She needed to go to a hospital.

"I don't know," she replied. "In the course I took, they just told us how not to drown. In all the stories, people who didn't drown got rescued. But they'd better hurry; we can't live much longer on dew. We can die from dehydration easier than drowning."

I wished she'd stop talking about dying every two minutes.

An eagle flew over us.

"There's another one," Marina said, scanning the tops of the trees. The eagle landed on a branch, the white of its head stark against the backdrop of the forest. It stared down at us. "I wonder if . . ." She perked up. "There! I knew it! We're saved!"

"What? Is it the helicopter? Where?" I stood up so fast I got dizzy.

"An eagle nest. This is where they set up the new cam. Now I know where we are! Wow, we're farther up the Cape than I thought. We'll never be able to walk to town. It's too far."

"What are you talking about? What's a cam?"

"There's a camera in that tree. The DNR just put it up so people could watch the eagles being born. All you have to do is go up there and signal."

She looked at me then with dismay because she had just remembered my confession.

My gaze ran up the height of the tree. At the same time, my stomach sank. It was so high.

"I can't," I whispered.

CHAPTER NINE

"Well, I can't do it." Marina pointed to her arm.

I thought of all I had done since the boat had gone over. About being in the water, and pulling Marina onto the board, and then getting to the shore. I had made a fire on my own. I never thought I could do that. I did it when I wasn't busy thinking I couldn't. I just did it. Seemed to me, the thing about surviving something is believing you can.

I looked way up the tree. All the way to the big ball of branches that Marina said was a nest.

"What about the eagles? Aren't they going to attack me?"

Marina shrugged. "I don't know. I've never climbed into an eagle's nest before."

"Well, that doesn't help."

"Maybe you should wear this. For protection?" She pointed to my immersion suit.

Slowly I pulled the suit on. My legs already felt wobbly and I hadn't even started climbing yet.

"There's no sound, just a camera, so don't bother talking," she called after me. "I'm also not sure if it's on all the time. I know they had to shut it down because of damage to the cables. Just jiggle it to make sure it's working. And hurry, it's going to get dark soon."

"Great," I muttered.

I stood beneath the lowest branch of the tree. It was like the highest parallel bars I'd ever seen. The lowest branch was way too far up to make it in a simple leap. I needed a springboard to mount.

I searched around and found a log with a broken end. I rolled it toward the tree and then propped it up on the trunk under the first branch. It wedged itself in as I shook it. Now all I had to do was run up the log and leap to that branch. The thought made me feel sick.

I stared up again, trying to judge the distance. Trying to ignore the pounding in my chest.

I rubbed my shaking hands on my suit, then clapped them together as if I were pounding off the chalk. I slowly backed up, moving branches out of the way. A simple move I'd done a million times. Except not nearly so high. Could I even reach that branch? What if I missed?

Don't think. Just do.

I took off at a sprint, ran straight up the log, and used my speed to leap into the air, swinging my arms over my head to give my jump more momentum. I stretched out my fingers as far as they would go, reaching, reaching.

I caught the branch with the tips of my fingers and somehow clung on. It was rough under my hands, and my skin scraped as I hung. I swung my legs upward and aimed for the next branch. Don't look down. That's all. Just keep climbing.

Of course, as soon as I thought about not looking down, I looked. The ground swayed beneath me. So far below already. I imagined it rushing up toward me, remembered the hollow sound, the last thing I heard before everything went black.

Stop thinking! Focus on the task. If I could keep my thoughts on just the climb, there would be no room for panic.

I pulled myself higher. Reached, stretched to the next branch, and the next one. My muscles trembled but they knew the motions. It was as if my arms and legs had their own mind and just did it. Stretch, reach, lunge, grasp, pull.

The bark left the skin on my palms raw, but I ignored it. Must keep going up. Branches started getting thinner closer to the top. But the worst part was the swaying. The tree swayed with the breeze up here, and with my weight. Every time I moved, the tree swayed more. My heart hammered in my chest.

Thump thump thump.

I could feel my pulse in the scratches on my face and hands. Finally, I was underneath the mass of sticks that was the nest. But that's when I realized what the hard part was going to be.

The nest was like a shallow bowl sitting in the center of a cluster of branches. It was as wide across as I was tall. I was going to have to reach far out to get around and over it.

Carefully, I pulled myself along the underside of the nest, grabbing the sticks and branches that stuck out. The muscles in my arms screamed as I hung sideways; my whole body shook. Slowly, I raised my head and peered inside. *Please let the camera be working.*

When my eyes came level with the nest, I was met by three angry heads. They shrieked and glared at me as I crawled onto the nest.

Blink. Blink.

"I'm just borrowing your camera," I whispered to them. "Don't call your mom and dad!"

I was expecting fuzzy chicks—*small* chicks. They were almost the same size as an adult eagle, but they didn't have the white heads. And they acted like babies. They huddled together, taking up most of the space.

The nest was big enough to sleep on. In fact, it looked more comfortable than the shelter I had made. Except for the dried-up carcass of something long dead. That explained the smell.

The camera was there on a branch, but I had no idea if it was working. I wasn't sure what I was expecting. Maybe for the screen to be like Stacey's camera phone, where you could see yourself. This camera was just a green, square box with a hood over the lens. I waved my arms in front of it while balancing on the branch.

"Help!" I yelled at it, before I remembered there was no sound. I swung my arms around and tried to show how we swam from the boat,

hugged a board, rode the waves onto this shore, and then how I made fire to dry us off and warm us.

All the while the chicks blinked at me, staring. I kept looking over my shoulder, terrorized by the thought of an adult eagle swooping down on me. Any second I expected to see the large wingspan.

Could they peck out my eyes? Most definitely they'd claw at me. Push me out of the nest. I'd fall down, down, down from the bar.

No. I wasn't on the bar. I was in a tree. And darkness was coming. I had to get down while it was still light enough to see.

I moved and a twig snapped. All three eaglets startled and started to screech. I heard loud wind sounds like flapping, and looked up to see two huge eagles circling over me. They both screamed back.

I craned my head looking up, but leaned out too far. My arms windmilled, and then I toppled off the nest.

CHAPTER TEN

I fell with a sickening feeling. My arms flailed wildly. Hands clutched, trying to grab something.

I caught a branch under my knee, missed the grip, and fell to the next one. I slammed into the branch but grabbed hold and stuck.

I hung from the branch, my body dangling. Then I pulled myself up and hugged the tree trunk. Pulse pounding.

Opening my eyes, I saw I had only dropped a short distance. I was still high in the tree. I was still alive! But I needed to get down.

I dropped from branch to branch, first carefully placing each hand, and then letting myself swing and hang. I had to trust my body. I was a gymnast and I could do this.

An eagle screamed above me. I glanced up and missed my next hold. I slipped. A branch caught me under the left arm and stopped me short. I clung tightly, breathing hard. Rough bark digging in. Focus!

Branch by branch, I made my way toward the ground. When I got to the lowest branch, I peered down at the log I had braced against the tree. How had I jumped that high? I couldn't let myself drop that far.

I sat on the branch, both legs dangling over the side. What was I going to do? I was stuck in the tree.

If I slid down the trunk with bare hands, I'd be flayed alive by the rough bark.

I patted my pockets and took a closer look at the belt on the suit. It was made with a wide band that looked like seat belt material. I pulled it out of the loops until I was holding just the belt, and then expanded it so it was as long as possible. Now I needed to get it around the tree trunk. I tried whipping it so the end would come around the trunk, but it didn't reach all the way. I kept trying to whip the buckle around the tree until, finally, I was able to grab it with my other hand.

I had both ends in my hands now. I just needed to jump. When I peered down at the ground, it swayed. I shut my eyes tight.

"Be brave. Let yourself go. You used to do this. You can do it again."

I eased my butt off the branch. Bracing my feet against the trunk, I leaned out, clinging to the belt. My stomach leaped up into my throat with the feeling of falling. I slid down the trunk, bark flying from my shoes. Before I'd even shut my eyes, the belt stopped short on the propped log and I let go. I dropped the rest of the way and landed.

Not on my head. On my feet.

I raised my arms and posed like I had just struck a perfect landing. My knees trembled; my legs hardly held me. I craned my head to look up into the branches.

"Yeah, I can!" I yelled.

"Did it work?" Marina shouted back. "Are they coming?"

"They're coming!" I yelled as I raced back to our camp. I could see the fire burning bright against the dimming light.

But no one came.

As darkness settled, we had to face another night in the shelter. Mosquitoes and black flies crawled in my hair, buzzed in my ears. Marina's wrist was now twice as swollen as it had been, and a really ugly color. And we were thirsty. I was feeling even worse after all that climbing.

"You're going to have to walk out of here and let them know where I am," she said quietly. "I can't walk that far."

The night was long.

I added wood to the fire to keep the bugs away. We listened to the whales and the seals and the owls and things that scurried in the dark behind us. Each new noise made us freeze and stare, wide-eyed, into the night.

Soon, the forest around us appeared in the pre-dawn light. We were still planning how I was going to be able to find help. How to follow the shoreline so I wouldn't get lost. I didn't want to leave Marina.

Once again, we heard splashes coming from the ocean. "Selkie coming to check on us?" I said, as I rolled over.

"Not seals," Marina said.

I looked out and my whole body zinged with energy. We turned to each other and laughed. And then Marina started to cry. She held out her good arm and we hugged.

A boat was coming straight toward us.

CHAPTER ELEVEN

Back home four months later

"There were dozens of calls," the reporter said, as I finished my story. He chuckled. "Complaints to the Department of Natural Resources about 'the kid in the tree' disturbing the eagles." He sat back. "Did you know that?"

"I heard." I took a big drink of my lemonade. Telling the story—just remembering it all—made me thirsty.

"Thank goodness for those nature lovers." Dad grinned from the loveseat next to me. "I'd never even heard of eagle cams before this. Who knew?"

"Well, thank goodness for the eagles," Mom said, placing a plate of cookies on the coffee table. "And for DNR for putting it up."

Dad reached to take her hand. She still got upset when I talked about it.

"I'm actually glad the whale attack rumors weren't true," the reporter said, earning a glare from Mom.

"Getting attacked by a whale wasn't the story here," he continued. "The real story is how you managed to not panic, save yourself, and save Marina, too!"

"We saved each other." I grabbed a cookie, still warm from the oven, and bit into it. The peanut butter center was gooey, my favorite. "I wouldn't have made it without Marina."

The reporter scratched his head with a pencil. "One thing I don't understand," he said. "You kept referring to yourself as overweight. You're obviously not."

"That was sixth grade. I'm back on the gymnastics team now. Coach says I 'got back on the horse.' He means the pommel horse. He thinks he's funny."

"And what about Marina? How was her wrist?"

"Oh, yeah. Broken. But she's better now. We video chat once a week. She's going to come to Ohio with her dad for a visit. We're both going to be marine biologists."

The grownups exchanged glances as if I weren't in the room. I knew they thought I sounded like a kid. But how could they understand I was serious? Having a seal look you in the eyes changes you.

"Wow, sounds like you have everything figured out," said the reporter.

"Dude," Stacey said as she stuck her head

into the room. "Dishwasher needs to be unload-ed and it's your turn. I am *not* doing it."

I turned back to the reporter. "I haven't got everything figured out. Who can understand big sisters?"

AUTHOR'S NOTE

There have been numerous tragedies in the ocean around Washington's Cape Flattery and Canada's Vancouver Island. The area has a list of hazards that make it complicated to forecast the weather accurately. Currents, undercurrents, near-shore currents, reverse currents, tides, prevailing winds, upwelling, and freshwater runoff are all factors that boat operators need to consider.

The area also has sizable waves coming from the Pacific Ocean at the mouth of the Strait of Juan de Fuca, and when they come against the direction of the current, it creates dangerous standing waves. Not only that, but something known as rogue waves—unpredictable walls of water that develop out at sea—can surprise boaters in calm waters.

The waters in this area are part of what is known as the California Current System, a current of cold water that reaches from Alaska down to California. Cold, deep, nutrient-rich water upwells in the summer months, attracting marine life—including whales—with an abundance of food. Commercial fishermen, sailors, and sightseeing tours all share the waters. But immersion in water colder than fifty degrees is dangerous for humans, and boaters must be cautious.

Even with all those odds, there are many stories of survival. I was amazed to read about a woman who fell off a boat in the Puget Sound area and swam for seven hours before she was found and plucked from the water by a passing boat. She credited her survival to the company of a seal who stayed with her for the whole ordeal. The one thing most survivors have in common is the will to keep going. That is what fascinated and inspired me to write this story.

While this story was inspired by true events, and every effort was made to keep to the facts, some details are fictional, including the names of the characters and some settings, as well as the presence of an eagle cam in the particular location of Cape Flattery. (There *are* eagle cams in the Puget Sound area.)

SO, WHAT CAN YOU DO TO SURVIVE IF YOU FIND YOURSELF IN A SIMILAR SITUATION?

U.S. COAST GUARD–APPROVED COLD-WATER SURVIVAL TIPS

Every minute counts in cold water.

1. MINIMIZE YOUR TIME IN THE WATER.

Act quickly. Your body loses heat twenty-five times faster in the water than on land, so get out of the water as fast as you can.

2. GET TO A SURVIVAL CRAFT.

Board a boat, raft, or anything floating. Turn a capsized boat over and climb in. Remember, most boats will support you even when they are full of water. If you can't get in the boat, climb on top of it and stay with it. That way, it will be easier for a rescue boat to spot you on the water.

3. STAY CALM.

Flailing around in the water causes the body to lose heat faster. If you don't have an exposure suit, hold your knees to your chest to protect your trunk from heat loss, and clasp your arms around your calves. This is called HELP (the Heat Escape Lessening Position).

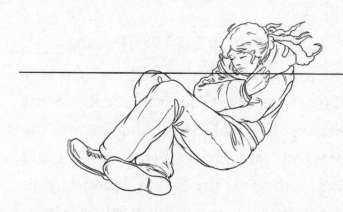

4. SAVE YOUR ENERGY.

Wearing a life jacket will help you save energy and will keep your body temperature from dropping quickly. Minimize the motion needed to keep afloat by helping to insulate the body.

5. KEEP YOUR CLOTHES ON.

Button, buckle, and zip up, and tighten collars, cuffs, shoes, and hoods. Wear a warm hat, like a fleece-lined skullcap, that will stay on your head in the water. Dress in layers of synthetic fabrics such as polyester fleece to keep from getting overheated or chilled from perspiration.

6. STAY PUT. DON'T TRY TO SWIM.

Don't try to swim unless your destination is very close. Ignore the shoreline; it is usually farther away than people think. Swimming disrupts the layer of warm water between your clothing and your body and sends the "warm" blood to your extremities, which cuts your survival time by as much as half.

7. DO THE HYPOTHERMIA HUDDLE.

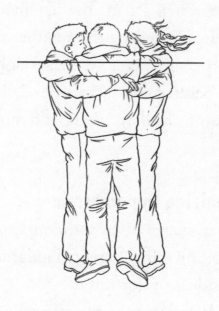

To preserve body heat, use the Heat Escape Lessening Position if you're alone, or if you're with a group, huddle with others. Rescuers are more likely to see you and rescue you faster if you're in a group.

Hypothermia

Though cold-water survival times vary from person to person, the colder the water is, the sooner hypothermia will set in. The likelihood of survivability is affected by the weather conditions and by a person's age, gender, weight, height, body fat percentage, fatigue level, immersion level, type of clothing worn, and survival gear available.

Recognizing Hypothermia

In the first stages of hypothermia, people can experience shivering, impaired judgment, clumsiness, and loss of dexterity.

In the later stages of hypothermia, body systems slow and eventually stop. Slurred speech, withdrawn behavior, muscle rigidity, and a cessation of shivering are signs of late hypothermia.

If left untreated, hypothermia will result in unconsciousness and death.

Treating Hypothermia

Rapid treatment of hypothermia is critical. If you identify someone as hypothermic, here's what you can do:

1. Call for help (call 911 or VHF-FM marine radio).

2. Restore warmth slowly.

3. Begin CPR (if necessary) while warming the person.

4. Give warm fluids.

5. Keep the person's temperature up by keeping him or her wrapped in a blanket.

Survival tips courtesy of the United States Coast Guard.

ACKNOWLEDGMENTS

In my research for writing this book, I collected information from many sources, including books, reports, and transcripts. I received helpful advice from a number of people, for which I am very grateful. Any errors in the story are my own.

I am grateful for the specialized advice I received from the following:

U.S. Coast Guard, Sector Puget Sound; Tammi Hinkle, Adventures Through Kayaking, Port Angeles, Washington; and Bruce Tomlinson, retired Ontario conservation officer of thirty years, Marine Enforcement Unit, Ministry of Natural Resources and Forestry.

Thank you to those who read the manuscript and provided excellent suggestions: Sylvia Musgrove, Jackie White, Marcia Wells, and Amy Fellner Dominy.

Thanks also go to Chris White and Steven White for reading the manuscript and giving me their expert opinions on where the illustrations should go.

ABOUT THE AUTHOR

Terry Lynn Johnson has lived in northern Ontario, Canada, for more than forty years. She grew up at the edge of a lake, where her parents owned a lodge. A nature enthusiast, she has explored Lake Huron with her family on their twenty-six-foot sailboat and has traveled more than two thousand kilometers on kayak expeditions in the Great Lakes, Alaska, and Nova Scotia.

She is a certified canoe instructor, and as the owner and operator of a dog-sledding business with eighteen huskies, she guided overnight trips and slept in quinzees.

She currently works as a conservation officer with the Ontario Ministry of Natural Resources and Forestry in the Northern Marine Enforcement Unit. She has seventeen years of hands-on experience and training working in cold-water marine environments and remote areas. She has trained with the Canadian Coast Guard and is qualified to operate vessels weighing up to sixty tons. Before becoming a conservation officer, she worked for twelve years as a canoe ranger warden in Quetico Wilderness Park.

In her free time, Terry enjoys snowshoeing, hiking, and dreaming up new ways to survive in the outdoors.

Here's a sneak peek at the next book in the
SURVIVOR DIARIES series: *AVALANCHE!*

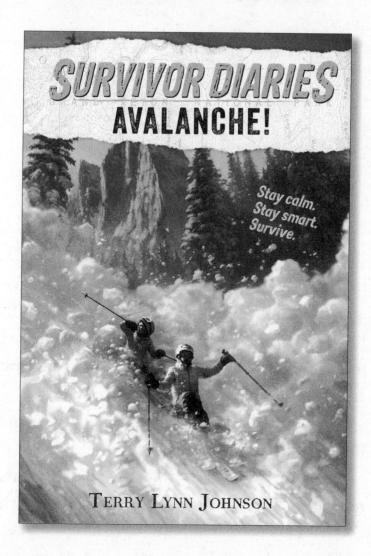

CHAPTER ONE

"Tell me how you survived the avalanche," the reporter said. He placed his phone on the kitchen table between us, then pressed Record. With his pen poised over his notepad, he looked at me expectantly. He smelled like grass and ink and summer tomatoes from the garden.

Without thinking, I glanced around for my brother, but he wasn't in sight.

"You sure you don't want to talk to Ryan, too?" Dad asked the reporter, filling his cup with coffee. "He's got a good eye for detail."

"Maybe later." The reporter smiled at me.

One tooth along the top was slightly crooked and stuck out. "I want to hear it from Ashley first."

"The avalanche wasn't even the worst part," I began. "But I'll never forget the roar. How fast it all happened. One minute we were skiing, the next we were being swept down the mountain at lightning speed. It just grabbed us and I couldn't stop myself from falling. I couldn't breathe. The snow was everywhere, a choking white blizzard in the air. Couldn't see—"

"Wait." The reporter stopped recording. "I explained to your parents, Ashley. I'm writing a series about brave kids like you who have survived in the wilderness. Readers will want to know everything you were thinking, everything you did, so they can learn what to do if it happens to them. Where were you? How did it happen? And why were you there? Try to tell me everything you remember."

He didn't look at Dad or anyone else. Only me.

I felt suddenly anxious about being part of a series about brave kids. I was used to just being Ashley Hilder, twelve years old, twin sister to the awesome Ryan Hilder. I had never been anything special before compared to him.

The reporter pressed the red Record button again. "Tell me your story."

I sat back in my chair, trying to conjure up the memory of that day. "It all started with the wolverines."

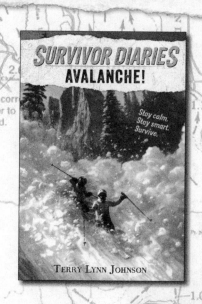
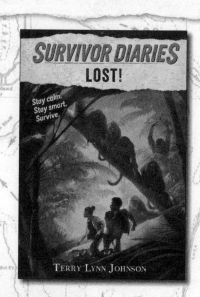

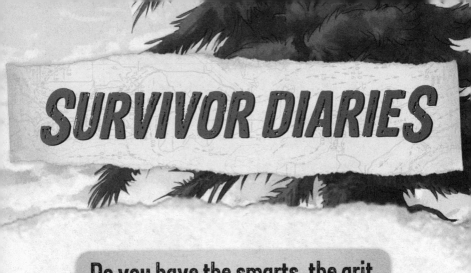

SURVIVOR DIARIES

Do you have the smarts, the grit, and the courage to survive?

— or —

Are you better off staying home?

YOU'VE READ THE BOOK, NOW PLAY THE GAME.
WILL YOU SURVIVE?

survivordiaries.com

"Why are you really reluctant to have your son work for me?" Jeremiah asked. "Or perhaps it is not just me? Perhaps you are reluctant to let him go?"

Pleasant looked up at him as if truly seeing him for the first time. His dark, wavy hair was the color of chestnuts. His eyes were the gold-and-green hazel of autumn leaves in his native Ohio and they held no hint of reproach, only curiosity. His expression was gentle and reflected only a deep interest in her reply.

"I will think on what you have said," she replied. "I respect that you have seen in Rolf perhaps some of your own youth, but I would remind you that he is not you—nor your son."

"No," Jeremiah whispered, glancing away again. "A friend then? Could we—you and your children and I—not be friends?" He arched a quizzical eyebrow and the corners of his mouth quirked into a half smile.

"Neighbors," she corrected.

He grinned and put on his hat. "It's a beginning," he said. "Good day, Pleasant."

"Good day," she replied without bothering to correct his familiarity. She watched him hop off the end of the porch closest to his shop and thought, *And perhaps in time, friends.*

Books by Anna Schmidt

Love Inspired Historical

Seaside Cinderella
Gift from the Sea
An Unexpected Suitor
A Convenient Wife
Christmas Under Western Skies
  "A Prairie Family Christmas"
*Hannah's Journey
*Family Blessings

Love Inspired

Caroline and the Preacher
A Mother for Amanda
The Doctor's Miracle
Love Next Door
Matchmaker, Matchmaker...
Lasso Her Heart
Mistletoe Reunion
Home at Last
The Pastor Takes a Wife

*Amish Brides of Celery Fields

ANNA SCHMIDT

is an award-winning author of more than twenty-five works of historical and contemporary fiction. She is a two-time finalist for a coveted RITA® Award from Romance Writers of America, as well as a four-time finalist for an *RT Book Reviews* Reviewer's Choice Award. Her most recent *RT Book Reviews* Reviewer's Choice nomination was for her 2008 Love Inspired Historical novel *Seaside Cinderella*, which is the first of a series of four historical novels set on the romantic island of <u>Nantucket</u>. Critics have called Anna "a natural writer, spinning tales reminiscent of old favorites like *Miracle on 34th Street*." Her characters have been called "realistic" and "endearing" and one reviewer raved, "I love Anna Schmidt's style of writing!"

ANNA SCHMIDT

Family Blessings

Love Inspired

Recycling programs for this product may not exist in your area.

LOVE INSPIRED BOOKS

ISBN-13: 978-0-373-82888-3

FAMILY BLESSINGS

Copyright © 2011 by Jo Horne Schmidt

www.LoveInspiredBooks.com

Printed in U.S.A.

Remember ye not the former things,
neither consider the things of old. Behold,
I will do a new thing; now it shall spring forth;
shall ye not know it? I will even make a way
in the wilderness, and rivers in the desert.
—*Isaiah* 43:18–19

For those who nurture the children—
woman or man.

Chapter One

Celery Fields, Florida,
Autumn 1932

Pleasant Obermeier dropped small dollops of batter into the oil sizzling over the wood-fired stove and expertly rolled each doughnut around in the oil until it was golden-brown before rescuing each and laying it on a towel to drain. Over the years that she had been the baker in her father's bakery in the tiny Amish community of Celery Fields, she must have made thousands of these small sweet confections. Like the loaves of egg and rye bread that she had already baked that morning, her apple cider doughnuts had remained a staple of the business in spite of the hard times that had spread across the country.

It occurred to her that little had changed about her daily routine in spite of the major changes that had taken place in her life these past three years. She still rose every morning at four and was at her work by five. Even so, her father, Gunther, still arrived before she did and had the fires stoked and ready to receive the morning's wares. The two of them had followed a similar routine since Pleasant was no more than a girl of fifteen. Now a woman of thirty-two—middle-aged by some standards—she had already been married and widowed and had taken on responsibilities she could never have imagined a few years earlier.

Three years earlier she had married Merle Ober-meier, a man ten years her senior. Then after Merle had died in a tragic accident two summers ago she had taken on responsibility for raising four children from his first marriage as well as responsibility for the large house and farm that he had left behind. But in spite of all of that, she had refused to give up her role as the local baker. There was something very comforting in the routine of the bakery. It was the one place where she could be alone with her thoughts. Even the few customers she was called upon to serve when her father was off making a delivery, or otherwise engaged as he was this morning, did not interrupt her revelry for long.

The bell over the shop door jangled and Pleasant hurried to dip up the last of the doughnuts and drop them onto the towel. "Coming," she called out in the Dutch-German dialect common to the community as she quickly rolled the still-warm doughnuts in sugar and set them on a cake plate. Before carrying the plate with her to the front of the shop, she automatically reached up to straighten the traditional starched white prayer *kapp* that covered her hair and smooth the front of her black bibbed apron.

But when she reached the swinging half door that separated the kitchen from the shop, she stopped. Her customer was a man—Amish by his dress—but someone she had not seen before. Celery Fields did not see many strangers. Their customers were mostly the local village residents and the farmers who raised celery in the fields that stretched out beyond the community. Occasionally, someone from the outside world—the *Englisch* world as the Amish called it—would stop as they passed through on their way to nearby Sarasota. But this was no outsider. This man was Amish.

She pasted on a smile. *"Guten morgen."*

He turned and she found herself looking straight up and into a pair of deep-set hazel eyes accented at the corners by the creases of a thousand smiles. Her earlier feeling of contentment was gone in an instant. Pleasant was wary of strangers—especially handsome male strangers. She had fought a lifelong battle against a streak of romanticism that for a woman like her was sheer folly. Tall, good-looking men like this one were not for her, regardless of how engaging their smile might be. She had long ago faced the fact that she was not only a member of a plain society—the Amish—but also that the face that looked back at her in her brief encounters with her reflection in a storefront glass was plain as well.

The cake plate teetered dangerously as the pyramid of doughnuts shifted and a few of the confections tumbled from the plate to the top of the counter. To make matters worse, both she and the stranger reached to rescue them at the exact same moment. His smile turned to laughter as their fingers brushed. But then their eyes met and his smile faded. He withdrew his hand as if it had been scalded. Certain that it was her expression of horror that had sobered him, Pleasant hurried to restore order. He was, after all, a customer.

"Clumsy," she murmured as she rescued two doughnuts that had made it to the floor and discarded them. When she stood up again, he had picked up the single doughnut still on the counter and seemed unsure of what to do with it. She held out a trash bin and after a moment's consideration he popped it into his mouth. Then he closed his eyes and savored the warm sweetness of it. "So you are the baker," he said.

Unnerved, she set the plate on top of the counter and covered it with a glass cake cover. "How may I help you, Herr...."

"Troyer," he said. "Jeremiah Troyer. I am Bishop Troyer's great-nephew." He smiled at her as if he expected this to be welcome news. He did have a most engaging smile.

"Are you and Frau Troyer visiting the bishop then?" she asked politely, refusing to permit his charming smile to disarm her while she gathered background information and was clear about what he wanted.

"I've just moved here," he replied. "And I am not married, Fraulein Goodloe."

"I am Frau Obermeier," she corrected. "My husband passed away two summers ago." She forced herself to meet his gaze. "Welcome to our community, Herr Troyer."

"I'm sorry for your loss," he said. "Is your father here?"

"Not at the moment. May I be of some help?"

He seemed to consider this and then plunged in to tell her his story. "Perhaps your father mentioned that I intend to open an ice cream shop," he explained. "I've also taken a position with the Sarasota Ice Company and bought the property next door." He waited for her to speak and when she said nothing, he continued, "I might have use for some of his wares in my ice cream shop, and when I spoke with your father last night…"

"You want to sell our baked goods right next door to us?" Pleasant's polite smile faded. In many ways Pleasant was a far better business manager than Gunther Goodloe had ever been. Gunther tended to be softhearted when it came to delayed payments or supplies not delivered as promised. Pleasant had no such problems. And when it came to the prospect of a competitor moving in on them, she…

The smile flashed again. "Actually, Frau Obermeier, I need cones for my ice cream and I was hoping that your father might help me concoct a recipe that would make my cones different from those of any potential competitors. But he assures me that you are the expert when it comes to baking."

"Ice cream cones," she murmured, fully understanding his interest now. This was business. Well, it would certainly be a change from the basic breads and rolls she turned out day after day. "How many were you thinking of ordering?"

Jeremiah laughed and the sound was like music in the otherwise subdued surroundings. Oh, he was a charmer, this one.

"Why, Frau Obermeier, we are not talking of a single order here. Once we come upon the perfect recipe, I shall need a steady supply of them."

Pleasant saw Merle's sister, Hilda, approaching

the bakery. Her heavyset sister-in-law huffed her way up the three shallow steps that led from the street to the door and entered. "Pleasant," she said, addressing Pleasant but looking at the stranger. "I don't believe I've had the pleasure. I am Mrs. Obermeier's sister-in-law, Hilda Yoder."

"I am Jeremiah Troyer and I'm pleased to meet you, Frau Yoder. Your husband owns the dry goods store?"

"Yes, that's right." In spite of the fact that Hilda often made a point of reminding others that pride was viewed as a sin by people of their Amish faith, she couldn't help preening a bit to have her husband known.

"I was coming to call on him next," Jeremiah reported. "And since Herr Goodloe is not here at the moment, perhaps I should stop back later this afternoon."

"That might be best," Hilda said before Pleasant could answer.

Jeremiah put on his stiff-brimmed summer straw hat and tipped it slightly toward Hilda and then Pleasant. "Give my regards to your father, Frau Obermeier," he said. "And please accept my deepest sympathies to both you ladies for the loss of your husband and brother," he added before leaving the shop and heading across the way to Yoder's Dry Goods.

Pleasant did not realize how closely she was watching him until Hilda lightly touched her arm and cleared her throat. "What are those boys up to now?"

Through the open front door Pleasant could see Merle's five-year-old twins—Will and Henry—wrestling with each other in the dusty street. "They'll spoil their clothes," Hilda chided, but Pleasant only laughed.

"Oh, they're just playing, Hilda. Clothes can be washed, you know."

"Of course, you would think that," Hilda replied stiffly, making it clear that in her view, Pleasant knew nothing about properly raising children—especially a pair of rambunctious five-year-olds. "It just seems to me with all you have to do at the bakery, you are certainly busy enough without adding extra loads of laundry to your chores." She clicked her tongue against the roof of her mouth. "I understand that Gunther intends to do business with the bishop's great-nephew and apparently it somehow involves you—some foolishness about needing you to make ice cream cones."

Before Pleasant could think of any appropriate response to her sister-in-law's comment, Hilda had left the shop, carefully skirting her way around the boys as she returned to the dry goods store.

"Boys, stop that," Pleasant called to the twins who rolled to a sitting position and blinked innocently up at her.

"Yes, Mama," they chorused.

Pleasant felt the familiar tug at her heart to hear any of Merle's children call her "Mama" without even thinking about it. That triumph—especially with Rolf and Bettina, the older two—had required a good deal of patience on her part and she treasured each and every use of the title. Always shy and withdrawn, even somewhat sickly while their father was alive, the two older children had blossomed under Pleasant's care. Rolf and Bettina never missed school and were often seen taking care of some chore or another around the large house. The twins—only toddlers when their mother died—had accepted her without question from the day she moved into the house.

Her heart melted as it always did in the presence of the identical boys. "Come here," she said, stooping down and holding out her arms to receive them. Giggling, they ran to her, colliding with her at the same moment so that they nearly knocked her off balance. "Look at the two of you," she fussed as she tucked their shirts into matching homespun trousers and slicked down identical cowlicks with fingers she wet on her tongue. "Now please try to stay clean," she pleaded as they scampered away.

It was at times like these that thoughts of Merle sprang to mind unbidden. He had had such a difficult youth as he often reminded her when he thought she was being too soft with the children. His own father had shamed the family by running away with his wife's sister when Merle was only a little older than Rolf was now. Merle had been forced to leave school and take a job in addition to managing the small family farm in order to support his mother and siblings. Knowing his painful past made the fact that Merle would never see how well his own children had turned out all the more poignant. And yet, she realized, that in the year she had been married to him, never had she witnessed a moment of such unconcealed love between Merle and any of his children as she had just enjoyed with the twins. Merle Obermeier had been a bitter man and in a year of marriage she had made little progress toward softening his ways.

She was about to close the shop's front door to prevent the dust from the street from blowing in when she saw Jeremiah Troyer exit the dry goods store and wave to her. She waited until he was in front of the bakery and then asked, "Did you need something more, Herr Troyer?"

"I came back to give you this," Jeremiah said, his tone easy and calm as he held out a folded piece of paper to Pleasant. "It's one of the recipes used by someone I knew back in Ohio. I'd like to consider something similar to this for the cones," he told her. "It's important to set one's product apart from that of the competition."

"You had an ice cream business in Ohio then?" she asked as she stepped onto the front stoop and accepted the recipe.

"Not exactly. You see, Frau Obermeier, as a boy I was ill with rheumatic fever, and my uncle—my father's eldest brother—thought it best that I take a job in town since I was too weak to work in the fields. The only person hiring was Peter Osgood, the pharmacist. He bought the cream and eggs for making the ice cream he served in the soda shop in the front of his drugstore from our farm. One day he mentioned that he was looking for a young man to help make the ice cream." Jeremiah shrugged. "I was already making the delivery of eggs and cream. It stood to reason that I might as well stay to do the work, and so I was hired. I was there for ten years."

Pleasant fingered the rough thick paper he'd handed her for a moment. His childhood held some similarities to that of Merle's thin and awkward eldest son, Rolf. "Mr. Osgood knows you have his recipes?"

Jeremiah laughed. "I didn't steal them. He handed them to me himself at the train station when he came to see me off and wish me well. In fact, you may have the opportunity to meet him one day. He's promised to come for a visit."

"And your father did not mind that you..."

A shadow of deep sadness flitted across his handsome features. "My father died when I was thirteen. My brothers and sisters and I were raised by our uncle."

"I see." Another thing that he and Rolf had in common. She looked up at him.

"And that's probably a good deal more than you need or want to know of my childhood," he said with a wry smile.

Pleasant pocketed the recipe and turned to open the bakery door. "I'll give this to my father when he returns and let him know that you stopped by." For reasons she didn't fully understand, she hesitated. "Good day, Herr Troyer," she said softly.

"And to you," he replied and he headed down the steps and on to the empty building he'd purchased to turn into an ice cream shop.

Almost as soon as Pleasant had entered the bakery, Hilda was back, her brow knitted into a frown of disapproval. "What was that paper he gave you?" she asked as she ran one finger over the display case and clucked her tongue at the dust she found there.

"A recipe for me to give Papa," Pleasant replied. "And now if you'll excuse me, Hilda, I have..."

"That man is trouble," Hilda muttered as she followed Pleasant into the kitchen. "He has this habit of laughing and smiling far too easily. In these hard times what does he find to be so happy about? You'll want to stay clear of him," she warned.

Pleasant decided to ignore this last remark. Ever since Merle's death, Hilda seemed to have assumed the need to speak for him. Pleasant could almost hear her late husband issuing the same warning to keep her distance. It occurred to her that Merle would not have liked Jeremiah Troyer. Pleasant could not say how she knew that or what the basis for Merle's dislike might have been. But she knew beyond a doubt that he would have offered her the same warning that his sister offered now. And as Hilda prattled on about the foolishness of even thinking of opening an ice cream shop in the middle of a depression, Pleasant could not help but think that perhaps she would be wise to take heed of such signs.

Amish communities around the country had long ago established the habit of holding their biweekly Sunday services in private homes or barns around the district. In fact, many districts were composed of no more than twenty-six households, making sure that each family would host services at least once during the year. In Celery Fields, they still had a way to go to reach twenty-six families. The community was still growing and for the second time that year, the service was to be held at Pleasant's house. The simple wooden benches stored on a special wagon and moved from house to house as the services did had arrived on Saturday and now stood lined up in the two large front rooms of the house.

In the two years that had followed her husband's death, Pleasant had made a number of changes that most everyone in the small community applauded.

For one thing, the citizens of Celery Fields no longer dreaded gathering in the house that Merle had always kept cloistered and shuttered even in the stifling summer heat. On the day of Merle's funeral, friends and neighbors had arrived to find the windows and doors of the house thrown open, exposing the somber and shadowy interior of the house to the light. Pleasant had stood together with Merle's four children on the wide front porch, greeting each new arrival. Further, when time came for setting up the benches—usually all crowded into the small front room at Merle's insistence—Pleasant had suggested spreading them into the adjoining dining room and giving people more room.

Then there was the matter of how she had handled the children—three boys and one girl. It was well-known that she had married Merle more because he was her one chance at ever finding a husband than because of any deep love for the man. For his part, Merle had made it clear that he had chosen her for equally practical reasons. She had managed her father's house after the deaths of her mother and her father's second wife. She had practically raised her two half sisters, and even now she continued to help her father in the family's bakery business. Merle had needed a mother for his four children and someone to manage the impressive house he'd built on the edge of the acres of celery fields he farmed. Theirs had been more of a business arrangement than a marriage. And that had suited them both.

Pleasant thought on all of these matters as she listened to the service, trying hard to keep her focus on the children and the responsibilities God had given her rather than the broad back of Jeremiah Troyer seated just two rows in front of her. When the service finally ended she hurried off to make sure that her oldest son, Rolf, had put out hay for the horses waiting to take the churchgoers home later, and then headed around the side of the house toward the kitchen.

On her way, she was struck by what a truly beautiful day God had given them. She took a minute to pause and close her eyes as she drew in a breath of the sweet warm October air. She could smell the herbs thriving in flowerbeds she'd planted herself all around the perimeter of the house. She almost felt as if she could smell the sun itself as the warmth of its rays bathed her face. She silently offered up a prayer of thanks for all of the blessings that God had seen fit to bestow on her as well as a plea for forgiveness for all the times she had complained about the life she'd been given. If she opened her eyes and turned away from the house and the bounty of its herbs and flowers, she knew that she would find herself looking out to the fields that stretched out for acres beyond the house. Merle's legacy for his children that had once thrived lay fallow now, the furrows parched and cracked. Still, the land and house were paid for so she thanked God that she and the children had food and shelter and, in these hard times, she felt truly blessed.

In the kitchen Hilda and several women were working in an easy and familiar rhythm. While the men reset the benches, the women prepared platters of fried chicken, mixed up a variety of salads and cut up pies still warm from the morning's baking. Pleasant joined her good friend, Hannah Harnisher, to help slice the heavy loaves of bread she'd baked the day before and lined up on one counter.

Hannah had once been married to Pleasant's brother, but after he died she had married Levi Harnisher. The couple had met a few years earlier after Hannah's son had run away with the circus—a circus then owned by Levi. Pleasant and Gunther had gone with Hannah to Wisconsin to retrieve the boy and the journey had forged a lifelong friendship between the two women—one they had not shared before that journey.

Pleasant had been different in those days. Life had dealt her a number of disappointments early on—her mother's death, her father's remarriage bringing two new siblings into the household. And then her brother had married the beautiful Hannah and the two of them had been so very happy. In those days, Pleasant had viewed each event as further evidence that she had been abandoned by those she loved. Then she had gone to Wisconsin with Hannah and along the way had gotten to know a group of women—circus folk—changing her outlook forever. With these new and unlikely friends she had discovered humor in the face of hardship and kindness in the face of the prejudice that is born of ignorance.

"Who was that man Gunther was sitting with?" Hannah asked.

"That's Bishop Troyer's great-nephew from Ohio."

"He's visiting then?"

"No, apparently he's come here to go into business." She could see that several other women—especially those who lived some distance from town and were eager to learn more about the handsome stranger they'd seen for the first time that morning—had leaned in closer to hear what she was saying. "An ice cream shop," she added, setting off a chain reaction of whispers as the news was repeated from one group to the next. The women were soon occupied speculating about the addition of an ice cream parlor and whether or not that was a good thing or something far too frivolous for an Amish community.

"Yes," Hilda added, "it seems that the bishop's nephew—great-nephew that is—has purchased the empty building next to the bakery and the storehouse behind."

As this new bit of information set off a wave of speculation among the others about whether or not the newcomer would also live in the building, Pleasant moved closer to Hannah and lowered her voice. "He has asked me—well, Father, really—to provide him with the baked cones he will use to serve his ice cream," she confided. "He expects to be in need of a steady supply."

Hannah's eyebrows lifted. "You'll be working even longer hours then. Hilda certainly won't approve of that."

"Well, what can I do? In these times, business has slowed to such a state that we almost never sell more than the basics. This is an order that we can't afford to decline and frankly, it will be nice to work on something besides rye bread and rolls."

"Perhaps Greta could…"

Pleasant laughed at the very idea that her youngest half sister might be any help at all. "Greta? That girl is a dreamer and it's all she can do to attend to the few chores she's responsible for at home. She would forget to check the ovens and no doubt burn the cones to a crisp," she said, but there was a fondness in her tone that spoke volumes. "And Lydia has all she can manage with the school."

Hannah pressed her hands over her apron. "I suppose I could help some," she said. "At least for a while."

Pleasant saw how her friend caressed the flatness of her stomach under her apron. "Oh, Hannah, you're expecting another child?"

Hannah's smile was radiant—more radiant than it had been even on the day when she had married Levi or the day when she had delivered twins—a boy and a girl, now three years old and the image of their mother. She nodded then put her finger to her lips. "Shhh. I'm fairly certain and I don't want anyone to know until I have the chance to tell Levi."

Pleasant could not have been more touched that Hannah was trusting her with this wonderful secret. It was a mark of just how much their friendship had grown.

"Caleb is going to soon feel outnumbered by little ones," she teased. Caleb was Pleasant's nephew—the boy who had run away with Levi's circus. Now as a teenager he was of an age to make one of the most important decisions of his young life. In the Amish faith—as in any Anabaptist group—baptism was an act of joining the church and as such was not performed until the person was of an age to be able to understand the covenant he or she was making with God. To prepare a young person for such a decision, parents often looked the other way while their teenagers took some time to explore the ways of the outside world. That time was called *Rumspringa* or "the season for running around." Of course, in some ways, Caleb had done that when he ran away with Levi's circus.

Hannah did not smile as Pleasant might have expected. Instead, she sighed. "I do worry about how he will feel about another baby in the house. After all, I remember what you said about your feelings after Gunther remarried and then Lydia and Greta came along. What if he decides to run away again?"

"Caleb will be fine," Pleasant assured her. "It's not the same at all."

Hannah's smile showed her relief. "I certainly have you to inspire me. The way you came into this house and made a true home for Merle's children. They love you as if you were their real mother, you know."

Pleasant waved away the compliment. "That was God's will. And God will show you and Levi the way as well."

Hannah squeezed her hand. "Thank you, Pleasant." She finished slicing the last loaf of bread, then added, "Bishop Troyer's great-nephew seems quite…nice. Is he…does he have a family?"

Pleasant knew the look her friend was giving her. It fairly shouted Hannah's idea that perhaps there might be a potential for romance for Pleasant here. "He is single and I'm sure there will be any number of our younger unattached women who will be happy to learn that."

Hannah watched Pleasant take ears of corn from a large pot and stack them on a platter. "It's been two years, Pleasant."

"You know my feelings on this matter," Pleasant reminded her.

"But why not at least open your heart to the possibility?"

"I have been married, Hannah."

"But have you ever truly been in love?"

Pleasant looked at Hannah for a long moment. Hannah had been twice blessed with true love—first with Pleasant's brother and then again with Levi. But other women—women like Pleasant—were called to other things. "Shh," she whispered and nodded toward one of the other women who had moved in closer to hear their conversation.

Then Hannah picked up two platters of sliced bread. "You'll bring the corn?"

Out in the side yard the men had just set the last of the benches for serving the meal. Hilda organized a parade of women, each carrying some platter, bowl or pitcher and headed across the yard. Pleasant looked at the stacked ears of sweet corn on the platter, but found herself remembering the plate of doughnuts and the ones that had fallen, and the touch of his hand.

And the way he had looked at her. Had he felt what she felt, if only for an instant?

She pushed the back door open with her hip, and although she heard the music of Jeremiah's laughter, she battled the temptation to glance his way. She refused to surrender to an old maid's fantasy that a man like that could ever be interested in one so plain.

Chapter Two

On Monday morning, after attending services with his great-uncle and aunt, Jeremiah stood at the front window of his shop. Along the unpaved road that stretched before him lay acres of celery fields on one side and a line of boxy houses—some of them little more than wooden shacks but every one of them pristine—on the other. At the far end of the street stood the large white house where services had been held. The home of the baker.

There was no reason that he could define about why he had been drawn to her like a moth to light. In the brief encounters he had had with her, he had noticed something in her eyes—a sadness and resignation that this was the life she'd been given and she needed to make the best of it. Jeremiah understood that feeling. He'd dealt with it from the day his father had died and he and his mother and siblings had moved in with his uncle. Watching Pleasant as she stood a little apart and observed the gathering of church members standing around her yard after services, he had wanted to tell her that things could change. She could change them.

It was a feeling he'd had before when meeting people for the first time, but never more intensely than he did in meeting Pleasant Obermeier.

Jeremiah shook off the thought and continued his survey of his new community. At his end of the street a town center of sorts had cropped up. There was a small wooden shack that served as the community wash house where the migrant workers who came to plant and later harvest the fields could wash themselves and their clothing. Next to that was a larger building that housed the local hardware store, and next to that was a building made of cement blocks and surrounded by a hodgepodge of machinery and parts. Next door to his property stood Gunther Goodloe's bakery. Yoder's Dry Goods occupied the largest storefront and the Yoders' modest house stood behind the store.

He lifted his face to the sun and thought that the small community in Ohio on the shores of Lake Erie that he'd left the day after his uncle's funeral seemed very far away. After years of living in the shuttered and isolated world that his uncle had fabricated as a proper Amish family household, he had sold his share of the family farm to his younger brother, packed his belongings and announced his intention to move to Florida and start fresh.

And the moment he stepped off the train at the base of Main Street in Sarasota and heard the rustle of palm branches high above him as he gazed out on the calm waters of the bay, he knew he'd made the right decision. He had gone immediately to the home of his great-uncle John who was his uncle's opposite in every way. Where Jeremiah's uncle had been a stern, unforgiving man,

John was a jovial and kind soul who, along with his wife, Mildred, welcomed Jeremiah with open arms.

He told them of his business plans and to his delight John had not only been enthusiastic about the idea, he had offered his financial support as well. In addition to serving as the community's beloved bishop, John had a furniture-making business that had attracted the attention of several wealthy businessmen and their wives in Sarasota. He had done very well for himself and Jeremiah respected the support and counsel his great-uncle could provide.

He explained to John how the advent of the chemical compound called Freon had made refrigeration commonplace in *Englisch* homes, but obviously because the Amish continued to avoid electricity and other modern conveniences, a source of ice to run their ice boxes and preserve their meats was essential.

"There's an ice packinghouse in Sarasota," John had told Jeremiah. "I know the owner and could speak to him on your behalf. After all, you'll be needing a paying job until you can get this ice cream business up and running."

Within a week of his arrival Jeremiah had accepted a job with the ice company and had finalized the purchase of the building next to the bakery as well as the small barn that came with it where he could set up his business and live in back of the shop. The ice packinghouse would, of course, be his main source of income, but he was looking forward to getting the ice cream shop up and running. Already his great-aunt Mildred had helped him furnish his living quarters with the essentials for getting settled.

"You need to concentrate on establishing yourself," she had insisted when he thanked her for everything she was doing for him. "You'd do well to focus your attention on your paying job first. An ice cream shop in these times…well, I don't know." Mildred was a sweet and gentle woman but had made it clear that she and John both questioned anything that smacked of frivolity. They were plain people—simple not only in their faith but in their daily routine as well.

"I believe there's a place for such a business even in these times, maybe especially in these times," Jeremiah replied.

"Your Uncle Benjamin taught you to make ice cream?" Mildred asked, her surprise evident as she laid out a handmade quilt on his single bed.

"In a manner of speaking. He was certainly responsible for my learning." He thought about the years spent working with Mr. Osgood. In addition to learning the business, his times at the shop had been some of the happiest of his life. The Osgoods had provided him with the encouragement and love that was often missing from his uncle's house. Indeed, the only person who had come to see him off at the train station was Mr. Osgood. The pharmacist had pressed an envelope into his hands. "An investment," he'd said.

Inside the envelope had been the recipes for all of Osgood's various ice cream concoctions and five crisp one-hundred-dollar bills. Jeremiah had arrived in Sarasota feeling like a rich man in every way.

Shaking off the memory, Jeremiah turned back to his work and finished taping the large sign that Mildred had made for him against the window. *Troyer's*

Creamery and Confection Shop—Opening Soon. Then he stepped outside to make sure the sign was straight and saw a woman coming out of Yoder's Dry Goods. She looked vaguely familiar but with the sun behind her, he couldn't be sure. He shaded his eyes with one hand and waited for her to come nearer. After all, Peter Osgood had taught him that the best way to build a business was to befriend as many people in the community as possible.

But then he saw that it was the baker's daughter. *Pleasant,* he thought and in looks she was all of that and far more. Her hair—what he could see of it under the starched white *kapp*—was the pale gold of freshly cut hay. At their first meeting it had surprised him that in sharp contrast to her fair skin and hair, her eyes were the color of the dark chocolate he used in making his ice cream. She moved with a natural grace worthy of royalty—or at least how he had always imagined titled people moving. And yet there was purpose in her step. She was carrying a satchel in each hand filled to the brim, her shoulders perfectly balanced by the weight of them.

Her expression was passive as she fixed her eyes on her destination—the bakery—and covered the ground necessary to reach it in long purposeful strides. She wore a solid blue ankle-length dress with the usual black apron and short cotton cape covering most of it. Most surprising of all, she was barefoot.

She was almost even with his shop before she saw him standing on the small wooden porch watching her.

"*Guten morgen,* Frau Obermeier," he said easily,

falling into the German-Dutch dialect of their shared heritage.

"Guten morgen," she replied but she kept walking. No time for visiting apparently, not even a moment.

"May I help you with those?" Jeremiah asked as he stepped off the porch and fell into step beside her. "They look quite heavy."

"I'm fine," she replied. "But thank you."

He bounded up the steps that led to the bakery entrance and opened the door for her. A bell jangled but no one came out to greet them or relieve her of her burden.

"Danke," she murmured as she entered the shop and headed immediately for the back room.

Everything about her posture, her failure to meet his eyes or smile, her single-mindedness about the contents of the satchels told Jeremiah that he should simply close the door of the bakery and go back to his own shop. Instead, he followed her into the large and spotless kitchen that held the lingering scent of yeast.

"Did you have the opportunity to look at the recipe I left with you on Saturday?"

"I did," she replied as she bustled around the kitchen putting things away.

Jeremiah decided to make himself useful by unpacking the satchels for her and handing her items such as cans of baking powder and bottles of vanilla. He did not miss the way she hesitated at first to take the items he held out to her. And then to his surprise she almost snatched them from him as if he might decide to run off with them. And not once did she look directly at him.

"We could go over it now if you have a few minutes,"

he said. "The recipe," he added when she glanced back at him over one shoulder.

"I have shown it to my father. He'll be here later. You can discuss it with him then."

"But you are the baker, are you not?"

"Yes, but…"

"Then I would like to discuss it directly with you." He had removed his straw hat and laid it on the long worktable that dominated the center of the room.

Still not looking directly at him she folded the cloth satchels and stored them in a basket under the table then began transferring a series of large flat pans, each covered with a cloth, to the table. The string ties of her *kapp* swung to and fro with the motion of her actions. She handed him his hat and went back to the side counter for another tray. It was clear that this was a process she had repeated hundreds—perhaps even thousands—of times. When she removed the cloths he saw that they held unbaked loaves of bread—rye from the looks of them.

"Frau Obermeier?"

"When my father returns, then we can discuss your order, Herr Troyer. Until then, I have bread to bake."

Jeremiah saw a series of hooks on the wall near the doorway that led to the front of the bakery and made use of one of them to hang his hat. Then he rolled back the long sleeves of his shirt.

Her eyes—definitely one of her best features—went wide with what Jeremiah could only interpret as shock. "What are you doing?" she demanded.

"I thought that as long as you wish me to wait until your father arrives that I could help you."

"Oh, so now you are a baker as well?"

Out of any other woman's mouth the words might have sounded teasing, even flirtatious. After all, Jeremiah was not blind to the fact that from the time he reached eighteen years and suddenly filled out the gaunt body that his earlier illness had left behind, he had attracted female admiration. His easy smile and determination to be everything his uncle was not had always resonated with females of all ages. But when Pleasant Obermeier spoke these words, they were no less than a condemnation.

Hoping to disarm her, he chuckled. "I'm afraid you would need to teach me that, Frau Obermeier. I had only thought I might move the trays to the ovens when you are ready."

"Thank you, but no. I can manage." She turned her back to him as she checked the heat coming from the large wood-fired ovens. "I'll let my father know that you wish to speak with him," she said.

"And you," he added as he retrieved his hat. "As the baker, you must have an opinion."

Her back still to him, he saw her shoulders slump slightly as if he had finally defeated her—or perhaps simply tried her patience beyond her ability to be polite. "Herr Troyer…"

"Jeremiah," he interrupted.

She turned to face him. "Herr Troyer," she repeated emphatically. "This is my father's business. If he asks me to be at this meeting, then I will be there. Until he makes that decision, I bid you a good day."

He had been dismissed. With nothing more to say, Jeremiah put his hat on and left the shop. But then the streak of impishness that had gotten him in trouble numerous times throughout his youth blossomed. He waited until a count of ten and then re-entered the shop, the bell announcing the arrival of a customer. He filled the time it took Pleasant to clatter a tray of breads into the oven and call out, "Coming," by considering the sparse but luscious selection of baked goods displayed in the shop's cases.

There were apple dumplings, whoopee pies that leaked their vanilla cream filling from between the chocolate cake sandwich like mortar from a freshly set brick wall, and the most mouthwatering-looking lemon squares that Jeremiah had ever seen.

The woman he assumed was responsible for all this temptation emerged from the back room with a welcoming smile that faded the moment she saw him. "Did you forget something, Herr Troyer?"

"I'd like a dozen of these, half dozen of those, and if you could add in a loaf of that rye bread you're baking."

"It won't be ready for…"

"I realize that. I thought perhaps you might be so kind as to drop it off on your way home later today. I'm right next door."

Pressing her lips together in a thin line of disapproval that did nothing to add to her appearance, Pleasant started filling his order. She packed two boxes, tied them with string and set them on top of the bakery case. When she had finished, he noticed that the small display of pastries he'd admired was almost completely gone.

"Will that be all?" she asked.

"I seem to have wiped out most of your…"

"I can always bake more," she said. "Would you like anything else?"

Jeremiah pretended to consider that question by looking around the shop. He plucked a bag of day-old rolls from a small table near the door and added it to the pile. "How much do I owe?"

When she punched in the amounts on the heavy brass cash register he thought she might actually bend the keys with the force of her strokes. He watched the numbers tally in the small window on top of the register and just before she hit the total key, he reached across the counter and stopped her by touching the back of her hand. "Did you add in the rye bread?"

"You can pay my father for that when he delivers it later today. At Goodloe's Bakery we make it a habit not to take payment until we are certain we can deliver what has been ordered."

"Meaning?"

"I might burn the bread," she said. "Or it might not have risen properly." She hit the key to total the sale and the cash register drawer sprang open. "Anything is possible," she added. "I might drop it on the floor or..."

The color that flooded her cheeks suddenly told him that they were sharing the memory of when she had dropped the doughnuts. He smiled and handed her the money. Without meeting his look she made change, slammed the cash drawer shut and dropped the coins into his outstretched hand. "Good day, sir," she said as she presented him with his parcels.

"And a pleasant day to you, Pleasant," he said as he accepted his order and headed for the door. Then he paused and sniffed the air. "I can see that I found a premiere location for my shop as well as my home if every morning I'm to be awakened by such wonderful smells."

Finally, the thin line of her mouth softened as her lips parted but she did not go so far as to actually smile. Pity, Jeremiah thought. Her smile was lovely.

Outside he found that he was in an even better mood than he had been upon first awakening that morning. Yes, he was going to enjoy life in Florida. It was impossible not to be in a good mood when practically every day was filled with sunshine. He closed his eyes and thanked God for the many blessings he had already found by moving to Celery Fields.

In spite of her determination not to surrender to her curiosity about Jeremiah Troyer, Pleasant edged toward the front window of the bakery and peeked out through the muslin café curtains to see where he might go next. To her surprise he was standing almost directly in front of the bakery, his eyes closed and his face raised to the sky above.

Was he praying? In the middle of the street?

And then with no warning, he opened his eyes and raised his hand in greeting to the Hadwells who owned the hardware store. He set the bag with the day-old bread and the larger box that held an assortment of pastries on the porch of his shop and carried the smaller box—the one that held six apple cider doughnuts—over to the hardware store.

He offered a doughnut to Mr. and Mrs. Hadwell and then called out to Harvey Miller who ran the machine shop to come and join them. Within ten minutes they had each taken a seat on one of the many nail barrels that lined the porch to enjoy the doughnuts. Gertrude Hadwell brought out tin cups and a pot of coffee and served the men. Jeremiah had his back to her but Pleasant could tell by his gestures and the rapt interest on the faces of the others that he was telling them some story.

"A tall tale, no doubt," she huffed as she dropped the curtain back into place and returned to the kitchen. The man had a way of taking over whatever space he might occupy. One might expect that of someone like Levi Harnisher, for example. Levi had once owned one of the largest and most successful circus companies in the country. And Pleasant would never forget the day he had walked right into this very bakery while she and Hannah were working and announced that he had sold the circus in order to return to his Amish roots and court Hannah.

Never in her life did Pleasant think she had ever witnessed anything so romantic as that. The love that shown in Hannah's eyes as she looked at Levi and his love for her that was reflected there was nothing short of breathtaking. And the memory of that devotion naturally brought to mind her relationship with Merle. Of course, she and Merle were very different from Hannah and Levi, who were romantics by nature. To the contrary, both she and Merle understood and respected the hard realities of life.

Jeremiah Troyer is a romantic, she thought and bit her lip as she focused all of her attention on rolling out crusts for pies instead of dwelling on the handsome newcomer who was to be their neighbor—and perhaps business associate. *Neighbor and business associate,* Pleasant sternly reminded herself, *and nothing more.*

If there was one lesson she had learned, it was that men were rarely as they presented themselves to others. Or perhaps it was that she was a poor judge of the male species. After all, she had foolishly thought that a young man from Wisconsin was flirting with her, calling at the bakery day after day just to see her. More to the point, the man she had thought Merle was before they married and the man he had turned out to be were not at all the same.

Hannah and others had tried to warn her, but she had insisted that they simply did not understand people like Merle and her—serious people who were devoted to their work and who understood the hard realities of life. But even she was not prepared for day in and night out of living with a man who saw little good in anyone or anything—including her and his own children.

The shop bell jangled and Pleasant sighed heavily as she wiped her hands on her apron and headed to the front of the store. "Did you need more doughnuts, Herr Troyer?" she asked as she stepped past the curtain separating the kitchen from the shop and saw Hilda standing there with all four of Pleasant's children.

"Pleasant, you must do something with this girl," her sister-in-law said as she pushed Bettina forward. "I am quite at my wit's end."

Chapter Three

"Bettina, are you all right? Has something happened?" Pleasant asked, coming around the counter and kneeling next to her daughter whose face was awash in silent tears.

"I didn't know they had wandered off," the girl said in a whisper as Pleasant wiped away her tears with the hem of her apron.

"Shhh," Pleasant murmured. "It's all right."

"It is not all right," Hilda thundered. "For it was your idea to give the child responsibility for making sure the twins are properly brought to my house before she and Rolf leave for school."

On weekdays, when the bakery was busiest, the twins stayed with Hilda who had seven children of her own. On Saturdays, they spent their day at the bakery with Pleasant while Rolf and Bettina took care of chores at home.

"I wanted to get the wash hung before…" Bettina began.

Pleasant stood up so that she was eye to eye with Hilda. Merle's sister had first watched over the children after their mother's death, taking them in so that Merle could tend his celery fields. And even after Merle and Pleasant married, she had continued to insist that the children spend their days at her home, persuading Merle that it was asking too much of them to accept Pleasant right away. But when Pleasant had accepted this arrangement without question and gone back to helping her father in the bakery, Hilda had done a complete about-face, complaining to Merle that Pleasant was ignoring the children, not to mention her duties as his wife and the keeper of his house.

Pleasant kept one hand around Bettina's shoulder as she tried to assure herself that only fear and panic would make Hilda speak so sharply in front of the children. "Hilda," she said quietly, "the children are all safe. She's only a girl and…"

"At her age their father was already working a paying job. At his age…" Hilda gestured toward Rolf. "He was…"

Pleasant touched her sister-in-law's arm. "Hilda, please," she murmured and was relieved when the woman swallowed whatever else she had been about to say.

Meanwhile, the twins had eased away from the drama and worked their way behind the counter where they had opened the sliding door of the bakery case and were helping themselves to some of the sweets that Jeremiah had not purchased. Bettina tugged on Pleasant's skirt and nodded toward the boys.

"Stop that this instant," Pleasant demanded as she moved quickly around the counter and picked up one twin under each arm like sacks of flour.

When she failed to take away the pastry each boy clutched, Hilda snorted. "You do them no favors by indulging them," she huffed as Pleasant deposited both boys closer to the door.

"Tell your Aunt Hilda that you're sorry for causing her worry and then apologize to your sister as well," Pleasant instructed.

"Sorry," Henry muttered even as he stuffed the last of his pastry into his mouth.

Pleasant grabbed an empty lard bucket she kept under the counter to collect waste and shoved it under Henry's chin. "Spit it out," she said in a voice that brooked no argument. The boy did as he was told and then burst into tears. Within seconds his twin had joined in the chorus and the racket they made was deafening.

Hilda threw up her hands. "Do you see what you've done?" she demanded and Pleasant prepared to defend her action until she saw that her sister-in-law had addressed this remark to Bettina.

Pleasant realized that if she didn't do something at once, her father—or worse—any customer who came in was going to find the shop crowded with crying children. "Let's all just calm down and have a nice glass of milk in the kitchen," she suggested just as the bell above the door jangled.

"Ah, Frau Yoder," Jeremiah Troyer said, ignoring the chaos of the overwrought children. "I thought that was you I saw coming down the road before."

Beyond caring why Jeremiah Troyer had invaded the bakery for a third time that morning, Pleasant seized the opportunity to herd all four children into the kitchen. She noticed that all sign of tears and protests had abated the minute Jeremiah entered the bakery. The children seemed quite fascinated by him.

"Sit there and be quiet," Pleasant said, indicating a long bench that ran along one wall. She was glad to see that even the twins seemed to recognize the limits of her patience. While she poured four glasses of milk and handed one to each child, she tried in vain to overhear the conversation taking place in the shop. Then she heard the opening and closing of the outer door and a moment later, Jeremiah stepped into the kitchen.

"May I have a word with Rolf, Frau Obermeier?" he asked.

"What about?" Pleasant asked.

Jeremiah gave her that maddening smile of his and tousled Rolf's hair. "With your permission, Frau Yoder has suggested that he might be a candidate to help out at the ice cream shop."

Rolf's eyes widened with a mixture of such surprise, unadulterated joy and pleading that Pleasant's heart sank. This was the most difficult part of being a parent. She was going to have to say no.

"I don't believe that would be a good idea," she said.

Rolf's face fell but he said nothing. Jeremiah's smile tightened. "I see. Perhaps this is not the right time." He glanced at Bettina and the twins and seemed to focus on their tear-stained faces. "Forgive me for the intrusion, ma'am. We can discuss the matter later." He nodded to the children and headed for the door.

"Wait a minute," Pleasant said, hurrying after him. He had opened the door and the bell was still vibrating when she caught up to him. "I know you mean well, Herr Troyer, but…"

"Are the children all right?"

Pleasant blinked up at him. "Yes, of course they are." *Why would he think otherwise?* She saw a flicker of doubt cross his expression and felt her defenses go on alert. "Herr Troyer, please understand that Rolf has his schooling and chores at home and…"

"As do many other children." The implication that other boys Rolf's age were working or learning a trade was clear.

"The children are my responsibility," Pleasant said tightly. "I will decide when the time is right that they should take on more than they must already manage."

Jeremiah looked away for an instant, out the leaded glass of the bakery door. "Of course, you know best, but if I may offer an observation as someone who was once smaller and not nearly as strong as others my age?" He seemed to wait a beat for her to grant permission and when she said nothing, he continued, "Do not deny the boy the opportunity to find his place in the world."

"He is only twelve," Pleasant protested. "Besides, he will one day have his father's farm to manage and…"

"I am not speaking of his life as an adult. I am speaking of his life now—the things that will surely shape the man he will one day become. There is a tempest building in that boy. A growing view of the world and those around him as unfair. He is fast approaching a crossroads where he will either accept his size as a challenge to be met or he will surrender himself to the belief that he has been unjustly punished."

Pleasant thought of Hannah's son Caleb and how he

had run away. Everything there had turned out for the best, but Rolf was different. Small and quiet—too quiet, she had often thought. And Merle had been especially hard on the boy.

"Why are you really reluctant to have your son work for me?" Jeremiah asked. "Or perhaps it is not just me? Perhaps you are reluctant to let him go?"

She looked up at him as if truly seeing him for the first time. His dark wavy hair was the color of chestnuts. His eyes were the gold-and-green hazel of autumn leaves in his native Ohio and they held no hint of reproach, only curiosity. His expression was gentle and reflected only a deep interest in her reply.

I am afraid, she thought and knew it for the truth she would not speak aloud. "I will think on what you have said," she replied. "I respect that you have seen in Rolf perhaps some of your own youth, but I would remind you that he is not you—nor your son."

"Nein," Jeremiah whispered, glancing away again. "A friend then? Could we—you and your children and I—not be friends?" He arched a quizzical eyebrow and the corners of his mouth quirked into a half smile.

"Neighbors," she corrected.

He grinned and put on his hat. "It's a beginning," he said. "Good day, Pleasant."

"Good day," she replied without bothering to correct his familiarity. She watched him hop off the end of the porch closest to his shop and thought, *And perhaps in time, friends.*

There had been one reason and one reason only that Jeremiah had gone to the bakery for a third time in the same morning. He had been sitting outside the hardware store sharing doughnuts with the Hadwells when Mrs. Hadwell had noticed Hilda herding Pleasant's children down the street. The girl was in tears and the three boys lagged behind her and their aunt, looking distraught.

Mrs. Hadwell had cleared her throat, drawing her husband's attention and then she nodded toward the little parade passing their store. Roger Hadwell glanced up and then turned back to the conversation he and Jeremiah had been having about remodeling Jeremiah's shop. But Jeremiah knew that look. He'd seen similar glances pass between neighbors and friends of his family his whole life. Louder than a shout it was a look that warned, "This is none of our business. Stay out of it."

And to his surprise, Jeremiah found it easier to comply with that unspoken warning than to call out to Hilda Yoder and ask if there was a problem. To his shame he lowered his eyes until Hilda had passed by on her way to the bakery, her fingers clutching the thin upper arm of Pleasant's daughter. But the scene stayed with him even as he headed back to his own shop and even after he forced himself to focus on the plans for remodeling the space. And when he heard one of the children cry out, he could stand it no more and headed for the bakery.

With no real plan in mind, he was a bit taken aback when he passed the bakery window and saw Pleasant thrust a bucket under the nose of one of the younger boys. Perhaps the child was ill. Perhaps he had misread the entire situation. He entered the bakery, closing the door with an extra force that he knew would cause the bell to jangle loudly. It worked. Everyone turned to him. Instinctively, he focused his smile on Hilda Yoder who scowled at the interruption while Pleasant said something about milk and took advantage of his arrival to take the children into the back room.

"What is it now, Herr Troyer?" Hilda snapped.

Jeremiah had no idea what he should say. He racked his brain for some reason why he might have needed to have dealings with the woman.

"I saw you come down the street earlier and then it occurred to me that you might be just the person to give me some advice." He suspected that giving advice was Hilda's stock in trade and when her scowl shifted from irritation to suspicion, he was pretty sure that he had guessed correctly.

"What sort of advice?"

Jeremiah chuckled. "I may know how to manage a business and make a decent ice cream, but when it comes to decorating the premises…" He shrugged. "I am quite at a loss." He could practically see the wheels turning in Hilda's brain and hurried on to press his advantage. "Clearly, I'm going to need tables and chairs and a serving counter and…"

Hilda nodded, her small light eyes flitting back and forth as if typing up a list. "Have you colors in mind?"

Jeremiah shrugged.

Hilda huffed out a sigh that, when translated, meant, "Men are hopeless," and set to work ticking off what he was going to need. "The place is a mess. You'll need cleaning supplies and then paint—a lemon-yellow I would think. Stop by the store this afternoon and I'll have Herr Yoder pull together those initial supplies. In the meantime, you can order tables and chairs and the counter from Josef Bontrager. He's an excellent carpenter."

"Frau Yoder, you are a blessing in disguise. How will I ever thank you?"

"You can pay your bills in cash and at the time of delivery," she informed him without a trace of humor.

"Of course. Thank you. I'll be by right after lunch if that's convenient."

Hilda nodded and headed for the door. She appeared to have forgotten all about the business that had brought her and the children here in the first place.

"I'll need a helper," Jeremiah said as he hurried to open the door for her. "Perhaps you know of a young boy who…"

"My older boys all work in the celery fields," she said, making the assumption that her sons would be at the top of Jeremiah's list. She glanced toward the kitchen. "Perhaps Rolf—he's too small for field work."

"Another excellent suggestion. Thank you," Jeremiah said as he ushered her out and closed the door behind her.

It had been a stroke of genius or more likely God's divine guidance that had made him ask her advice on a helper. The one thing he understood was that Hilda Yoder took great pride in seeing herself as invaluable to others when it came to handling their affairs. He did not consider what he might do if she were to suggest that he hire one of her seven children. But as things turned out that should have been the least of his concerns. He had been totally unprepared for Pleasant Obermeier to reject his offer. He had seen the dead and baked fields behind her house. Surely she could use the money the boy could bring home.

He stood for a moment looking down the road at the large white-washed house with its tin roof and wrap-around porch where she had lived with her late husband and where she now lived with his four children. He glanced back at the bakery where, according to his great-aunt Mildred, she had spent a good portion of her life helping her father run the business even after she had married Merle Obermeier.

Jeremiah had lived most of his life in a house where dreams were frowned upon and only hard work was respected. And until he had gone to work for Peter Osgood, he had followed that regimen, burying his dreams in order to try and please his uncle. Now he could not help but wonder what dreams Pleasant had put aside in order to care for first her widowed father and then her half sisters and finally the widower and his four motherless children.

He remembered how, after his father had died, his own mother had abdicated the raising of the children to her brother-in-law. That was to be expected for Jeremiah's father—a kind but timid man—had always bowed to his older brother's wishes as well. How many times had Jeremiah wished that his mother would stand with him when he tried to challenge his uncle's rigidity?

Oh, Pleasant, he thought, *do not make the mistake my mother made.*

But it was hardly his concern, he reminded himself. He had a job to attend to as well as a business to get up and running. His fascination with the baker and her children was nothing more than that—idle curiosity, and as his uncle had reminded him more than once and emphasized with the back of his hand, idle thoughts were the devil's workshop.

Chapter Four

Pleasant had underestimated the amount of time she would have to devote to creating the ice cream cone recipe. In spite of the fact that the bakery's business had dwindled to the basics—breads, rolls and the occasional pie or dozen cookies—she was still busy from dawn to well after dusk. Merle's house was a large one and required constant cleaning to keep it presentable. With four growing children there was a great deal of washing and ironing to be done on top of the cooking she did at home and the upkeep of the kitchen garden she relied upon for fresh produce to feed herself and the children.

Then there was the celery farm itself. Over the years, Merle had acquired a great deal of land—land that needed to be plowed and planted and harvested. Land that this past spring had barely produced a saleable crop and that now in the fall was nowhere near ready to be planted. After her husband's death, Pleasant had turned the management of the farm over to her brother-in-law. Hilda's husband, Moses, was a shy, quiet man—nothing like Hilda. But he had a head for business and managed

the farm as well as his dry goods store with an exper-
tise that set Pleasant's mind at ease. Still, he would
not make a decision without first consulting with her
and Rolf. For as she explained to Jeremiah, the farm
was Rolf's future, in spite of his father's doubts that he
would ever amount to anything as a farmer or businessman. She worried about Rolf. Merle's constant badger-
ing of the boy had taken its toll, and of all the children,
he had been the hardest to bring closer. Whenever she
tried to show her appreciation for some chore he had
done without being asked or commented on his high
marks in school, his dark eyes flickered with doubt and
distrust.

It had been a week since Jeremiah Troyer had
stopped at the bakery and asked to interview the boy
for a job in his ice cream shop and Pleasant had been
unable to forget the look that had crossed Rolf's face
when she'd turned down the offer. Just before he'd lowered his eyes to study his bare feet, she had seen a
look of such disappointment come over his features
and there had been a flicker of something else. For one
instant he had looked so much like his father.

Memories of the rage that had sometimes hardened
Merle's gaze came to mind now as Pleasant rolled out
dough and plaited it into braids for the egg bread she
was making. She paused, her flour-covered hands
frozen for an instant as the thought hit her. What if
Jeremiah had been right? What if Rolf turned out to
be as bitter and resentful as his father had been? Could
such things be passed from father to son like the color
of eyes or hair? Or was it possible that circumstances
might guide the boy in that direction? Certainly Merle's

resentment had begun early in life and in spite of his success in business and the love he had shared with his first wife, he had remained until the day of his death a man who looked at the world with hostility and ill will.

"Well, not Rolf," Pleasant huffed as she returned to her task. "Not my son."

But how to set the boy on a different path?

She wiped her forehead with the back of one hand and blew out a breath of weariness and frustration. *How, indeed, heavenly Father?*

She walked to the open back door of the bakery, hoping to catch a breeze before she had to face the hot ovens again. Next door she saw Jeremiah Troyer replacing a wooden column that supported the extended roof of his shop. She thought about the Sunday when he had easily lifted two of the heavy wooden benches used for church services—one under each arm. She continued to observe him as he fitted the column in place and anchored it, drawing one long nail after another from between his lips and pounding them in until the column was locked in place.

Who would teach Rolf such things? Her father? Perhaps. But he was getting on in years. He tended to leave the heavy chores to the carpenter, Josef Bontrager, who was always willing to help because it gave him an excuse to see Greta. She thought about the way Jeremiah's ready smile and easy laughter were so different from Merle's personality. Might it be enough to simply expose Rolf to this different breed of man? To let him see that not all men were like his father had been? That there were other ways he might decide to go?

Without realizing that she had done so, Pleasant opened the screen door and stepped outside. Jeremiah gave the porch post a final test for steadiness and turned when he heard the squeak of the screen door. The hammer he'd used in one hand, he raised the other hand to his hat and tipped his head in her direction. "Pleasant." He acknowledged her with a quizzical smile as he squinted against the morning sun. "Was there something I could do for you?"

Flustered to find herself outside and engaged in this exchange with him, Pleasant reverted to her usual defense. She thinned her lips and frowned. "Not at all," she replied. "The ovens give off such heat. I just needed a breath of fresh air."

Jeremiah nodded and turned back to his work. He set down the hammer and picked up a broom. Meticulously, he rounded up the wood shavings and sawdust left from shaping the porch column to match its mate.

"You know if you'd like, Rolf could paint that column for you when he comes home from school later," she called.

Jeremiah stacked his hands on the tip of the broom handle and leaned his chin on them as he studied her. "That would be appreciated," he said.

Pleasant nodded and turned to go back inside the bakery's kitchen. *It's a start,* she thought.

"I could still use an assistant," Jeremiah called and her step faltered. "Maybe we could see how painting the porch post works out and then…"

"My offer is simply that of a neighbor wishing to help another neighbor," Pleasant said stiffly.

"Got that part," Jeremiah said, moving closer, twirling the broom handle through his fingers and grinning. "But you'll soon learn that I don't give up easily, Pleasant."

It was the second time he had used her given name that morning. It was as if he were testing her. She smiled sweetly, the way she had seen her half sister Greta smile when she was determined to have her way. "And in time you will learn, Herr Troyer, that I do not make decisions lightly and I will always do what I think is best for my children."

She turned to leave but realized that he was propping the broom against the wall and intended to follow her inside.

"How's the cone recipe coming?" he asked as he held the door for her and then followed her into the kitchen.

"I expect to have some samples for you to try by the end of the week," she said. "They would best be tested with ice cream since the flavors will have to mingle."

He nodded and took a seat on one of the stools that Gunther kept in the kitchen.

Make yourself at home, she thought, exasperated by his assumption that his presence was welcome.

"How about this? You let me know as soon as you have something that you think might work and I'll make up three different flavors so we can try the various combinations. We can have a tasting party."

She opened her mouth to refuse, but then thought, *Why not?* It would be a special treat for the children. "All right," she replied, placing the braided egg loaves on pans.

His silence was unusual so she glanced up and saw him studying her, a half frown on his forehead and a half smile on his lips. "You do surprise me, Pleasant," he said and then the smile won and blossomed into a full-fledged grin. "End of the week then."

And the man actually winked at her as he pushed himself to his feet and left her standing there, a pan of unbaked egg bread half in and half out of the oven.

Jeremiah sat at his desk and watched the Obermeier boy painting the porch column. He was meticulous in the work, going back over a section that did not meet his standards for perfection. Jeremiah remembered his own painstaking attention to detail in the years he'd spent living with his father's brother. For him it had come from knowing that if he failed to do a job to the exacting standards his uncle had set for him, he would have to do it again or worse, he would be punished.

Had Rolf's father been a man like Jeremiah's uncle? Did that explain the boy's reticence?

"Maybe the kid's just shy," Jeremiah muttered as he pushed his chair away from the desk. He had to stop seeing his uncle in every adult and himself in every quiet child. He took down his hat from the wooden peg near the door and went outside. "Good job," he said.

Rolf stepped away for a moment and surveyed his work. "Missed a spot," he muttered and bent to cover it before turning his attention to the next side of the square column.

"How's school?" Jeremiah sat on the edge of the porch.

"*Gut.*" Rolf lapsed naturally into the Pennsylvania Dutch that Jeremiah assumed was most often spoken at home.

"What are you studying?"

Sticking with his native tongue, Rolf listed the subjects. "Arithmetic, history, geography."

"Your classes are conducted in English?" Jeremiah assumed this might be the case since it was a common way to prepare young people for dealing with those outside the Amish community.

"Ja."

"Does your mother use English at home?"

The paintbrush faltered for a moment. "My stepmother does—yes."

Jeremiah considered the correction. Did it mean that Rolf resented Pleasant or simply that he felt a loyalty to his own mother? "I was about your age when my father died. Tougher on you, I expect, losing both your parents."

This time, Rolf looked at him as if trying to decide where this conversation might be headed. "Mama is good to us," he murmured, his tone slightly defensive.

Jeremiah let the silence settle around them for a long moment. "Do you like ice cream, Rolf?"

"Ja."

"Me, too. I've been working on a new flavor. How about tasting it for me and telling me what you think?"

Rolf continued his long brush strokes. "I should ask permission first."

Jeremiah covered a smile by glancing away toward the bakery. "That's probably best. Your sister's helping out at the bakery, is she?"

Rolf nodded. "After school she watches my brothers until Mama gets everything ready for tomorrow's baking, then we all go home together."

"Well, then the way I see it we've got ourselves a bunch of tasters. You finish up there and go get your mama and sister and brothers while I go get dishes and spoons and the ice cream."

"You want me to bring them over here?" The kid's eyes widened.

"Well, sure. I mean that's where the ice cream is."

Rolf's hand shook slightly as he returned to his painting, now going over an area he'd covered adequately.

"Or I could go over and get the others while you clean up here. Looks to me like you've finished." Without waiting for the boy's reply he headed for the kitchen entrance to the bakery.

Through the open door he could hear the lively chatter of the twins and the clatter of the large metal pans and bowls that Pleasant used for making the breads and rolls she baked each morning. As he got closer, he could hear the low murmur of voices—Pleasant's and the girl's. Bettina, he reminded himself.

"Hello?" he called as much to give fair warning of his approach as to deliver a greeting.

Two pairs of small feet padded across the bakery floor at a run while everything else went silent.

"Well, hello there," he said when the twins lined up at the door and stared out at him. "Is your mother here?"

"Is there a problem, Herr Troyer?" Pleasant glanced anxiously past him to where Rolf was cleaning the paintbrush.

Now why would she automatically assume that?

Jeremiah thought. "Actually, I've come to ask another favor."

She waited, wiping her hands on the dish towel she held while the twins glanced from him to her and back to him.

"If we can be of help," Pleasant said, "we're more than…"

"I have this new flavor of ice cream I've concocted—vanilla with bits of mango mixed in. I wondered if you and the children might taste it for me and give me your honest opinion."

The twins did not wait for her reply, but opened the screen door and burst out onto the back porch of the bakery seemingly ready to follow him anywhere as long as he held to his promise of ice cream.

"Boys," Pleasant chided, then turned her attention back to Jeremiah. "I thought we had agreed on the end of the week. There is no possible way that I will have anything ready by…"

"You'd be doing me a great favor," Jeremiah continued as if her protests had nothing to do with the topic at hand. "While you're developing the cone recipe, don't forget that I need to be working on special flavors for the ice cream. We can't just offer the standard flavors, after all. Besides, I tend to be far too lenient when it comes to my own tastes for flavors."

Bettina had joined Pleasant on the porch and she was smiling up at him. "What other flavors have you invented, Herr Troyer?" she asked.

Jeremiah removed his hat and scratched his head for a moment. "Well, let's see now, there was the time

I thought maybe there might be a market for frog's leg chocolate."

All three children giggled and miracle of miracles, he was pretty sure that Pleasant was fighting a smile.

"You made that up," Bettina said.

"You're right. I did. But I actually did think about adding prunes to vanilla once." He made a face that had the twins convulsing with laughter. "So you see I'm not always the best judge when it comes to these things."

"I wouldn't want to spoil the children's supper," Pleasant hedged.

Jeremiah shrugged. "My guess is that you were planning to give them dessert with supper?"

"Well, yes, but…"

"So what if they have dessert first?"

Her mouth worked as she tried to find an answer to this unorthodox logic. "I…without the promise of…"

"They might not finish their peas and carrots?" Jeremiah guessed and Pleasant nodded. He frowned as he studied each child in turn. "Rolf, come over here a minute, would you?"

The boy's bare feet sent puffs of sandy dust flying as he ran across the dry dirt yard. "Yes, sir?"

"Am I to understand that sometimes you children have to be coaxed to finish your vegetables?"

Rolf and Bettina nodded. The twins studied the ground. Jeremiah sighed.

"So you see, Herr Troyer, ice cream at this hour…"

All four children looked up at her, their eyes wide with protest as they realized they were about to lose this opportunity. "But Mama, if we promised?" Bettina pleaded.

Pleasant folded her arms across her chest and studied each child. "No. There have just been too many times…"

Jeremiah was almost as disappointed as the children were. He didn't know why it meant so much to him but it did. "Your mother is right," he began.

"Unless," Pleasant interrupted, "Herr Troyer would agree to come for supper and bring some of his ice cream along for dessert."

The children whooped with delight at what they clearly considered an acceptable solution.

Pleasant was watching him though. "You do like vegetables, do you not, Herr Troyer?"

"What kind?" he asked and hoped the answer would be green beans or perhaps carrots.

"Brussels sprouts," Pleasant replied and he knew that the look of disgust that had flickered over his face for an instant was exactly what made her smile. "May we expect you at five-thirty then?"

Chapter Five

Have I completely lost my mind? Pleasant thought as Jeremiah walked back to his shop, whistling a nameless tune. But she put the thought aside as the children clamored around her.

"Ice cream! Ice cream!" the twins chanted as they marched up and down the small porch.

"He said I did fine work," Rolf reported shyly, his eyes still following Jeremiah until the shopkeeper disappeared inside his back door.

"I don't think he likes Brussels sprouts though," Bettina mused. "Did you see the look on his face? Maybe we should have the beans, after all."

"We're having the sprouts," Pleasant said. "And speaking of supper, we need to get home. Boys, stop that marching and go along home with your sister. Rolf, would you stay and help me finish closing up for the day?"

"Yes, Mama," all four children chorused and then they grinned up at her, their eyes shining with anticipation.

"And stop at your grandfather's, Bettina. Ask him and Greta and Lydia to join us for supper."

Bettina squealed and held hands with the twins as the three of them ran down the dusty road. "It's like a party," Pleasant heard her say.

"Would you like to see the job I did for Herr Troyer?" Rolf asked as he helped Pleasant finish putting away the pans and bowls and scrub the counters.

Pleasant saw the worried look the boy gave her. His father had always insisted on inspecting any task assigned to the boy and more often than not he had found something not quite to his liking.

"You said that Herr Troyer was pleased with the work," she reminded him.

"I know but Papa…"

"Your papa taught you well, Rolf," Pleasant hurried to reassure him. "I can see from here that you did a fine job. If I didn't know which was the newer post I wouldn't be able to tell the new from the old. Now let's finish up here and get home or our company will be there ahead of us."

It was an exaggeration, of course, but it made Rolf smile and the boy seemed unusually relaxed later as the two of them walked past the other shops and then the celery fields and other homes to the end of the road.

"I like Herr Troyer," Rolf murmured when they had almost reached their house. "He's sort of like Herr Harnisher, Caleb's father."

The two men were nothing alike—at least outwardly. Levi was a good man but he tended to be quiet and reserved while Jeremiah Troyer seemed to delight in getting to know people of all ages and backgrounds. But

Rolf had a point. The two men did share a nature that invited others—even children and strangers—to open their hearts to them, share confidences and let down their guard of the normal Amish tendency toward reserve.

Of course, her view of the ice cream maker was that he was a business associate of her father's—nothing more. All right. He was also a neighbor and member of the congregation, but nothing more than that. Still, he had made Rolf glow with a pride of accomplishment that in spite of the Amish tendency to frown on such self-satisfaction, pleased her. Besides, until he was fully baptized and had joined the faith, Rolf was not yet truly Amish. He had been born of Amish parents but as a child he was not yet fully a member of the faith so a little pride was not a bad thing, she decided.

"Rolf, perhaps from time to time you could help Herr Troyer as he gets ready to open his shop. There's a great deal to do I expect and after all…"

Rolf was looking up at her, his expression one of disbelief. "Do you mean it?" His voice quavered as if he didn't dare give voice to his hope.

"Helping a newcomer to our community is what our people do as a matter of course, Rolf."

The smile that split his face was his father's smile—a smile she and the children had rarely seen. But she had only a second to bask in its radiance before the child threw his arms around her waist and hugged her, his hat sailing unheeded onto the ground. "Oh, thank you, Mama," he said, his voice muffled against her apron.

She smoothed his hair and relished the warmth of

his thin arms clutching her. "You'll still have to manage your chores here and your schoolwork," she reminded him. "And you're to take no payment. These are good deeds—neighbor helping neighbor. Do you understand?"

"Yes, Mama." He looked up at her. "May I tell Bettina?"

"You may tell her that I have given permission for you to help Herr Troyer from time to time if he asks. This is not a job, Rolf."

He had rescued his hat and dashed away almost before the last word left her lips and she watched him go, running into the house, calling out for his sister. *At last,* she thought, realizing that she had finally broken through to the last and most reticent of Merle's children. And she had Jeremiah Troyer to thank for it.

It was pretty obvious that Pleasant had given him an extra large helping of the sprouts, Jeremiah thought as she handed him his plate. Her father sat at the head of the table, slicing a pot roast that smelled as good as it looked. He would place a slab on a plate from the stack in front of him and then pass it to Pleasant who would add potatoes and the dreaded green vegetable.

"Bread, Herr Troyer?" Bettina asked with a sweet smile. "Sometimes it helps take away the taste," she confided in a low whisper when Pleasant's attention was drawn to the twins who were busy jostling one another for more room at the crowded table.

Pleasant's half sisters, Greta and Lydia, sat across from Jeremiah, eyeing him under the fan of their pale lashes. Rolf sat to one side of him and Bettina to the other. And once everyone was served Pleasant took her place opposite her father at the far end of the table.

"Shall we pray?" Gunther asked and in unison every head bowed and silence filled the room. Even the twins were quiet.

"Amen," Gunther intoned after a long moment and the room erupted into the sounds of flatware on china, the twins' chatter and water from a pitcher splashing into the empty glass that Gunther had just drained. "How are things coming along?" he asked, directing the question at Jeremiah.

"At the shop? Fine. Good."

"How about your job at the ice plant?"

"That's worked out better than I could have hoped," Jeremiah said. "My employers are especially pleased with the number of orders for block ice that I've gotten from people living here in Celery Fields. That business had fallen off considerably once the *Englisch* started using refrigerators instead of ice boxes."

Gunther nodded. "*Ja.* Better to buy from one of our own even if you are working for an *Englisch* company."

"And the cones?" Jeremiah asked and Gunther looked down the table at his eldest daughter.

"I...that is..." Pleasant's cheeks turned a most becoming shade of pink as every person at the table paused in midbite and looked her way. With an almost visible effort she composed herself and turned her attention to Jeremiah. "I apologize, Herr Troyer. We've had some extra orders at the bakery this week and..."

Gunther frowned. "When's your opening?" he asked Jeremiah.

"I haven't set a date yet. I was hoping to be open by the first of November."

"Less than a week," Gunther said to Pleasant.

"Plenty of time," Jeremiah assured her and turned his attention to Lydia. "Fraulein Goodloe, I understand you are the schoolteacher for the community's children."

"Yes," she replied with a shy smile. "I am blessed to have been chosen."

Her sister Greta glanced at him and when Jeremiah smiled at her she almost choked on the food she was chewing.

Perhaps it would be safer if he concentrated on his own plate, empty now except for the pile of Brussels sprouts and the round roll that Bettina had urged him to try. He picked up his knife and fork and cut into a sprout, put half of it in his mouth and then followed that with a bite of the roll and chewed.

He was aware that Bettina was watching him and when he swallowed and repeated the process she whispered, "Told you so."

"More pot roast, Jeremiah," Gunther boomed.

"Thank you but, no. I have more than enough to finish here and I want to save room for ice cream."

The twins started to speak up but Pleasant silenced them by pointing out the untouched vegetables on their plates. "Only those who clean their plates get ice cream," she reminded them.

Jeremiah couldn't help feeling a little sorry for the boys. On the other hand, they only had two sprouts each to finish while he was still facing half a dozen. He squared his shoulders and picked up his fork. Slicing each sprout in half, he wolfed them down, chasing them from his mouth with the rest of the roll and gulps of cold water until there were only two left.

He glanced at the twins who immediately saw the challenge he was sending them. Pleasant had sliced their food into bite-sized pieces. Henry nudged Will and both boys grinned at Jeremiah and the race to finish first was on. Everyone except Gunther seemed to have caught on to the game. Rolf and Bettina sat forward, silently cheering their brothers to victory. Lydia and Greta glanced uneasily from Jeremiah to Pleasant, apparently waiting for her to say something. Instead, she slowly finished the last of her supper, as if unaware that anything was amiss. But Jeremiah saw her ease a bite of the vegetable that had been hidden under some gravy forward on Henry's plate lest he miss it. The boys won and their victory was crowned by Gunther's deep belch—the Amish man's compliment to his wife or daughter for a good meal.

Pleasant stood and began removing plates that had been wiped so clean Jeremiah thought they would need only a minimum of scrubbing. Lydia, Greta and Bettina helped, making short work of clearing the table. Pleasant took small clear plates from an open shelf and handed them to Bettina. "We have Herr Troyer's ice cream and your favorite pie, Papa."

"Ah, shoo-fly pie." Gunther sighed patting his ample stomach.

"We can have both?" Henry asked.

"Ice cream *and* pie?" Will chorused.

"A taste of ice cream," Pleasant replied not looking

at Jeremiah. "Remember, we are only giving our opinion to Herr Troyer."

The twins nodded solemnly and waited for their sister to serve each person a dessert of a slice of still-warm, shoo-fly pie topped with a small mound of mango ice cream. Will shoveled the ice cream into his mouth then looked at Henry for his opinion.

"Well?" Jeremiah asked.

"I'm going to need another taste," Henry announced.

"Me, too," Will said.

"I agree. Seems to me if we're to have any hope of coming out even between the pie and the ice cream we're all going to need more," Gunther said passing his plate forward.

Jeremiah took some ice cream and pie onto his fork and tasted it. He savored the mix of flavors. The cool subtle vanilla with the sweet bits of mango mingled with the molasses, cinnamon, nutmeg and ginger of the pie filling. "This is it," he murmured, taking a second bite and imagining the flavors mixed with chocolate ice cream or butter pecan or... "This is the cone we need. Shoo-fly cones," he announced.

It was ludicrous, of course, Pleasant thought later as she washed the last of the dessert plates and paid little attention to her half sisters chattering on about the handsome—and eligible—Jeremiah Troyer. The unique flavor of shoo-fly pie came from the pie filling, not the crust. How did he expect her to turn a pudding-like filling into something sturdy enough to hold ice cream? And yet the challenge had been there in the way his eyes had sought hers across the table.

But this was no game such as the one he had played with the twins to finish their vegetables. This was a business challenge, one that could mean the difference between a substantial increase in business for the bakery and none at all if Jeremiah decided to go elsewhere. She paused in her washing to gaze out the kitchen window. Although the sun had set, she knew that she was facing the fields—the empty barren fields, the fields that would not only yield little if any produce but would surely yield even less income.

The drought that was choking much of the country had not spared Florida and this season's crops had been sparse indeed even for those who had been wise enough to plan for such contingencies. After the disastrous spring harvest, Moses Yoder had warned her that after paying the field hands there would be little left from the sale of the crops. Then over the unusually hot summer months, strong westerly winds combined with the drought to blow away a good portion of the soil. In fact, dust was so thick in the air that most people in the community had taken to keeping their windows closed in spite of the heat. It was either that or dust furnishings and wash floors daily. Others had managed to eke out a small harvest, but not Pleasant.

"Do you think he left a girlfriend back in Ohio?" Greta asked and it took a moment before Pleasant realized that the question had been directed at her.

"Who?"

Greta rolled her eyes. "Herr Troyer. Who have we been talking about since he and Papa left?"

"I have no idea," Pleasant replied. *And I have no time for girlish fantasies.*

"Are you truly going to try and create a shoo-fly ice cream cone?" the more practical Lydia asked as she took the stack of dessert plates from Pleasant and placed them back on the shelf.

"Of course," she snapped impatiently, exhausted by all the many problems she faced. But then she softened her tone and smiled at her half sister, the schoolmarm. "After all, that's the assignment."

Lydia gave her an uncertain smile. "You've taken on so much since Merle died, Pleasant. You need some help."

"She needs a husband," Greta said with all the certainty of one who was enough of a romantic to believe that any problem could be solved through marriage to the right man.

"Greta!" Lydia admonished, her voice a warning.

"I had a husband," Pleasant reminded Greta, whose mouth had formed a perfect circle with the realization of what she'd just said.

"Oh, sister, I am so sorry."

Pleasant accepted the apology with a wave of her hand. "It's late and the evening was an interesting one. Your mind is on other matters."

Greta grinned, her good spirits restored. "Like Jeremiah Troyer?" She sighed. "Did you see his eyes?"

Lydia heaved a sigh of resignation and wrapped her arm around her younger sister. "Herr Troyer is too old for you, Greta, so stop daydreaming about his eyes. Besides, what would Josef Bontrager say if he could hear you now?"

"Oh, I'm just having a little fun. Anyone could see that the only one of us Herr Troyer was looking at tonight was Pleasant," she added with a mischievous smile.

Pleasant laughed. "Go home both of you. It's late and I still have work to do."

Long into the night she sat at the kitchen table scribbling notes as she tried to come up with the formula for creating a crisp cookie cone from a recipe for pie filling. When the rooster crowed at four, she startled awake and realized she'd fallen asleep at the table. She stretched and then pumped water into the kitchen sink to splash on her sleep-laden eyelids. She stirred the embers of the fire in the wood stove and set a pot of barley oats on top to simmer.

Bettina would finish making breakfast for her brothers, wash the dishes and get the twins to Hilda's on her way to school. Meanwhile, Rolf would milk the cow, feed the chickens, collect the eggs and deliver them to the bakery on his way to school. As Pleasant let herself out of the house and started down the road to the silent and dark bakery, she thanked God for the blessing of these children. They might not be hers by birth, but they were hers by circumstance and not a dawn passed that she didn't plead with God to show her the way to guide them properly.

The eastern sky showed only a glimmer of the day to come as Pleasant passed the dry goods store. She glanced up and saw a dark figure sitting on the front stoop of the bakery. She hesitated. It was not uncommon these days for homeless transients to find their way to the village and plead for food or money. Most were harmless, but she'd heard some disturbing stories.

She kept her distance and called out to the man. "Hello? May I help you, sir?"

The man started and she realized he'd been dozing. He stood, stretched and then started walking her way. "I had a thought about those shoo-fly cones," Jeremiah Troyer said and Pleasant let out a relieved breath that she hadn't realized she'd been holding.

"It's you? At this hour?"

He was close enough for her to see his grin in the leftover light of the moon and stars that had still filled the predawn sky. "Couldn't sleep," he admitted as he fell into step with her and followed her around to the back door of the bakery. "Do you want to hear my idea?"

Do I have a choice? she thought as she tallied the number of loaves she still needed to get baked and ready for Gunther to deliver in just a few hours to the Sarasota grocer he'd contracted with. "Of course," she replied as she prepared to stack wood from the supply outside the back door into the skirt of her apron.

"Let me do that," Jeremiah said relieving her of the two logs she'd already gathered.

She held the door open for him. "Just stack them in the wood box next to…"

He was still standing outside the door. "You don't lock the door?"

"No," she replied. "Papa believes that if someone wants in, a locked door won't matter."

"But what if someone were waiting?"

"Someone was," she reminded him. "This morning."

"You know what I mean," he grumbled as he dumped the load of wood into the wood box and then turned his attention to poking the fire that Gunther had already started for her.

"What's this idea of yours?" she asked, realizing that if she was to get her regular orders filled she would first need to deal with Jeremiah.

He looked back over his shoulder at her, his face lit by the flames of the fire. "What if instead of adding the molasses and spices to the dough of the cones, we made up a kind of filling and dipped the cones into it before adding the ice cream?" His smile faltered when she did not immediately respond. "Well, what do you think?" He stood and shut the iron door to the stove and dusted off his hands.

"I think you would end up with a soggy, sticky mess," she replied matter-of-factly as she uncovered a mound of dough she'd left to rise overnight and pounded her fist into its center.

"Oh," he said. "Well, what if…" He seemed at a loss to finish the thought. "You're sure it wouldn't work? A kind of a syrup?"

In the shadows of the kitchen it was hard to see his expression now that he had moved away from the fire, but the disappointment in his voice spoke volumes. Pleasant felt a twinge of sympathy for the man. After all, he had clearly been up most of the night just as she had. "You've only just come up with this idea of shoo-fly cones, Herr Troyer. Perhaps it's not too much to expect that it may take a day or so to perfect it?"

He stood next to the worktable and drummed his fingers on its surface. "Patience has never been one of my virtues, I'm afraid." He glanced around. "Should I light some lamps?"

"No need to waste the kerosene. It will be light soon, Herr Troyer, and the work I'm doing does not require light." *Although perhaps being alone with a man in the shadows does,* she thought and was about to reconsider his offer when he let out a sigh that could be translated as nothing but exasperation.

"Look, Pleasant, I guess I can understand the Herr Troyer business when we're in public or with your children, but when it's just the two of us and we're working toward the same end wouldn't given names be… easier?"

"I just…"

"Try it—Jer-e-mi-ah." He sounded out each syllable as if teaching her a new language.

To her surprise and consternation she felt a bubble of laughter tickle her throat. "Jer-e-mi-ah," she repeated in an exaggeration of his instruction and she was very glad that he could not see her smile.

"Excellent," he announced. "Now try it in a sentence."

She stopped kneading the dough. "This is foolishness," she said. "I have work to do."

"This is foolishness, Jer-e-mi-ah," he repeated. "I have work to do, Jer-e-mi-ah."

"You are trying my patience, Jer-e-mi-ah," she chanted and pounded the dough with fresh enthusiasm. She heard the clink of harness and the muffled hoofbeats of a horse outside. "That will be Rolf come to bring the milk and eggs," she said as she wiped her hands on a flour sack towel and headed for the back door.

"Should I hide in the wood box, Pleasant?"

"Don't be silly. You'd ruin your clothes. Hide under the table there."

She went out to help Rolf, but not before she distinctly heard him murmur, "Well now who would have thought that Pleasant Obermeier has a most pleasant sense of humor?"

Chapter Six

Pleasant went about her regular chores at the bakery almost without thought. Her mind was now fully occupied in coming up with a workable recipe for the cones. While she waited for the loaves of bread and the few pies and pastries she kept in the front display case to bake, she played with some scraps of leftover dough. First she wadded them into a smooth ball and then rolling the ball flat as she tried to decide how thick a cone might need to be. Then she turned her attention to the real issue—how to incorporate the ingredients that made a shoo-fly pie so rich and sweet into the dough.

She took a bit of ginger, cinnamon, nutmeg and cloves, and ground them into a fine powder using a mortar and pestle. The fragrance of the combined spices filled the air and she savored their rich exotic scent. No perfume devised by man could ever compete with that. She mixed dark brown sugar in with the spices and set them aside. Then she picked up the jug of dark molasses and studied it as if the answer to her quandary might be found in simply holding the container.

"How's it coming?"

She had been so engrossed in thought that she'd failed to hear Jeremiah's step on the porch outside the kitchen door. "Slowly," she admitted.

Apparently, he saw that as his invitation to come inside. He considered the ingredients lined up on the worktable. Pleasant scraped up the dough and kneaded it back into a ball. "Let me show you something," she said as she rolled out the dough, then lifted an edge. "Do you think that's thick enough or too thick?"

"Looks just right to me."

"Good. Then the problem becomes how to take the dough, the spices and the molasses and put them together."

"May I?" Jeremiah reached for the bowl of powdered spices and when Pleasant nodded, he sprinkled a small amount across the surface of the dough. "Will that work once you bake it?"

"I think so, but let's see," Pleasant said as she slid the pastry dough onto a pan and placed it in the hot oven. "There's still the problem of the molasses," she reminded him.

"Do we really need molasses?"

"If you want to advertise the cones as 'shoo-fly' cones you do," Pleasant said. "Molasses is the heart of any recipe for shoo-fly pie."

"*We* do, Pleasant. This is a joint venture—a partnership."

The aroma of the spices was enhanced by baking as Pleasant checked the oven to be sure the pastry did not burn.

"Is it done?" Jeremiah asked, coming closer to peer into the oven.

"Yes." She tried not to think about how disconcerting it was to have him so close to her. His actions were perfectly innocent—he was excited about the prospect of coming up with a recipe that worked. It had nothing to do with any desire he might entertain to be closer to her.

She removed the pan from the oven and carried it to the worktable. "Let it cool," she admonished when he reached to break off a piece and then juggled it from hand to hand like a hot potato.

He grinned and popped it into his mouth. "Mmm," he murmured, eyes closed and a smile on his lips. "That's delicious."

Pleasant broke off a small bite and blew on it before putting it on her tongue. He was right. The spices and brown sugar had added something special to the bland taste of the pie dough. "We still need the molasses," she said.

Jeremiah's smile widened to a grin. "Yes, *we* do," he said. "But it's a good start. I'll leave you to it. Let me know if you come up with anything you need me to taste." He took his hat from the peg by the door and headed back across the yard to his own shop.

Pleasant picked up the rest of the pastry and nibbled at it as she watched him go. Greta was right about one thing. Jeremiah Troyer was one handsome man.

It was later that night, long after the bakery and other businesses had closed for the day, that Jeremiah came up with the answer. It happened when he was painting the last of the shop's walls and accidentally dropped a scrap of cardboard into the bucket of paint. He fished it out and held it for a moment, letting the excess paint drip off it. It reminded him of what Pleasant had said about his idea of dipping the cones in molasses.

"A soggy sticky mess," he muttered to himself as he carefully deposited the sodden cardboard in the dustbin. He continued painting and thinking about the molasses. And then it hit him and he was so excited to share the idea with Pleasant that he set his paintbrush to soak in a jar of turpentine, grabbed his hat and left for her house at a jog.

The house was dark except for a single amber light in an upstairs window. He glanced at the sky, pitch black and clouded over. All the way back down the street, not a light shone from any house. It was late. He looked back at Pleasant's house. The upstairs light was out now. Dejected, he turned to go but then heard the unmistakable squeak of a screen door opening and closing and followed the sound around to the back of the house.

"Pleasant?" he called in a whisper.

"Who's there?" Her voice held no fear, only curiosity. She was silhouetted by a single lamp in the kitchen as she dumped out a pan of water over the porch railing.

"It's me—Jeremiah. Sorry to bother you so late and all, but I had this idea."

No answer but she did not move away from the door.

"About the molasses," he continued. "What if we mixed a little into the batter? Not so much as to make it impossible for the dough to harden after baking, but..."

A dog barked and a horse snorted in the neighboring yard. Pleasant glanced toward the sound and then took a step back into the house. "It's late, Herr Troyer. Surely this can wait."

He sighed and advanced a step closer. "It's Jeremiah, remember? And yes, it can wait but I won't get any sleep and I doubt you will either thinking about the possibility, wondering if maybe…"

"All right," she said impatiently, still glancing around as if fearing to be caught at something illegal. "I'll try mixing up some samples tonight and let you know in the morning. That's the best I can offer, Jeremiah." This last was delivered in a whisper that pleaded with him to understand the position he was putting her in and pleased him enormously with her inclusion of his given name.

"Fair enough," he whispered back. "Thank you, Pleasant. See you in the morning."

Recognizing that trying to sleep would be an exercise in futility, Jeremiah spent the rest of the night completing the painting and scrubbing the wood floor of his shop. By four in the morning he had placed the half dozen iron-legged round tables and matching chairs around the shop's freshly stained counter and unpacked and washed the sundae dishes and tall soda glasses that would line the glass shelves behind it.

The sky in the east had just turned a paler shade of charcoal when he went outside and took up his position on the front stoop of the bakery. And only minutes later he saw her coming down the dusty road. She was carrying something—a tray, he thought and pushed himself to his feet to go and meet her.

"Well?" he asked when they were not three yards apart.

"I have some samples," she said and handed him the tray. Then to his surprise she just kept walking to the bakery.

"Wait. Aren't we going to try them?"

"I have tried them, Jeremiah, and I have other orders to fill. You'll let me know what you think."

He caught up with her, balancing the small tray with the dish towel spread over its contents. "What did you think?"

"It doesn't matter what I think. You are the customer here. It only matters if you are satisfied."

"But…"

"I have work to do, Jeremiah, and as you predicted I did not get much sleep last night, so please, let me get to it." She did not wait for his response, but instead walked up the front steps of the bakery and went inside closing the glass-paneled door firmly behind her.

Jeremiah took the tray to his shop and set it on the counter. When he removed the cover he found five triangular cookies. He picked one up and broke off a small piece, taking note of its rich deep brown color and the unmistakable scent of cinnamon as he bit into it. In quick succession he performed the same ritual with the other four samples. Some were paler in color—a golden tan flecked with darker bits of the spices in one case— and others were even darker than the first sample. The thing they all had in common was that they were delicious, and while he could distinguish subtle differences in them, he could not possibly choose one over the other.

He saw Rolf driving the wagon loaded with eggs and milk from the farm to the bakery, his sister and the twins riding with him this morning. *"Guten morgen,"* he called as he exited his shop, bringing the tray of cookies with him. "I wonder if I could trouble you children to help me with a small problem."

Rolf and Bettina exchanged a glance. As usual Bettina spoke for the two of them. "We have school and the twins are late for Auntie Hilda's and…"

"This will only take a minute," he promised as he handed Bettina the tray. "Would you and your brothers taste each of these and tell me which one you prefer?"

Bettina broke off small pieces and passed them around to her three brothers. Each child accepted the bite, chewed it thoughtfully and then waited for the next sample.

"This one," Bettina said pointing to the rich dark brown sample.

"Me, too," the twins chorused.

"And you, Rolf?" Jeremiah asked.

"I like them all," he admitted. "But if you're going to make ice cream cones with one of them, then that one."

Jeremiah grinned. "It's unanimous then. Let's go and tell your mother so she can start baking and I can change that sign to post an actual date for the grand opening."

The idea for using her recipe for molasses cookies as the foundation for making the cones had struck Pleasant just after three that morning. Why hadn't she thought of it before? She tried different ways of incorporating the spices into the recipe until she had found what she considered to be as close to the taste of shoo-fly pie filling in a cookie form that could be achieved. When Jeremiah entered the bakery, the children trailing behind him, and held up the darkest of the cookies she'd given him to sample, she could not help but smile.

"This one," he announced. "It's unanimous."

All four children nodded.

"Go on with you," she fussed, shooing the children out the door. "You'll be late for school and your Aunt Hilda will wonder what's keeping the twins."

"But we won't tell her," Bettina said with a conspiratorial glance at Jeremiah. "No one must know about the shoo-fly cones until the grand opening. Isn't that right, Herr Troyer?"

"That's right. It's a secret," he added, focusing his attention on the twins. "Remember?"

Solemnly the twins nodded, then giggled as their sister led them from the bakery.

"I'll unload the milk and eggs," Rolf mumbled.

"I'll give you a hand," Jeremiah said, following the boy out to the street. "Wouldn't want to make you late for school," he added with a glance back at Pleasant.

Relieved and pleased—in spite of her lack of sleep—to have finally given Jeremiah the product he needed, Pleasant turned her attention to her regular baking. Almost by rote she took up the mound of dough she'd left to rise overnight and began dividing it into smaller lumps. From outside she could hear the metallic drumbeat of the milk canisters being moved from the wagon to the back stoop and the occasional jingle of harness as the horse impatiently stamped a hoof or shook off an annoying fly. Rolf and Jeremiah were talking, but in such low tones that she could not make out the words. She heard Jeremiah laugh and it made her smile. It occurred to her that he would be a good parent—kind and patient. *Not like Merle was,* she thought and shook it off as disloyal.

After a moment, she heard the clop of the horse's hooves moving around the side of the building. She sighed. Rolf had gotten so caught up in his conversation with Jeremiah that he had forgotten to bring in the eggs.

"Wait," she called, running to the back door and pushing open the screen just as the wagon disappeared. "The eggs," she explained when Jeremiah looked up at her.

"These eggs?" he asked, holding up the wooden crate that they used to transport the eggs from the henhouse to the bakery every morning. He grinned. "I told the boy to get on to school. After all, I wouldn't want to be responsible for making him have to explain himself to your sister. She strikes me as a no-nonsense, and no-excuses, teacher."

"Lydia is an excellent teacher," Pleasant replied, unable to keep the shadow of defensiveness from her tone. She couldn't help wondering if in time, Jeremiah Troyer would come to understand that life here was difficult and people were quite serious about their work.

"I'm sure she is and as such she would find it hard to believe an excuse such as 'Sorry I'm late, Fraulein. I had to taste some ice cream cone samples.'" His voice had risen to a ridiculous falsetto with the excuse.

Pleasant fought a smile and held the door for him to
carry in the egg crate. "Just set it there," she said, mo-
tioning to a side counter. "Thank you for helping Rolf
with the delivery. He takes his studies very seriously
and really hates being late—for anything."

"A good quality." She could feel his eyes on her as
if he were studying her. "You're a good mother, Pleasant."

"They are good children."

"You and your husband had no children together?"
He sucked in a breath and added, "I apologize. That is
not my business."

She focused on filling the row of tin loaf pans lined
up like toy soldiers along the edge of the long worktable. "It's all right. No, we were not blessed. We were
married only a short time before his accident."

"My great-uncle John said he was kicked by a
horse?"

"Yes."

"I'm sorry for your loss. It must be hard for you and
the children."

"Yes."

"My mother…after my father died…she…his death
was very hard on her," he said. "I don't think she was
strong enough to manage the way you seem to have
done."

"Your family went to live with your father's brother?"

Jeremiah nodded and she did not miss the way his
normally amiable features hardened in a way that reminded her of Merle's face whenever he thought of
something unpleasant. "My uncle." He bit off each

syllable as if the words left a bad taste in his mouth. He turned his attention to studying the contents of the shelves that lined the kitchen walls. An uncomfortable silence settled over the room like the fine flour dust that covered every surface.

"May I ask you a question?" Pleasant ventured.

"Of course."

"Why have you never married?" She felt the heat rise to her cheeks. She must be overtired to ask such a thing and wished with all her being that she could take back the words. It was the kind of thing Greta would ask, although her younger half-sister would do so with a flirtatious lilt to her voice.

But Jeremiah seemed unmoved by the personal nature of her question. He chuckled and shrugged. "Some men are not meant to settle down."

"You're very good with children," she said.

"I like children. They give me hope for a better future for all of us." He smiled. "Young Rolf, for example. And Bettina. She will be an exceptional young woman." He pushed himself away from the counter where he had been leaning and watching her work. "By the way, I asked Rolf to come by the shop after school. I have some work to be done—washing the front window and such. Is that all right?"

"Did he agree?"

"Not really. He said we'd have to ask you first. So I'm asking."

"It's all right as long as he is home before dusk to take care of his chores there." Pleasant cracked an egg and shifted the halves back and forth until the white had run into a small dish. She set the yolk in a second dish then dampened a pastry brush with the egg white and brushed the tops of the loaves of uncooked bread. She was aware that Jeremiah was watching her and her hand shook. "Was there something else?"

"Well, yeah. I mean, don't you want to talk about the next steps for making the cones? Now that we have the recipe we have to figure out how best to create the actual product."

"I thought that I would…"

"Do you have a waffle iron?" He glanced around the shelves of the kitchen as if searching for the instrument.

"Yes, at home," she replied.

"Peter Osgood had this way of making cones on a waffle iron and then rolling them into a cone just at the right moment."

"That sounds like a lot of work," Pleasant said as she set the tin loaf pans into the oven and then wiped away drops of perspiration from her temples with the back of one hand. "How many cones will you need for your grand opening?"

He shrugged. "How many folks live here—I mean, in the Amish district?"

"Counting children? Around a hundred and twenty."

She watched as he mentally calculated the need. "A gross then just to be on the safe side."

She tried not to show her surprise. "You know best, of course," she murmured.

"But you don't agree?"

"It's just that with hard times and all, even the people here have had to watch pennies. I don't think you can really count on every single person buying ice cream from you on your opening day."

His eyes twinkled when she might have expected a frown. "But what if the ice cream were free?"

"Free? You cannot do business by giving away your wares, Jeremiah."

He chuckled. "Ah, Pleasant, once they have a taste of my ice cream and your shoo-fly cones? Why, we'll have regular customers for as long as we're in business." He picked up the last piece of her samples and studied it for a moment. "Do you think you could make a smaller version? A size just large enough to hold about a heaping tablespoon of ice cream?"

"I suppose, but why…"

"If we did smaller cones, people could sample more than one flavor of ice cream. We could do a survey and see which flavor was the most popular, and then…"

He glanced at her and then popped the last bit of the sample cookie into his mouth. "I see that you remain unconvinced, but mark my words, come the grand opening and you're going to be making me a gross of cones every week just to satisfy the people living here in Celery Fields, Pleasant." He grinned at her. "And that doesn't begin to count the *Englisch,* who will come once I hand out samples to the guys down at the ice plant."

"Speaking of which, shouldn't you be on your way to work by now?"

Jeremiah headed for the door, then paused to tip two fingers to his hat in a mock salute. "One gross," he repeated as he left the bakery. "You'll be convinced

I'm right once you see them line up for ice cream," he called.

Pleasant was convinced of only one thing—as she had suspected all along, Jeremiah Troyer was a dreamer.

Chapter Seven

The grand opening of Troyer's Creamery and Confection Shop took place on a Saturday afternoon in early November when most of the community's residents traditionally gathered in town to do their marketing and other shopping for the coming week. And as he had predicted, the line for free samples of Jeremiah's ice cream stretched out the door and down the street past Yoder's Dry Goods and the hardware store nearly to Pleasant's house. The weather was perfect—sunny without a hint of the usual humidity so typical of Florida. A perfect day for ice cream.

Everyone—even Hilda Yoder—seemed to agree that Jeremiah had planned the perfect opening for his new business. "It's all so very exciting," Hilda gushed when she peeked into the back door of the bakery.

And it certainly sounded that way. Pleasant could hear children racing up and down the street squealing with delight over their favorite flavor. And outside the steamed-up kitchen windows and open doors, she caught glimpses of adults laughing and visiting as they licked ice cream from the tiny cones that Pleasant had created for the occasion.

Of course, Pleasant was so busy in the bakery kitchen turning out batch after batch of regular-size cones that she had to rely on the reports of her half sisters and the children. Lydia and Greta had been recruited by Gunther to help with the baking. They also carried trays of still-warm cones from the bakery to the creamery and then returned with empty trays that they set to refilling. Bettina stirred batch after batch of the batter while the twins sat with their grandfather and tallied up the number of outgoing cones on the hand-operated adding machine he kept on his desk in one corner of the kitchen.

From time to time Pleasant was aware of Jeremiah's laughter wafting between the two shops as he stood at the makeshift counter he'd set up on his shop's front stoop and scooped up ice cream for his customers. He had recruited Rolf to help him and assigned Hannah's son Caleb the task of making sure that no child got into line for a second sample ahead of someone who had not yet been served. And after less than two hours, Jeremiah had sent word that he was going to need more regular-size cones. It seemed that after tasting a sample, people were insisting on buying a full-size cone filled with their favorite flavor and Jeremiah was clearly determined not to disappoint anyone.

In spite of her exhaustion, Pleasant did not mind the ongoing work. She felt as if she were helping to create something that had nothing to do with waffle cones. She was working with Jeremiah and her family to offer the people of Celery Fields a kind of a reprieve from the months of poor crops and hard times that had plagued the small community for over a year now. Jeremiah Troyer had given the people of Celery Fields a great deal more than ice cream. At least for this one afternoon, he had given them a glimpse of better times to come. He had dished up hope.

"Jeremiah says we can stop now," Greta announced as she clattered an empty metal tray onto the table and collapsed on a bench. "He's completely run out of ice cream." There was a rumble of excited chatter from outside and Greta was instantly on her feet grabbing Bettina's hand. "Come on. He's going to announce the winning flavor."

Gunther and the twins hurried after Greta and Bettina, leaving a long tail of adding machine paper curled across the desk. "Are you coming?" Pleasant's father asked but she noticed that he did not wait for her reply.

She walked to the front of the bakery and stood in the open doorway. The crowd had clustered together in front of the creamery and Jeremiah was standing in the midst of them, his smile rivaling the sun for brightness. He held up his hands calling for quiet.

"Thank you, my friends," he said as the chattering throng grew quiet and mothers hushed their small children. "You have made me feel welcomed from the day I arrived, but never more so than today. The flavor you have chosen as the most popular today is…" A hush fell over the crowd. "Plain old vanilla," Jeremiah announced and those gathered around him broke into applause. "I feel so blessed," he continued once the crowd had quieted again. "I would like to ask my great-uncle Bishop Troyer if he would lead us all in a prayer of thanksgiving." He made room for John to join him and as every head bowed, Jeremiah looked over to where Pleasant was standing. And just before she bowed her head, Pleasant had the oddest feeling that everyone else had melted away and there was only Jeremiah—and her.

Forgive me, she prayed silently, shocked at her romantic foolishness. She forced her attention away from the memory of Jeremiah's gaze meeting her own. The half smile that had not quite blossomed across his handsome features. The question that seemed written in his expression. But try as she might to take in the words of thanksgiving that the bishop was offering, she could not seem to keep herself from peeking out beneath lowered lashes. She told herself it was only to confirm her silly imaginings. She saw that Jeremiah had bowed his head as well, but his eyes remained fixed on her.

The success of the opening of the creamery and confectionary had been far beyond anything Jeremiah had imagined. The people had come, drawn no doubt by the promise of free samples. But then they had returned, counting out their pennies to pay for a second cone of ice cream, sharing this larger treat with sweethearts or spouses or grandparents. For every full-size cone he sold, Jeremiah gave away another free sample. He had barely had time to look up but was aware that Pleasant kept a steady supply of freshly baked—and still warm—cones coming his way. Right up until he scraped the last scoop of ice cream from the bottom of the container, Rolf was handing him one cone after another.

"That's it," he said as he filled the last of the small sample cones and handed it to a little girl, a miniature of her mother in a dark cotton dress, a black apron and a stiff white *kapp* that hid most of her brilliant red hair. He turned his attention to Greta. "Go tell your sister that she can stop for today. We are out of ice cream."

Greta took off at a run while Rolf solemnly set about to clean the ice cream scoops and the pails that had held the various flavors. From the porch of Yoder's store, Jeremiah heard a groan as the little girl announced that she had just been given the very last cone. He stepped forward prepared to apologize, but then the crowd had let out a cheer and toasted him with raised half-eaten shoo-fly cones. He could not recall a time in his life when he had felt such happiness and he wondered for one brief moment if indeed his success here would have finally been enough to convince his uncle that he was not the failure the older man had always labeled him.

He shook off the thought and scanned the crowd. He saw his great-uncle and called him forward, but it was not the community's bishop that he'd wanted most to share this day with. It was the woman who had helped to make it all possible. It was Pleasant Obermeier. In her quiet efficient way, she had delivered everything he had asked of her—the unique recipe that would set his business apart, the cones perfectly formed and to whatever scale he required, and a steady supply of them. All without complaint or excuse. She was a remarkable woman and he wanted to thank her but she was nowhere among the men, women and children who crowded around his shop.

Jeremiah frowned and then a movement at the entrance to the bakery caught his eye. She was leaning against the doorjamb, her arms folded into her apron, a bemused smile on her face as she observed a scene that had to be unlike anything she'd ever witnessed in the community before. Suddenly, the distance between them seemed far too great and he wanted to go to her, to tell her what her help had meant to him, to share this moment with her.

She looked over at him and he felt for a moment as if she had understood, but then she frowned and bowed her head, shaking it slightly as if admonishing herself for some wrongdoing. He wondered what this woman could ever do wrong. He thought about the way that she was raising four children—none of them her own. He recalled the way Gunther was practically incapable of making a decision without uttering the words, "We'll see what Pleasant thinks." He thought about the Hadwells and the way they had hinted that Merle Obermeier had been a difficult man.

He felt a bond to Pleasant that had nothing to do with ice cream cones. He marveled at her strength, her boundless energy, her courage to face whatever God might bring her way. As a boy he had often wished that his own mother might take a stand in favor of her children and against the tyranny with which his uncle had reigned. He bowed his head in shame. His mother had done her best to maintain peace in a house that broiled with constant turmoil.

John Troyer took his position as bishop seriously and when asked to pray, he tended to drone on for some time. Most people had grown used to it and kept their heads bowed but in spite of the invitation he had extended for his great-uncle to offer a prayer, Jeremiah seemed incapable of keeping his attention focused on the words. Instead, he kept his head lowered but looked at Pleasant. She was not a beauty in the usual sense. She was too tall, too thin and far too earnest. But, oh, on those rare occasions when she smiled, how it lit her features. Her deep brown eyes sparkled and there was the hint of a dimple in the left corner of her mouth.

She caught him watching her and he looked away, turning his attention from her to the sorry state of his boots as he felt the heat of embarrassment rise to his cheeks. He had to take care, he reminded himself. More than once he had shown interest in a woman for her work ethic or her talent for quilting or cooking and his interest had been misinterpreted. It would not do for a woman like Pleasant—a woman who by all reports had a disappointing history in matters of the heart—to think that his interest was in any way…romantic.

"Amen," the crowd murmured in unison and then broke into smaller groups as they made their way back down the main street toward their buggies and wagons. "Amen," Jeremiah whispered, then turned to give John the traditional one-pump handshake Amish men shared. "Thank you."

"Thank you," John replied. "I'm not sure you understand how much this day has meant to the people of this community. It's been a long time since they were able to enjoy such an afternoon. God has blessed us all."

"I should go and settle my account with Gunther," Jeremiah said, nodding toward Pleasant's father who had returned to the bakery and was now holding a long streamer of paper. "Looks like I might have quite a tally there."

John laughed. "You'll join us for services tomorrow and Sunday dinner? We're meeting at Levi Harnisher's farm."

"I will," Jeremiah agreed. "Have a good evening, Uncle."

"And you."

Jeremiah watched his great-uncle head for home and realized that he was postponing the inevitable. He needed to go to the bakery and meet with Gunther and he still had not properly thanked Pleasant for what she had done to make the day such a success. He'd seen a wild orchid blooming in the tree behind the creamery, but such a gift would be far too open to misinterpretation—by her and anyone who might witness him giving it to her. No, a simple thank you was all that was called for.

He walked to the bakery planting each footstep in the soft sand of the street as if to break stride might cause him to lose his nerve and return to his own shop. "Herr Goodloe," he called out as he reached the steps leading up to the bakery entrance. "I expect you have a bill to present."

Gunther was grinning widely. "Indeed I do and you may just regret giving away all that free ice cream."

Jeremiah smiled and held out his hand. "Let's see the damage," he said. The count of full-size cones had reached several dozen and the smaller sample cones came to more than a gross.

Jeremiah let out a long low whistle and Gunther chuckled. "Told you," he said, then he sobered. "Thank you, Jeremiah. I won't pretend we can't use the money. It's a blessing in so many ways."

"I thought that the bakery was still…"

Gunther shook his head and glanced toward the door, then lowered his voice. "It's the farmers that are suffering. Those that joined the cooperative in the first place will be all right—they'll struggle but they'll make it."

"And Pleasant?"

Gunther looked away. "Moses Yoder tells me that with the mucklands pretty much dried up, the crops will suffer. The other farms—those that are part of the cooperative—have the advantage of the drainage system built a few years back. But Merle was one stubborn man when it came to having anything to do with outsiders." He sighed heavily. "Unless we have an unusually wet month, there's not much sense in Pleasant trying to plant a winter crop."

"I had no idea," Jeremiah said and felt ashamed of the triumph he'd been feeling over his own good fortune. "What can I do to help?"

Gunther shook his head. "We'll get past this. Pleasant knows she and the kids always have a place with me and they own the house and land free and clear, although certainly there's no market for selling a house or land these days. But she's stubborn. Her mother was the same." He smiled at the memory, then he grasped Jeremiah's hand. "The kids know nothing though and they had a hard enough time of things when their father was alive. I know Rolf is helping out some at your place, but…"

"I wouldn't discuss such a thing with the boy—or anyone," Jeremiah assured the older man.

Gunther smiled with relief. He was something of a talker and Jeremiah expected that he regretted having revealed so much.

"Now then," Jeremiah said, "shall we settle this account?"

Gunther grinned and led the way into the bakery's kitchen. Pleasant busied herself directing her half sisters and Bettina in cleaning up from the day's baking and preparing the kitchen for a fresh start come Monday morning. She glanced at him and nodded but said nothing as Jeremiah followed Gunther to his desk in the corner and took a seat.

"Check my figures," Gunther advised as he pushed a paper filled with penciled calculations across the desk to Jeremiah.

"Looks fine," Jeremiah replied, barely glancing at the paper. His mind was still reeling with the notion that while he had been pushing her to come up with a recipe for ice cream cones, she had been facing serious problems of her own and never said a word. Oh, once or twice she had alluded to the need to attend to her own business, but he had assumed she meant getting the standard bakery orders filled. It had never occurred to him that she might be talking about the huge tract of land her late husband had acquired and left for her to manage with Moses Yoder's help. No wonder half the time the woman looked as if she could use a good night's sleep.

He opened the small tin box that he'd used as the cash box for the opening and counted out the money he owed Gunther. "I'll be closed tomorrow, of course, and I think Monday as well." He laughed. "It will take some time to make more ice cream and I'll have to work on that between my shifts at the ice plant and making my regular deliveries. If you could deliver half the week's order of cones on Tuesday and then the rest on Friday, that ought to work out fine."

"Ja," Gunther replied as he stashed the money in a worn cloth bag and placed it in a desk drawer that he locked.

"Will that be all right, Pleasant?" Jeremiah asked.

She glanced up from scrubbing the last of the pots. "Of course," she replied, the words clipped and impatient as if he had expressed some doubt in her ability to deliver the goods.

Jeremiah could not help but wonder what had happened in the woman's past to make her so defensive, so quick to assume that she was being questioned. She turned her attention back to her work, quietly instructing Bettina in how best to dry the large container without dripping water all over the floor. Where her tone with him had been abrupt and defensive, he noticed that when she spoke to the girl her voice was soft and gentle and she was quick to give Bettina a smile when she followed instructions to the letter.

Gunther pushed his chair away from the desk and stood up. "It was a good day for the ice cream business," he noted as he offered Jeremiah a handshake.

Jeremiah stood as well and accepted Gunther's hand, knowing that what went unspoken was the fact that the two of them had just launched a kind of partnership that was sure to benefit both their businesses. "And the bakery business," he added with a smile.

He was reluctant to leave until he had thanked Pleasant properly for all her help. Yet at the same time he didn't want to embarrass her by doing so in front of her father, half sisters and the children. He decided it might be best to write her a note and leave it for her to find on Monday when she came to open the bakery for the day. "Have a good evening," he said, including everyone in his leave-taking. "I'll see you all at services tomorrow?"

"Yes. At Levi's farm," Gunther said as he walked with Jeremiah to the door.

Jeremiah glanced back toward the sink, but Pleasant was focused—as always it seemed—on her work.

Men, Pleasant thought as she scrubbed a nonexistent stain from the sink. Her father and Jeremiah had congratulated one another as if the success of the day had been entirely their doing. She was well aware that jealousy was unworthy of her and she would surely regret the uncharitable feelings she entertained at this moment, but really. Did it not occur to either one of them that she and Bettina and Lydia and Greta had contributed to the day's triumph? Certainly if they had failed to keep up with Jeremiah's constant need for more cones, he could have found an alternative. After all, she had seen the glass sundae dishes and soda glasses that lined the shelves in his shop. But still, for the sake of the others, the man surely could have given some sign that he recognized their efforts.

Pride goeth before a fall, she chastised herself. The arrangement to make ice cream cones was a business collaboration between her father and Jeremiah.

Simple as that. She was the baker in her father's business. Period.

But she could not erase the memory of how Jeremiah's eyes had lit up the day she presented him with the sample cookies. She could not forget how he had come to her house—not her father's—in the dead of night because he had come up with an idea for making the cones. And she had thought often about the hunched lonely figure sitting on the step of the bakery in the predawn darkness waiting for her to deliver the news of whether or not she had been successful.

"Mama?"

Pleasant looked over her shoulder at Bettina standing with Rolf and the twins. It was clear that they had asked something and were waiting for her reply.

"I'm sorry," she said, drying her hands on a damp dish towel. She smiled at them. "Are you four ready for some supper or have you completely spoiled your appetites with ice cream?"

"Aunt Hilda and Uncle Moses have asked us to come for supper," Bettina reminded her.

The invitation had gone completely out of Pleasant's head. "I promised to bring dessert," she murmured.

"It's all right," Bettina assured her. "I boxed up the last dozen sugar cookies earlier so they wouldn't get sold as everything else did."

Rolf glanced at the clock on the wall behind them. Hilda—like her brother Merle—did not like for anyone to be late.

"We'll have to hurry then," Pleasant said, smoothing back the twins' hair and scrubbing their faces with the damp dish towel. "Where's your Grandpa Gunther?"

"He's outside talking to some people. He said we should go on and he would make sure everything was closed up."

Pleasant nodded. She knew that this meant her father would collect the money that Jeremiah had given him and that he'd locked away for safekeeping in the desk. He wouldn't leave it in the bakery overnight. Times were too uncertain to trust that some vagrant might not come looking for food and decide to see if there was any cash on the premises while he was at it.

"All right, then we'd best hurry." She held hands with the twins and followed Rolf and Bettina out the door and up the street to the home of Moses and Hilda Yoder. The house was not as large as Merle's house, but in many ways it was far more welcoming. The Yoder children were all playing in the yard when they arrived and Pleasant sent her four children to join them while she took the box of cookies and walked around the side of the house and into Hilda's kitchen.

"I'm sorry we're late," she apologized, even though they had made it with minutes to spare. "It took longer than I thought to…"

"Moses needs to see you in the front room," Hilda said without preamble. "Supper can wait."

Pleasant set the box of cookies on the sideboard and walked down the short passageway that led from the kitchen past the stairway to the front of the house. Moses Yoder was seated in the overstuffed chair near the fireplace. When he saw Pleasant, he set aside the newspaper he'd been reading and rose to greet her. "Come sit here," he invited, indicating Hilda's rocking chair opposite him.

His tone and demeanor gave Pleasant every indication that he was about to deliver news she didn't want to hear.

"It's the farm," she said as she collapsed wearily into the rocking chair and faced him.

"Yes. I'm sorry, Pleasant, but I see no possibility that we can salvage it. Perhaps if Merle had been willing to join the cooperative, there would be some way…"

"I understand," she assured him and set the chair to rocking as she stared blankly out the front window. Outside, she could hear Merle's children laughing and squealing as they played a game of hide-and-seek with their cousins. She had done the one thing that would mark her as a failure in Merle's eyes more than anything else. She had failed to protect the farm that had been the mark of his success as a husband and father. The land that he had preached to Rolf would one day be his. The legacy that even as she laid her husband to rest, Pleasant had promised him she would protect.

Moses cleared his throat. "The drought can't last forever," he said, although what comfort this might offer Pleasant she couldn't fathom. "And you own the property free and clear."

She glanced at him and saw his misery. "Moses, you have done what you could and I am grateful for that. Please don't blame yourself. This is God's will and while it may be difficult for us to understand now, in time…"

"What I'm saying, Pleasant, is that perhaps in a year or so, the land will have value. Until then you have the house and you have the community."

She understood that he was telling her that her neighbors would help out. If there were repairs to be done, they would help. It was their way. "If we have a wet winter, then perhaps…"

Moses shook his head. "Even so, it will take more than one season before the soil is revived enough to support crops of any sort, Pleasant."

She nodded. "Thankfully, our needs are small," she whispered even as she thought of the four growing children. But she forced a smile as she met Moses's gaze. "We'll be fine. Thank you again, Moses."

"We are here for you, Pleasant," he told her. "You know that. The entire community."

"I do and I thank God for that blessing." She stood up and he did as well. "I should help Hilda," she said and fled from the room before her brother-in-law could see the tears that had already begun leaking down her cheeks.

Chapter Eight

At services the following morning, Pleasant felt as if she were literally dragging herself along. At supper the night before, Hilda and Moses had exchanged several meaningful glances, but had blessedly allowed the chatter of the children to dominate the conversation. And she was grateful to them for that. It certainly was not Hilda's habit to be so respectful and on reflection, it made Pleasant think that her loss was far more devastating than she had yet realized.

Exhausted as she had been after a day filled with endless baking, she had stayed up long after the children were asleep going over and over her household accounts. She had taken away what little remained of the money that in the past had flowed into her accounts from the sale of the crops. Before the drought that had been a sizeable sum, but over the past year it had dwindled significantly. She had never taken anything from the bakery. That was her father's business and it had provided for her before her marriage to Merle, but after that, her husband had provided whatever she or the children might need. And after his death, the legacy he had left behind had continued to fill their needs.

But now the resources for bringing cash into the household had dried up with the land that stretched uselessly beyond her back door for acres and acres. It was worthless now according to Moses, unlikely to come back to life any time in the foreseeable future. The bakery was barely bringing in enough to cover the cost of supplies and provide for Gunther and her half sisters. Of course, with the business that Jeremiah was bringing them there was always the possibility that the two families could pool their resources and make do. But Jeremiah Troyer was a dreamer and the likelihood that he would need the steady supply of cones he had ordered was remote at best.

Yes, the grand opening had gone well beyond anything she might have imagined, but that was one day and the reality of the times told her that it could not possibly last.

Pleasant went over and over the numbers and in the end came up with the same result. She and the children would become dependent on others—their charity, their hand-me-downs, their pity. *I hate this,* she had thought miserably as she laid her head on her folded arms and fell asleep.

She had awakened at her usual hour on Sunday, her back stiff from sitting in the hard kitchen chair all night. She had made breakfast for the children and supervised their preparations for attending services. For herself, she had taken only a cup of strong black coffee. If they were going to have to cut back then she was determined to make sure that the children had plenty to eat. By the time Rolf had driven them to the Harnisher farm in the buggy, they were already late and Pleasant was feeling jittery and out of sorts and hardly in the mood to consider what God might need of her in the days to come. For it was their way, she sternly reminded herself as she climbed down from the buggy and herded the children across the yard, to come to worship in a spirit of understanding how they might best serve God—not how He might remove their burden.

One lesson that Jeremiah had learned growing up in a small community was that even pious people could not resist the temptation of gossip. So when he arrived for services at the Harnisher farm the next morning, he wasn't surprised to see people gathered in small groups, their heads inclined toward one another, their combined whispers sounding like the hum of bees as he parked his buggy and walked across the yard. What confused him was that their conversation seemed to focus on something serious rather than the retelling of the grand opening of his shop a day earlier as he might have expected. Even the children seemed subdued as if they had gleaned from their parents and other adults the need to speak only in whispers and to sit quietly together rather than running about.

Fearing that some tragedy had befallen one of the church members, he went inside the modest home looking for his uncle. Along the way he realized that he was scanning the faces of the similarly garbed women looking for Pleasant. There was no sign of her. Had she taken ill? Or perhaps it was the children. He quickened his step moving down the hallway from the rear entrance of the house to the front.

"Guten morgen," Levi Harnisher greeted him.

Jeremiah had met the Harnisher family when he and Levi had discussed arrangements for Levi to provide the cream that Jeremiah would need to make his ice cream. Levi had laughingly told him that he had tried his hand at raising the celery and other produce that others had raised with great success. "Then my Hannah—and several others—suggested that with my background in handling animals for the circus it might be wiser to concentrate on raising horses. Later, I added the dairy herd. How can I help you?"

Jeremiah had felt an immediate bond with the man and took no time at all to lay out his need for a steady supply of fresh cream.

"That I can do," Levi had assured him and they had settled on the deal with a simple handshake.

And because Jeremiah trusted Levi not to think he was prying but simply concerned, he asked the question that was uppermost in his mind. "Has something happened to Mrs. Obermeier?"

Levi raised his eyebrows and Jeremiah realized that it was indeed odd for him to be inquiring about the widow so directly.

"It's just that folks seem to be abuzz about something and I thought I heard her name mentioned and I noticed she's not here for services."

His explanation seemed to satisfy Levi who was nodding as he glanced toward the lane that led from the main road to his farm. "She's with my wife." He nodded toward a closed door down a short hall. "She had some bad news yesterday." He hesitated, then added, "It's the farm. Her late husband refused to join the Palmer co-operative. He was a stubborn man."

"But surely her late husband made some provision— if not for her than for the children."

"It's a long story, but several years ago the Palmer family of Chicago came here for the winter and bought a large tract of the muckland that borders the land that Merle bought a few years later. The Palmers put in miles of canals for drainage purposes and started selling pieces of the land off to individual farmers with the understanding that those farmers would join the Palmer Farms Growers Association."

"Sounds like a good deal."

Levi glanced toward the room where his wife, Hannah, had emerged and was signaling to him. "It was a good deal and for those who took it, the arrangement was a lifesaver. But Merle was one stubborn man and determined to go it alone. And for a number of years he did all right for himself, but he never put in the canals and drainage that might have saved his land during these hard times." He shook his head. "Excuse me, Jeremiah. My wife needs my help."

Out in the yard church members had divided by gender. The women filed in through the back door while the men entered from the front. Separately they took their places on the hard wooden benches that had been unloaded from the wagon used to transport them from home to home and set up in the Harnisher's front room. Jeremiah lingered near the front hallway watching for Pleasant until he heard the congregation start to sing the opening hymn. He had the urge to walk down the hall to see for himself that she was all right. But that would only embarrass her and provide fresh fodder for the community's rumor mill.

He took his place at the end of the second row of benches closest to the front door. As the hymn ended and John and the preacher entered the room, he thought he heard the creak of a door opening and closing. A minute later he saw Pleasant lead the twins to a place in the last row of benches. Bettina and Rolf had already squeezed in on benches occupied by older girls and older boys, respectively. Jeremiah slid over to make room for Gunther, who sat down next to him with a heavy sigh and a weary smile.

By tradition, Amish services ran for three hours, but on this particular Sunday the service seemed interminable to Jeremiah. He had trouble concentrating on the sermons—the first being something about loving your neighbor while the main sermon delivered by his great-uncle John was on the topic of accepting that God would provide—in hard times and good. He couldn't help wondering if that promise was bringing Pleasant any comfort at all.

But his main problem with concentrating on the service was that he was overcome with guilt. How many times over the past weeks had he gone to the bakery—or even her farmhouse—thinking only of what he needed? When had he ever stopped to think about the responsibilities she had taken on in raising her late husband's four children by another woman? Had he once considered what she might be facing because of the drought and the crops that had failed?

Not once, he thought as he hung his head and studied

the polished planks of the Harnisher's floor. He owed her far more than the note of thanks he had placed on the bakery door that morning. He owed her an apology.

Having settled on a plan, Jeremiah was restless for the remainder of the service. So much so that twice others glanced his way and he realized that he was impatiently tapping one foot. He stilled his foot with an apologetic glance at those next to him and forced his concentration to the sermon.

As soon as the service ended, the women—Pleasant with them—headed off to the kitchen to lay out the communal meal they would all share. Older children took charge of their younger siblings while the men set up the benches for the meal. Because some of the benches would be stacked double to form tables, there would not be enough seating for everyone and so they would eat in two shifts. All of this happened without the need for instruction. It was a ritual the congregation had performed for countless Sundays over the years.

Jeremiah helped set the tables and seating all the while keeping an eye out for Pleasant. His need to see her and apologize was nearly overpowering. And yet he knew that to go to the kitchen, to ask to speak with her in front of others, would be the worst possible thing he might do. It would not only embarrass Pleasant, it would raise questions about what kind of man he was. After all, he was still something of a stranger in Celery Fields and Amish communities throughout the country differed widely in what traditions and interpretations of the unwritten laws of the faith—the Orndung— dictated. Something that might hardly raise an eyebrow back in Ohio might be grounds for real concern here in

Florida. Either way, he was fairly sure that a single man taking an unmarried—even widowed—woman aside for a private conversation would definitely not be in the realm of proper behavior.

So when he saw Pleasant Obermeier emerge from the kitchen carrying a large bowl of potato salad, he headed in the opposite direction and forced himself to keep his distance for the remainder of the meal.

Pleasant had endured the genial chatter of the other women trying to disguise their pity. She was well aware that everyone knew what had kept her awake most of the night and made her late for services. She was also aware that this was their way of being sympathetic and supportive. She saw it in their eyes filled with the questions they would not ask. What would she do now? Could she find a buyer for the land or perhaps the house?

"If only Merle had…" one woman began in a hushed voice.

"Perhaps the Palmers," another woman whispered.

But Moses had told her that the land was useless for growing anything and what would the wealthy Chicago family want with a house that was already badly in need of painting and repair?

"We should have a frolic," Hannah announced as a silence fell over the food preparations and everyone seemed at a loss for some way to show Pleasant their concern. "Tomorrow at Pleasant's house?"

The other women hesitated, glancing uncertainly at Pleasant. A frolic was what Amish women called an occasion when they gathered at one of the group's houses and spent the entire day cleaning or cooking or quilting or sometimes all three. The shared work and opportunity to socialize gave the occasion its name.

"The bakery," Pleasant gently reminded her friend.

"Oh, the bakery can last one day without you," Hannah insisted. "Besides, you've always said yourself that Mondays are slow and after the grand opening of the creamery yesterday, I doubt anyone has the money to buy extra baked goods."

"I'll say," Hilda Yoder exclaimed. "I told my brood that if they wanted ice cream then they were facing vinegar pie for a month."

Several women nodded and all eyes returned to Pleasant. She saw Hannah's suggestion for what it was—a way for the women to do something for her without it seeming like charity. "I suppose," she said slowly, "I do have laundry that piled up what with spending so much extra time at the bakery and all." And then she smiled for the first time since hearing Moses's report. "And Papa suggested I needed to get some rest. A day away from the bakery might be just the medicine I need."

The women smiled and were soon engaged in plans for the gathering. Before long, they had come up with a list of things they would do that went well beyond washing and ironing, and would take much longer than a day's hours to accomplish.

"Well, what we don't finish at Pleasant's we can simply move to my house or Hilda's or someone else's," Hannah said. "Our Monday frolic," she announced. "It could become a regular thing."

Pleasant laughed and shook her head. "I think that

husband of yours has influenced you to think in the same grand scale of things that he used when he owned the circus, Hannah."

Her friend blushed as she did whenever Levi was mentioned, even after all this time. Pleasant could not help but wonder if any of the other women gathered around her had experienced such a depth of pure devotion that Hannah shared with Levi. Was that unusual, she couldn't help wondering. Or was the cold silence that she had shared with Merle more the norm? Or more likely most marriages fell somewhere in between. It hardly mattered since she was now widowed and unlikely to ever marry again—at least not for love.

You didn't marry for love when you married Merle, she reminded herself. No, she had married for companionship and security. A companionship that had never blossomed and a security that was now as fragile as the fine dust blowing off the dried up fields that surrounded her home.

"Excuse me," she murmured, still struggling with the overwhelming burden that the news about the farm had thrust upon her. "I need to check on the twins," she added, picking up a bowl of potato salad as she hurried from the room.

The men glanced up from their conversation as she set the bowl on a makeshift table, but then looked immediately away. She supposed that they were also talking about her. She looked around for the children and saw that Bettina was sitting on the porch surrounded by the twins and other small children, telling them a story. She would make a wonderful teacher one day.

She looked for Rolf and saw him with Hannah's son Caleb and some other boys out near the barn.

And then she saw Jeremiah. He was walking out toward the barn. She saw how Rolf's face brightened when he saw Jeremiah coming his way. The time that Rolf had spent helping Jeremiah had been good for the boy. Perhaps she had made a mistake in not accepting Jeremiah's offer to hire the boy for regular chores. At least then she would be able to count on Rolf's continued exposure to the businessman's good influence. And now that the creamery was officially opened, the likelihood that he would be stopping by the bakery or farmhouse to talk about cone recipes was remote.

She would miss that. As exasperated as she had sometimes been with him, his visits had always left her feeling a little lighter, a little more hopeful. Perhaps she would speak with Rolf, assure herself that he could manage his schoolwork, the chores at home and help out at the creamery. After all, work with Jeremiah would teach the boy a trade and now that the farm was for all intents and purposes not the future that Merle had imagined for his eldest child, Rolf would need to find some way to earn his living.

Bettina could teach until she married and Rolf could go into business—perhaps take over the bakery, she thought and silently thanked God for showing her a path that just might lead to a secure future for Rolf and Bettina. The twins had time. She breathed in the warm air and felt better. They would be all right. With God's help she would find a way for her children to be safe and none the wiser of the calamity that had befallen them.

Having decided on a plan, she joined the other mothers in gathering the children and helping the little ones fill their plates, then refilling the serving dishes so that the adults could eat. In the familiarity of routine, the afternoon passed and soon her father was driving them back to the farm.

As soon as he called for the horse to stop in the yard, the children scampered out of the buggy and ran off to change out of their good clothes.

"Pleasant," Gunther said as she climbed down from the buggy, "you can always move in with me," he murmured, his eyes looking straight ahead instead of at her.

"I know that, Papa, but we're going to be all right," she assured him.

He flicked a glance at her and then his mouth tightened as he resumed his gaze into space. "The bakery does a steady business. Perhaps…"

The bakery business had suffered along with every other business in Celery Fields. The standing orders from restaurants and small grocers in nearby Sarasota that had been the mainstay of their business had dwindled to only half what they had been a few years earlier. Without Lydia's small stipend as the community's teacher, Pleasant knew that her father and half sisters would be struggling to make ends meet. "These are hard times, Papa," she said. "But we've seen them before and we no doubt will see them again."

He nodded.

"The thing is before hard times can come again we must have some better times," she said, reminding him of what he had so often told her mother. "Otherwise, it's just hard times all the time." She reached up and placed her hand over his leathery skin. "We're going to be fine, Papa. All of us." And even as she spoke the words she felt an unexplainable comfort in hearing herself voice them.

On Monday, Jeremiah had decided that he would wait until after Rolf made his morning delivery to the bakery and the children were off to school before he went over to speak with Pleasant. He wasn't due at the ice plant until later that morning and he had rehearsed his speech several times, changing the words when he thought he was perhaps being too forward or showing that he might have listened to gossip about her.

He'd been up since before dawn but there had been no sign of her. Then he heard the familiar rumble of the wagon's wheels and went to the window. Gunther and Rolf unloaded the milk and eggs and carried them inside the bakery while Bettina held the reins and waited patiently in the wagon. There was no sign of the twins or of Pleasant. Perhaps the boys were ill, although they had certainly seemed fine after services.

He saw Rolf exit the bakery, nodding at some instruction that Gunther had offered, and then the boy climbed into the wagon with his sister and headed back to the farm. Jeremiah knew the routine. Most days Bettina would have taken her younger siblings to the Yoder house while Rolf delivered the milk and eggs. Then the two of them would return the wagon and then walk to the small wooden building behind Hadwell's hardware that served the community as its one-room schoolhouse.

Jeremiah collected his hat and strolled over to the

bakery's kitchen door. As he passed a window, he saw Gunther sitting at his desk going over some orders.

"*Guten morgen,* Gunther," he called from outside the screen door using the Dutch-German that the older man seemed to prefer.

"Come in, Jeremiah," the older man boomed.

"Is everything all right?" Jeremiah asked. "I saw Rolf and Bettina earlier but not the twins. Are they ill?" It seemed best not to ask about Pleasant directly although in his heart that was the question uppermost.

Gunther smiled. "*Nein.* The women are having a frolic at Pleasant's today and she kept the twins with her since Hilda Yoder will be there and probably bringing her youngest three as well."

Jeremiah felt a mixture of relief and disappointment. Relief that she was all right and disappointment that he would have to wait yet another day to see her and apologize for being so insensitive in the past. Gunther was rambling on and Jeremiah forced himself to pay attention.

"…expect the boy will be stopping by after school today. Unless, of course, you've changed your mind." He eyed Jeremiah, one gray bushy eyebrow arched.

"Changed my mind about…?"

"The job. Taking Rolf on as a helper in your business."

"I thought that Pleasant was not in favor of that idea."

Gunther shrugged then leaned in closer. "She would never want me to say so, but I gather that with the farm a loss and all, she's looking for some way to give the boy training that might stand him in good stead down the road. He's twelve now and the years go by fast. She understands that he's going to need a trade to make his way."

"I see."

"I told her he could work for me here, but she won't hear of it. Says he needs to work for somebody who isn't family. I reminded her that I'm not family except through marriage and really not even then when you consider that...."

"She wants Rolf to work for me?"

"Rolf wants to work for you," Gunther corrected. "She's just decided to give the idea her blessing."

Jeremiah's respect for Pleasant knew no bounds. No doubt her late husband had planned that his eldest son would take over the farm one day. No doubt Merle Obermeier had thought he was setting his son up for life when he bought the land and built the house. No doubt he'd envisioned one day when Rolf and his wife would manage the farm while he and Pleasant moved into a smaller dwelling next to the larger farmhouse to live out their later years.

But from what he'd been able to gather from Levi Harnisher and the comments of others the previous day, that wasn't going to happen. It would take years before the land could be brought to the point where it might yield crops again and in the meantime, Pleasant had already begun to consider how the future needed to change for Merle's children. "Have the boy stop by the creamery after school," Jeremiah said. "We'll see what we can work out."

Gunther nodded. "He's a good lad. A hard worker and bright."

"Then I'm certain that we can come to some arrangement that will suit," Jeremiah said. "You're sure that Pleasant approves?"

"Told me about it herself," Gunther replied. "Talked to the boy as well."

"All right then. As long as Pleasant is in favor."

Gunther shrugged. "What choice does she have?"

Rolf appeared at Jeremiah's back door later that afternoon. The boy kept his eyes on his shoes from the moment Jeremiah led him to the front of the shop and invited him to sit opposite him at one of the half dozen small round tables. "I understand that you would be interested in working for me, Rolf."

"Yes, sir," he murmured and it came out as more of a guess as to what might be the appropriate response than with any assurance.

Jeremiah leaned back in his chair, rocking it on its back legs as he studied this boy who reminded him so much of himself at the same age. "You understand that there are conditions?"

"Yes, sir."

"You will be at the shop every Saturday morning at seven and weekdays as soon as you are finished with school…"

"I could skip school," Rolf ventured, hoping to please.

"No, sir. If things work out I expect that you will be working the cash register from time to time and I want you to know your figures."

"Yes, sir," Rolf replied, his eyes growing wide at

the very idea that Jeremiah might entrust such a duty to him.

"If you are late, then I will dock you two hours pay."

"Yes, sir."

"At first you can wear your everyday clothes. You'll be mostly working in the back, churning the ice cream, washing dishes and the like."

"Yes, sir."

Jeremiah could not help but notice that with every response the boy sat a little straighter, spoke with more conviction and met his eyes more directly.

"Later—assuming business picks up—I'll need you serving customers and you'll need to make sure that you and your clothes are absolutely clean—especially your hands and under your fingernails."

"Yes, sir," the boy said and Jeremiah would not have been surprised if Rolf had snapped to attention and saluted him.

"Then we have a bargain?" He offered Rolf a handshake.

Rolf grinned and pumped Jeremiah's hand once. "Thank you, sir."

Jeremiah stood and Rolf scrambled to his feet as well. "Tomorrow after school and Saturday at seven o'clock sharp," he reminded him.

"Yes, sir." It was clear that Rolf was anxious to leave and share the good news with others.

"Rolf?"

"Sir?"

"Don't you want to know what the position pays?"

Rolf blushed slightly. "I forgot," he murmured.

Jeremiah named an hourly figure that made the boy

look up at him in total disbelief. "Will that be agreeable?"

"Yes, sir."

"And if things work out, then on Saturdays you may take your choice of any leftover ice cream and share it with your family. I like to start the week fresh," Jeremiah explained.

Rolf looked as if he was about to explode with all the news he now had to share with his family. "That would be fine, sir," he managed, edging toward the door.

"Good. I'll see you after school tomorrow then."

Jeremiah couldn't help chuckling to himself as he watched Rolf run the entire distance from the ice cream shop to the farmhouse. He imagined him bursting into the house fairly exploding to share his news. He imagined Pleasant's delight and wished that he could witness the way her smile would surely ease the small lines of worry between her eyes—at least for a little while.

But certainly there was no smile in evidence when she appeared at his door not twenty minutes later.

"Exactly what do you think you're doing, Herr Troyer?" she demanded.

Chapter Nine

The very fact that Pleasant had made the trek from her house to the creamery, through town for everyone to observe with not a single thought for the way this would set tongues wagging once again, was clear evidence of how upset she was with Jeremiah. She did not break stride even when Moses Yoder called out a greeting. Nor did she so much as glance at the bakery where her father was closing up for the day.

She marched straight onto the front stoop of the creamery and pounded on the frosted glass of the front door, setting the closed sign that hung on a hook to rocking. She had not asked for his charity. No, she had sent Rolf to apply for a position that had been offered.

She knocked again.

The door opened and he stood there all six feet and more of him with his broad shoulders and that maddening smile that seemed a permanent part of his expression.

"Pleasant," he said, his eyes lighting with surprise and pleasure. "I…"

She brushed past him. "Please close the door," she

said and took the moment that it took him to do so to try and compose herself. She laced her fingers together and held her hands stiffly in front of her waist.

"You're upset," Jeremiah said and she almost laughed at the understatement.

"My family neither needs nor wants your charity," she burst out, forgetting everything she had planned to say, the calmness with which she had planned to say it.

"I don't understand." He pulled out a chair and offered it to her.

She ignored the gesture. Instead, she began to pace. "I don't know what you heard yesterday at the Harnishers. I have to believe that your intentions are only good, but you have overstepped."

"Your son applied for a vacancy at my shop. It is my understanding that he did so with your full approval. I interviewed the boy, found him up to the job and offered it to him. What exactly is the problem?"

"And you pay all of your employees so well?" She did not wait for an answer. "He is a boy who will run errands for you and do other chores—chores for which if they were his farm chores he would not expect to be paid. Even if he performed such tasks for a neighbor and the neighbor gave him a reward it would be a token—nothing more."

"This is not a household chore or neighborly errand. I have offered Rolf a job, Pleasant, with regular hours and regular duties. I have made that perfectly clear to the boy. He will work hard for the wages he earns and he has been told that if he fails to live up to the conditions I have set for the position, his pay will be docked. Again, what exactly is the problem?"

She felt confused. His words made sense and yet...

"Would it help if I were to start the boy at a lower wage until he proves himself?"

"No—yes—I don't know," she said and sank down into the chair he had pulled out for her.

He took the opportunity to take a chair opposite her and rest his elbows on the table leaning closer. "What's this all about really, Pleasant?" he asked and his voice had lost all of the businesslike tone with which he'd been presenting his arguments.

She studied her hands for a long moment not daring to look at him, not wanting to see the expression of concern that she knew softened his eyes. "I...tell me what you heard yesterday," she murmured.

"When I arrived I heard some snatches of conversation—about you and the farm. I asked Levi Harnisher what was going on and if you were all right. He told me about your late husband's refusal to join the Palmer family's cooperative and how he had not dug the canals that would help keep the land fertile in times of sustained drought. That's it."

"My husband always thought—never thought that it would get so bad. 'It's Florida,' he used to remind me. 'The rains will come,' he would say." She picked bits of dough from under her fingernail. "He was so wrong," she whispered and did not notice the tear that plopped onto the back of her hand.

But Jeremiah noticed. He pulled a clean white handkerchief from the pocket of his homespun trousers and laid it on the table between them.

"Thank you," she whispered as she picked it up and dabbed at her eyes.

"I wanted to apologize to you, Pleasant," Jeremiah said.

"No need."

"Not for this business about hiring Rolf. I need the help and I honestly had no idea of what a proper wage would be so I offered him what Peter Osgood paid me."

"What then?" she asked and looked up at him.

"Ever since I arrived I have been single-minded about setting up my business. It was selfish of me to consider only my needs and give no thought at all to what you might be facing. So when Gunther mentioned that you had given Rolf permission to apply for a position as my helper, I thought I had found a way to repay you without insulting you for all the work you did to make my grand opening a success." He smiled. "Guess I messed that up. But I want you to understand that I have always had every intention of hiring a boy and your son had shown traits that seemed to make him the perfect candidate for the job."

"I do understand that and I need for you to understand that I had my reasons for reconsidering your original offer to Rolf," she admitted. "I'm—we're—grateful for the opportunity."

"It seems to me that there's no real harm done here. I need help. Rolf seems eager to learn a trade. You're protecting his future by trying to prepare him for something other than farming."

He was making so much sense that Pleasant was having trouble remembering why she had been so upset in the first place. "Pride," she murmured.

"Excuse me?"

She stood up. "I let my pride get in the way," she said. "Thank you, Jeremiah. Rolf tells me that he's to

report for his first day of work after school tomorrow."
She moved toward the door and he reached around her
to open it for her and walked with her out to the street.
Across the way at Yoder's Dry Goods a figure moved
away from the window and Pleasant sighed wearily.

"Now it is I who must apologize, Jeremiah," she said.
"It seems that my impulsive action in coming here without the buffer of my father or the children could cause
you some problems." She glanced toward Yoder's.

He smiled. "Do I look worried?"

"No, but perhaps you should be. After all, the people
of Celery Fields are your prospective customers."

"Let me take care of that, Pleasant. It seems to me
that you have more than enough on your mind at the
moment. Get some rest."

His last words had been uttered as gently as a caress
and on her way home, Pleasant couldn't help thinking
that she felt more hopeful than she had earlier. Earlier, she had been torn between instantly understanding what the money that Jeremiah had offered would
mean for them as a family, and her determination that
she was the one responsible for providing what her children needed. But Jeremiah would hire a boy whether or
not that boy was Rolf. He needed the help and because
it was a job that carried certain responsibilities, it was
only fair for the boy he hired to be paid. "He is thinking
of his business—his needs, not yours," she told herself.
And by the time she arrived at the farmhouse she had
convinced herself that Jeremiah Troyer was not a man
who offered charity. He was a businessman who would
do what it took to be successful in a business that was

by anyone's measure risky. Still, he would be a good influence on Rolf.

At supper all four children were unusually quiet—even the twins. *Little wonder,* Pleasant thought. The way she had stormed out of the house without a word almost before Rolf could finish delivering his news. She saw Bettina and Rolf exchange a look and then glance her way.

"Well," she said, forcing a brightness to her tone, "it would seem that we have something to celebrate tonight, but first let us bow our heads in silent prayer remembering to thank God for the many blessings he has shown our little family." She folded her hands in her lap and the children did the same. The twins squeezed their eyes closed but Pleasant saw Bettina glance at Rolf. Rolf only shrugged in reply.

"Amen," Pleasant murmured. She started to dish up meat and potatoes onto the stack of plates in front of her. She passed the first two to Bettina who cut up the meat for her younger brothers and then placed the plates in front of them. "Herr Troyer tells me you are to start work after school tomorrow," she said, handing Rolf his plate.

"I don't have to," he said, "if you've changed your mind, I mean."

"Nonsense. You have taken a position and you will do your best." She handed Bettina her plate and then placed meat and potatoes on her own while Bettina passed around the side dishes—green beans and sliced tomatoes and the day-old bread that had not sold at the bakery. "Has he described your duties to you?"

"He said at first I would be working in the back,

churning the ice cream and washing the dishes from sundaes and sodas he makes out front."

Bettina snickered.

"What's so funny?" Rolf challenged.

"You washing dishes," Bettina managed between giggles.

Pleasant smiled. "She has a point, Rolf. Getting you to wash or dry a dish here at home is what I believe you once referred to as 'women's work?'"

Rolf smiled sheepishly. "Papa used to say that. I just picked it up from him."

"Well, perhaps tonight after supper you might want to help your sister with the dishes. You might learn something."

Rolf's eyes widened with protest and Bettina grinned. "Happy to have your help," she said.

For the rest of the meal they talked about Rolf's new job and how he would manage that along with his schoolwork and chores around the farm. And by the time the children went to bed, Pleasant was certain that allowing Rolf to take the job at the creamery had been the best possible decision. Not only had it helped to build Rolf's self-confidence, it had also affected the other children. As the brother and sister were doing the dishes, Pleasant overheard Bettina assure Rolf that she would help him with his chores at home. Later, as she settled the twins in for the night, Will had announced that he and Henry were perfectly capable of collecting the eggs every morning.

"How about the two of you feed the chickens while Rolf collects the eggs?" Pleasant suggested. "Of course, that means that you two sleepyheads must be up with the sun and dressed and ready without Bettina having to scold you. Can you do that?"

The tow-headed boys nodded solemnly, and Pleasant gathered them to her, hugging them both and thanking God once more for the blessing of these children giving her life meaning and purpose. It was not all she had ever wanted, but she knew now that the children were all she would ever need.

Over the next several weeks, Jeremiah could not seem to get Pleasant's farm out of his mind. The tragedy of such a large tract of land lying fallow and useless stayed with him. The sight of those empty fields that she faced at the start and end of every day had to be a constant and painful reminder of what she had lost— the secure future that her late husband had planned for her and the children. According to local gossip, Merle Obermeier had been a stern man but a good provider. He had been deeply in love with his first wife, the mother of his children. And he had married Pleasant to provide those children with the nurturing that, by all accounts, he was incapable of providing.

"If you ask me," his great-aunt Mildred revealed one day when she stopped by the creamery to bring him cloths she'd made for the tables, "every time Merle looked at those children he saw their mother and it broke his heart. In time he had no heart left—not for loving those precious little ones and certainly not for loving another woman."

"But Pleasant was in love with him," Jeremiah assumed.

Mildred shrugged. "Not at all. Let's just say that for

the two of them it was a marriage of convenience. And that's all I'm going to say on that matter, Jeremiah. You've driven me to gossip and I won't have it."

"I apologize," Jeremiah told her. "You're right. It's the boy." Rolf had been working at the creamery for nearly a month by then.

"He's not working out?" Mildred asked sympathetically.

"On the contrary. He does his work perfectly and he's quick to learn any new task. But if I stop him to make a suggestion or even to urge him to take his time, he reacts as if…"

"You might scold him? Or perhaps even raise your hand to him?" Mildred nodded as if such a reaction were perfectly understandable.

"Exactly, and yet I've given him no cause to believe that I would ever…."

Mildred sighed. "You don't have to, Jeremiah. His father was a strict disciplinarian, especially to Rolf and his sister." She shook her head. "One thing's certain— those little ones were blessed the day Pleasant came into that house." She smoothed the last cloth into place and surveyed her work. "There. Makes the place look more inviting," she said.

"It does indeed," Jeremiah said. "*Danke, Tante* Millie."

"Come by for supper tonight. The bishop has invited the Palmer brothers to dine with us."

"The owners of the cooperative?"

"That's them. Every few months or so the bishop likes to have them over just to catch up on what they might be planning next." She winked. "Forewarned is forearmed is your great-uncle's motto," she said and waved as she left the shop.

The encounter had netted him a cache of questions—about Merle Obermeier, about Rolf's relationship with his father, about what business move the highly successful Palmer family might make next. As the bishop, John Troyer was the unofficial head of the Amish community and Jeremiah could see the wisdom of staying in touch with their *Englisch* neighbors, especially when those neighbors were part of a dynasty that had built fortunes in Chicago and now along the Gulf Coast of Florida.

But as things turned out, Jeremiah didn't have to wait for supper at his great-uncle's home. For that very afternoon two men—clearly outsiders—walked through his front door and ordered ice cream cones with double scoops of vanilla for one and chocolate for the other.

They were dressed in the kind of business suits that outsiders favored—coat with lapels and buttons, vest draped with a pocket watch chain for one and plain for the other, trousers that hung with a sharp crease marking the length of each leg. Their starched white shirts accented the subtle color and pattern of their silk ties.

"How's business?" one of them asked when Jeremiah delivered their cones to the table by the window where they had taken seats.

"Gut," Jeremiah replied. "Good."

"Do you have a minute?" One of the men pulled over a third chair indicating that Jeremiah should join them. "Allow me to introduce myself," he added. "I am Potter Palmer and this is my brother, Honore. We represent the Palmer Farm Growers Association. Many of your neighbors here are members."

"*Ja.* I am familiar with the cooperative." Jeremiah waited a beat then added. "I am Jeremiah Troyer."

"Good ice cream," Honore said.

"Danke."

"I believe you also work at the ice plant in Sarasota?" Potter asked.

An innate instinct to protect his business made Jeremiah instantly suspicious. "How can I help you gentlemen?" he asked, meeting their gaze directly.

Potter's smile reflected an element of respect. "How familiar are you with the process involved in growing and harvesting celery, sir?"

"Not very. But then I am not a farmer."

Honore chuckled. "Neither are we. We—like you— are businessmen. It is the balance sheet that is of most interest to us. Am I right?"

Jeremiah leaned back in his chair and waited for more.

Potter Palmer continued to work on his ice cream as he explained the situation. "When the celery crop is harvested, it is imperative that the produce be cooled almost immediately, as soon as the stalks leave the ground if possible. We have the equipment to manage that, of course, but for our Amish members there is some hesitation to make use of our methods because it involves the use of electricity. They would rather sacrifice yield than go against your traditions."

"And in these times," Honore added as he polished off the last bite of his cone and wiped his fingers on his napkin, "yield is already compromised."

"I understand," Jeremiah said, although he certainly did not understand what this might have to do with him.

"Are we to understand that in addition to your position at the ice plant and your shop here in Celery Fields, you also have a delivery business serving your Amish neighbors with blocks of ice?"

"*Ja*. Yes, sir. I buy the ice from the plant and then sell it. People of our faith do not believe in electricity and we must rely on block ice to preserve our food."

The brothers glanced at one another. "We would like to discuss a somewhat similar business arrangement with you, sir," Honore said as he pulled a paper from an inner pocket of his suit jacket and handed it to Jeremiah. "This is our order for the delivery of ice for the cooperative."

"For those members of the Amish tradition," Potter corrected. "It is a standing order as you can see for as long as you can meet our needs and assuming we can negotiate a fair price for your product and services."

Jeremiah studied the paper. It was an order that could secure his business for years to come. "Why come to me?" he asked. "Would I not be taking business from my employer?"

"On the contrary, the ice company would benefit. Several of our Amish members resist dealing with outsiders and their crops can suffer in the process. But they would accept our processing standards if you delivered the ice—one of their own."

"How have you chosen me?" Jeremiah asked and saw a hint of respect for his caution flicker across the brothers' features.

"Levi Harmon…"

"Harnisher," Potter corrected his brother. "When we first met Levi, he was a highly successful owner of a circus and his name then was Harmon. Apparently, when he decided to return to his heritage, he took back the family name. But I'm afraid Levi will always be Harmon to us."

"You know Levi?"

The brothers laughed. "We've known him for years," Honore said. "Believe it or not, we used to attend the same parties and charity events. Of course, that was before."

"He's a good man and has an excellent head for business," Potter said. "We value his opinion. He was the one who suggested you and that we would only be increasing our standing with our Amish members by finding a way that they could feel they were doing business with one of their own." He arched an eyebrow. "The question is—are you interested?"

Jeremiah looked up at the brothers. He had heard their story. The heirs to a massive fortune built on shrewd business deals made by their ancestors in Chicago were not particularly interested in endearing themselves to their Amish members unless there was a profit in the bargain for them. He smiled.

"Yes, I am definitely interested, but I must speak directly with my employer at the ice company. I want to make very sure that they are all right with this arrangement."

The brothers exchanged a look and Potter reached for a gold fountain pen that he carried in his breast pocket.

But instead of accepting the pen, Jeremiah folded the paper they had laid out for him. "I just need a day or two to fully consider the arrangement and whether or not I can provide the service you need." He saw by the look they exchanged now that he had surprised them and that, as he had suspected, they had underestimated him.

He stood up. "I'll have an answer for you by Thursday if that is agreeable."

The brothers stood as well and Honore reached for his wallet.

"Please, gentlemen," Jeremiah said, "accept your first of what I hope will be many servings of Troyer's ice cream with my compliments."

Honore smiled and put away his wallet. "You make a good product, sir. And that cone—unusual flavor there."

"Shoo-fly," Jeremiah said.

"Pardon?"

"The flavor in the cone is based on a recipe for shoo-fly pie. The woman who runs the bakery next door created the recipe."

Potter glanced out the window to the bakery. "Merle Obermeier's widow?"

"Yes." Jeremiah felt himself instantly on guard again as the brothers once again communicated with one another by a glance rather than actual words. "Do you know her?" he asked, hoping to translate that veiled glance.

"Knew her husband," Honore said.

"Briefly," Potter added and frowned as if the memory were an unpleasant one. But then he gathered himself and extended his hand. "Thursday then," he said in a more jovial tone as his brother laid an engraved business card on the table. "Thank you for the ice cream."

"Yes," Honore added. "I'm going to tell my wife that perhaps for her next social event your shoo-fly cones and ice cream might be a unique dessert."

Jeremiah escorted the two businessmen to the door. Outside, he saw that Pleasant was out sweeping the constant film of sand from the bakery's porch and steps. She glanced over briefly but showed no curiosity about the outsiders coming out of his shop or in the car that pulled around from the side of Hadwell's hardware and idled in front of the creamery until both men got in. He saw a figure move away from the window of the dry goods store and knew that probably Hilda Yoder had also observed the visit.

Roger Hadwell had no such need to hide his curiosity. He strolled across the street and stood next to Jeremiah watching the car drive away leaving a trail of dust that would make Pleasant's sweeping an exercise in futility.

"The Palmers?"

"Ja."

Jeremiah was thinking about the way the Palmer brothers had glanced at each other when they mentioned Merle's name. He wondered if they thought that he—like Obermeier—would refuse to work with them. He wondered if his hesitancy might cost him an opportunity.

"What did they want?" Roger asked.

Jeremiah fingered the paper he still held in one hand. "Ice cream," he replied as the dust settled and once again the road through Celery Fields was deserted.

Chapter Ten

In spite of the need to watch every penny, Pleasant was determined that the children's anticipation of the Christmas season would not be dampened. On Christmas Day, they would spend their time fasting and praying together and reading from the Bible. But on the day after Christmas—or Second Christmas as it was known—they would visit family and friends and share a day of feasting and gift giving.

When Merle had been alive she had made the mistake of showing him the cards that her friends from the circus had sent. These outsiders did not know that the Amish did not believe in such an exchange of greetings, but to Pleasant it was the gesture that counted. Merle had been shocked that she had even opened the cards and had quickly taken them from her and thrown them into the fire. But after his death she had kept the cards and opened them with the children on Second Christmas, regaling them with stories of her adventure with the circus.

Merle had also not allowed the exchange of gifts within their family and had barely tolerated Gunther's insistence on giving the children some small token when the two families gathered on the second day for dinner. But a year after Merle's death, when they had been on their way home from sharing supper at Gunther's, Bettina had sighed and said, "I wish we could exchange gifts, Mama. It would be such fun to draw names and plan what to give."

And that night as she tucked the children in, Pleasant had handed each of them a paper with another sibling's name on it. "Shhh," she had cautioned. "You have a whole year now to plan your gift, but you cannot tell." Her gift that year had been knowing that after she had gone back downstairs, all four children had slipped out of their beds and gathered in Bettina's small bedroom to whisper and giggle over this new tradition. And she suspected that long before morning dawned at least the older two had figured out who had which name.

But perhaps the highlight of the season was the annual program presented to the entire community by the children. Traditionally, such programs were held in the schoolhouse and attended by the parents of the children enrolled in the school. Lydia had assigned each child in her classes a part to play and the excitement among the children was palpable. Rolf was to be the narrator of the reenactment of the story of the birth of Jesus while Bettina was to recite a poem for the occasion and both children were determined to do their very best. Every evening just after supper, Bettina recited her poem for Pleasant, and Rolf silently read through the Scripture passages he would read as his classmates reenacted the story.

It was on such an evening on the day before the

pageant that Bettina's rehearsal was interrupted by a knock at the door. Pleasant glanced at the clock on the mantel—now decorated with fresh greens—and wondered who might be calling at seven o'clock on a weekday evening. "Who's there?" she asked before opening the door, mindful of the stories that persisted of the occasional vagrant or transient going from house to house and sometimes even robbing those homes if they were desperate enough.

"Pleasant? It's me—Jeremiah."

As seemed to be her habit these days any time she saw Jeremiah or heard his voice or the sound of his laughter, her heart leaped. And being a natural worrier, her second thought was that something had happened—someone fallen ill or a fire perhaps. She opened the door as the children gathered around her. "What's happened?" she asked as she pulled the children closer.

"Happened?" He looked perplexed and actually glanced around as if he thought he might have missed something. "Why, nothing."

Relieved but at the same time irritated with him for calling at such an hour, she did not move away from the door to let him in. "Then why have you come?"

He smiled. "And greetings of the season to you as well," he said softly. "May I come in a moment? I have something for Rolf."

Pleasant stepped aside to make room for Jeremiah to enter. Once fully inside, he took a moment to glance around, settling his gaze on the cypress boughs and eucalyptus that adorned the fireplace. "Smells like Christmas," he said. Then he noticed the open Bible that Rolf had been studying and the typed copy of Bettina's poem. "I'm sorry to disturb you, but a few days ago when he was practicing his part during a break at the shop I noticed that Rolf was having some trouble reading the small print in his Bible. I thought these might make it a bit easier for him."

From the pocket of his homespun trousers he produced a small leather case, snapped open the hinged lid and held up a pair of wire-rimmed eyeglasses. "They were my father's," he explained. "He used them to magnify the words when he read Scripture to us." He handed the glasses to Rolf. "Try them on."

As always, Rolf glanced first at Pleasant, seeking permission, and when she nodded, he accepted the glasses as if they were something fragile and precious. Carefully, he hooked them over his ears and peered up at her. "They make you look fuzzy," he reported.

Jeremiah laughed and reached for the Bible. "They are for close work like reading. Slide them down your nose a bit and look over the tops when you want to look at your mother."

Rolf followed his instructions.

"Now try reading this," Jeremiah said as he handed the boy the Bible.

Silently, his lips moving, Rolf read the text. Then he grinned and peered up at Pleasant. "They make the words bigger," he reported. "I can see them clearly now."

Pleasant had known that Rolf 's eyesight was not as good as it should be when she noticed his habit of squinting as he did his homework, but eyeglasses were expensive. She had planned that the income from the celery harvest would cover the need to buy shoes for all four children and eyeglasses for Rolf but there had been only enough income to pay the workers and buy the feed she needed for the chickens and other livestock.

"You shouldn't wear them except when you need them for reading," Jeremiah instructed. "You can keep them in this case between times." He handed Rolf the closed leather case.

"And you must take special care that they not get broken or lost," Pleasant added. "Herr Troyer has loaned you these glasses until we can have you fitted for a pair of your own." Pleasant spoke to Rolf but her purpose was to make it clear to Jeremiah that his gift was far too generous to be accepted as permanent. "Thank you," she said turning her attention to Jeremiah.

He glanced down at his shoes, suddenly shy. "I just thought—I mean he was squinting so and…"

She realized that the children had drifted back into the front room and now Rolf was eagerly reading the story from the Gospel according to Luke aloud while his siblings sat on the floor around him like a makeshift audience. She was alone in the hallway with Jeremiah. Outside the still-open front door, the last rays of the sunset had disappeared. Inside the hallway they were wrapped in the shadows cast by the single kerosene lamp and the fire that crackled in the front room.

"Gunther has invited John, Millie and me to join your family for Second Christmas," Jeremiah said.

"I'm glad," she replied and found that she meant it. The idea of sharing the day with him felt like a gift.

"Well, I should be going." He stepped onto the porch and started down the stairs.

"Will you come to see the children perform?" she asked, knowing that it was unusual for anyone who did not have a direct connection to the schoolchildren to attend the pageant.

He turned and although he was completely in shadow now, she thought she could almost hear his smile when he spoke. "I wouldn't miss it."

On the night of the pageant, the schoolhouse was filled to standing room only. Jeremiah had arrived late, having been delayed with a delivery of ice cream to the home of Potter Palmer for that family's annual Christmas Eve party. He could not help noticing the difference between the trappings that marked an *Englisch* Christmas and those of the Amish. The Palmer residence was festooned with greenery both inside and out. As he drove his wagon up the long driveway he could see a large decorated Christmas tree framed in the front window, and another smaller tree in a window that he passed on his way to the rear of the house.

In the kitchen, the cook and a housemaid were engaged in a lively discussion of what age was old enough for children to stop believing in the myth of Santa Claus. He had never understood the purpose of creating a tale of some magical creature whose job it was to determine whether or not a child had been good enough to deserve to find a stocking filled with gifts on Christmas morning. Christmas was a religious celebration and the idea of a gift was that it came unexpectedly to be sure. But a gift was the product of hard work, an expression of appreciation and love from one person to another.

He unloaded the wagon and followed the Palmer's butler to the large refrigerator where the ice cream would be stored until needed. Then on his way back to Celery Fields, he shook his head in wonder at the need for these outsiders to add their own secular interpretations to what had to be the greatest story ever told. Outside the small schoolhouse, he paused for a minute to consider the natural beauty of poinsettias and hibiscus in bloom, their colorful leaves and blossoms far more beautiful than the artificial lights that adorned the Palmer's Christmas tree.

The town was quiet, shops closed and what citizens weren't already inside the schoolhouse were no doubt gathered in their homes or at the homes of neighbors quietly—and simply—enjoying the blessings of the season. He could not deny the twinge of envy that ran through him in that moment. A family—mother, father, children—was possibly one of God's most precious gifts. It was also a blessing that he had long ago decided he would not seek, at least in the traditional way.

His reasons for opening the ice cream shop had been many. He had certainly understood how people would see that choice as unusual and perhaps even foolhardy given the times. But what he saw was the opportunity to surround himself in his daily life with families—parents, children, grandparents, cousins—without running the risk that he might one day turn out to be like his uncle. He certainly had seen some of the early signs that he was as capable of turning into the same hard and bitter—and sometimes cruel—man that his uncle had been. He had a quick temper that along with his small size had landed him in more than one fight with peers when he'd been a boy. And the older and bigger he had become, the more often he had had to restrain himself from striking back when his uncle unfairly punished him or one of his siblings.

No, he would not marry, he thought as he stepped inside the crowded schoolhouse.

And then he saw Pleasant.

She was seated on one of the benches where the children sat to receive their lessons. Will and Henry sat to either side of her, their short chubby legs swinging back and forth, evidence of their excitement. Pleasant smoothed each boy's cowlick and then turned their attention to the front of the room where Rolf had just stepped up to the simple wooden lectern that Lydia Goodloe used when teaching her students.

Self-consciously, he unfolded the stems of the eyeglasses and hooked them over his ears. There was a titter of snickers that was instantly shushed by mothers around the room. Jeremiah saw Lydia signal Rolf to speak louder as Levi and Hannah's son Caleb and a girl that Jeremiah recognized as the oldest of Hilda and Moses Yoder's children, slowly made their way to the front of the room. The girl cradled a doll and sat on a small stool while Caleb took up his place just behind her. Jeremiah folded his arms and leaned against the back wall of the classroom as the story unfolded. But his attention was not on the pageant. It was drawn again and again to Pleasant Obermeier, whose profile he could observe without her knowing and who was surely the most beautiful woman in the room.

He found himself mentally running down the list of eligible men in the community, wondering if Pleasant might not marry again someday. But he found that he could not imagine her with any of those men. More than that, he found that he did not wish to imagine her with any other man and that thought stunned him.

Between his great-aunt Mildred and Roger Hadwell's wife, it had not taken long to learn the story of Merle Obermeier's similarities to Jeremiah's uncle when it came to how he ran his household and raised his children. Once when Jeremiah had surprised Rolf practicing his part for the pageant instead of scrubbing out the large tins that held the ice cream, the boy had instinctively raised his hands in a protective gesture. Jeremiah had recognized that stance. He had used it often enough himself when his uncle had raised a hand to him.

"Those tins aren't going to scrub themselves," Jeremiah had commented and then gone back inside his shop. Through the window he had watched Rolf as he regained control of his rapid breathing, glanced around nervously and then closed his Bible and went back to work. Later, he had taken Rolf aside and quietly explained to him that if there was work to be done, he needed to attend to it as they had agreed. Once the tasks he'd been hired to complete were done, then he could use his time for homework or practicing his role for the pageant. And he had not missed the way the boy seemed almost weak with gratitude.

He turned his attention back to Pleasant, her features soft in the candlelight that illuminated the room as she watched Bettina take her brother's place at the lectern and deliver the poem she had memorized. And as Bettina spoke the poem aloud, he saw that Pleasant had sat forward a little and was mouthing the words along with her. Jeremiah suspected that she was probably unaware that she was doing this and that made the moment all the more poignant. She was a good mother and he had no doubt at all that she had been a good wife.

At first, Pleasant thought that Jeremiah had decided against attending the pageant and told herself that she was disappointed for the children. But then when the program ended she had turned to greet a neighbor and seen him. In fact, he was watching her and he had not looked away when she met his gaze. Instead, he had pushed himself away from his position leaning against the wall and started working his way through the throng of parents and children toward her.

Her first instinct was to flee, as if somehow his approach represented some danger to her. But she found that she couldn't move for the close quarters of benches and people and so she waited for him to reach her. Along the way, he paused to greet the Yoders and the Harnishers and others so that when he finally reached her and the twins, she had convinced herself that she had been mistaken to imagine that he had been watching her at all. He had simply made eye contact as any friend or neighbor might and she was a romantic fool.

"I'll get your glasses from Rolf," she told him and headed immediately for the front of the room where Lydia was surrounded by the excited participants of the program. She had to gain control of her emotions

when it came to Jeremiah Troyer. In the weeks that had
passed since the opening of his ice cream shop, she had
fallen into the habit of being far too aware of his ac-
tivities. At first she had told herself that she was only
concerned about Rolf and that her son live up to his
responsibilities. But Rolf had quickly settled into his
new job and kept up with his schoolwork and chores at
home as well.

Then she had tried convincing herself that they were
in business together. She made the cones for his shop
and it was only natural that she would be aware of when
he might be coming to pick up the week's order or drop
off a payment for her father. But the truth was that she
looked forward to those occasions as she might well
have looked forward to some beau coming to call when
she was younger.

No, the plain fact was that she was drawn to Jeremiah in a way that no woman of her age or station in
life should be. She had permitted herself to fall back
into the romantic foolishness that had been her undoing
before she married Merle. Yes, her life these days was
difficult and lonely, and she would not deny that having
someone to share her many responsibilities with would
be a blessing. But a companion only—not someone like
Jeremiah whose very smile could set her heart racing.

When she reached Lydia and the children, she took
out the case for the glasses and handed it to Rolf. "Don't
forget to say thank you," she murmured as her son reluctantly removed the glasses and carefully laid them
in the case. Then he looked up at someone standing
behind her.

"Thank you, Herr Troyer," he said. "They really helped a lot."

"Then keep them until you get fitted for a pair of your own," Jeremiah said. "I'm sure your teacher here would agree that if they help you with your schoolwork they are well worth wearing."

Lydia nodded. "You didn't stumble once in the reading tonight, Rolf. I have to agree that perhaps what I have thought might be a failure to learn your words has instead been a problem with seeing."

Rolf, Lydia and Jeremiah turned to Pleasant for her approval and agreement. "The glasses are a family heirloom, Lydia," she explained. "If they would be broken or damaged…"

"They can be replaced," Jeremiah said, his voice soft. "Although they are my father's glasses, it's the memory that is precious not the item." He smiled at Rolf and ruffled the boy's hair. "Besides, they make you look quite wise and grown-up," he added.

Rolf blushed and looked up at Pleasant. "They do help, Mama."

She could see that she was outnumbered and besides, what was the real problem? Was it that they were borrowed glasses? Or that they were evidence of her inability to afford glasses? Or that they somehow tied her family to Jeremiah? "Very well," she said. "But when you are not wearing them, they are safely stored in their case, all right?"

"Yes, Mama." Rolf's smile erased any doubt she might still be harboring. She would find a way to get him the glasses he needed and in the meantime she would not allow pride to keep her from accepting a neighbor's help.

She glanced around and saw that most people had started to file out of the classroom. "We should go," she told the children. "Tomorrow is going to be a full day."

"And the day after that," Bettina said with a twinkle in her large blue eyes. "Presents," she whispered to the twins who squealed with excitement and made a beeline for the door. "Come on, Rolf," Bettina urged as the two older children followed the twins up the aisle and out the door.

It seemed only natural for Pleasant to follow them, but when she realized that Jeremiah was walking out just behind her, she turned back to Lydia. "Coming?" she asked.

"Not just yet. You go on. I want to finish cleaning up here so everything is ready for the next school day."

"Perhaps Jeremiah could help," Pleasant suggested.

"No, thank you. You both worked all day already. I'll see you tomorrow, Pleasant, and you the day after, Jeremiah," she added with a smile.

Pleasant considered her half sister for a moment. She was such a lovely young woman—always thinking of others and that did not begin to take note of her outer beauty. She was the image of her late mother— the woman that Gunther had fallen madly in love with after Pleasant's mother died. The woman that Pleasant had so resented in those early years. But now she saw in Lydia what her father must have seen in Lydia and Greta's mother—a sweetness and beauty that was unmatched. And as she made her way out into the night, she could not help but wonder why Jeremiah Troyer had not seemed to take note of her half sister.

So when he fell into step with her as she and others made their way through the village and on to their homes, she found that God had given her a new purpose. Frankly, she did not understand why she hadn't seen it before. Clearly the woman that God had led Jeremiah Troyer to Florida to find was not Pleasant, but rather the beautiful and eligible Lydia. And if he had yet to recognize that then perhaps it was God's will that she help him see the light.

"Lydia is such a gifted teacher," she ventured as she and Jeremiah followed the stream of townspeople from the school.

"Hmm," Jeremiah agreed but it was clear that his thoughts were elsewhere, no doubt on business, Pleasant thought.

"She spends far too much time at the school and with the children, though," she added. "Just for this pageant alone she was working hours and hours."

No response. He walked beside her, his hands clasped behind his back.

"Guten abend," Hannah called out as Levi turned their buggy down the road that led to their farm.

"Merry Christmas," Jeremiah called back. "And to you, Pleasant," he added.

They had come to his shop and home and Pleasant felt compelled to make some last effort to bring her half sister's many virtues to his attention.

"Lydia would make a good wife," she blurted and then immediately clasped her hands over her mouth. It had been what she was thinking but not at all what she had intended to say.

He was looking at her but she could not see if he was smiling or shocked. "I expect she would," he said agreeably as if they were discussing the weather. "Did you have someone in mind, Pleasant?"

Now he was making fun of her—and rightly so. She had made an utter fool of herself. "It's an observation," she said. "Good night, Jeremiah," she added and hurried away, calling for her children to watch for buggies and wait for her.

"Merry Christmas, Pleasant," he replied and she was sure that she caught a hint of amusement in his tone.

Honestly, she chided herself as she hurried to catch up to the children—and put more distance between herself and Jeremiah, *you are becoming a busybody.* If he had any interest in Lydia then he was perfectly capable of pursuing that interest without her clumsy attempts at matchmaking. And certainly she had enough to worry about without concerning herself for one second with his personal business. Besides, it was Greta who had been mooning over the man, not Lydia. And the very idea that Greta would turn her affections from Josef Bontrager to Jeremiah was laughable. Those two were meant for each other.

No, Jeremiah Troyer was not for any one of the Goodloe women—not Greta, not Lydia and most definitely not her.

Chapter Eleven

It had been some time since Jeremiah had felt quite so lighthearted and at the same time confused. He had little doubt that it was the lovely widow Obermeier who was the cause of his jumbled emotions. He had made it all the way past thirty years and stuck to his decision formed early on that he would never marry, never allow himself to fall in love. From what he had observed over the course of his life there were far too many risks involved in taking such a step.

His parents, for example, had been deeply devoted to one another and the house he had known as a young boy had been filled with laughter and happiness. But then his father had died and his mother had changed, falling into a chasm of grief and sadness from which she had never recovered. His grandparents had been solemn people who frowned on any evidence of levity or the normal high spirits of children. It had not taken long after the family had moved in with his father's brother for his uncle to make clear his disapproval of such antics. If words did not make the point then he more often than not would resort to the switch. And it had not taken long at all to turn Jeremiah's siblings into the obedient, somber-faced offspring that his uncle seemed to prize.

Only Jeremiah had fought back—not physically, but emotionally, holding fast to the memory of that earlier time and that home filled with love and laughter. For a long time he dreamed of the day when he would marry and start a family of his own. But as the years went on and he learned more of his uncle's past, he came to understand that the man his uncle had become was not the man he had always been. The worries of life had changed him and his determination to assure that his children and those of his dead brother would have a secure future became the one thing that drove him.

For some time, Jeremiah had thought that he could be different, but the longer he lived in his uncle's house, the more the memory of life in his father's house faded. He had no idea how his father had managed to give his children a sense of security and responsibility and at the same time an understanding of the joy of life. Then one day he found himself chastising his younger brothers for some task not performed up to the high standards their uncle had set for them. He had heard in his voice the anger of his uncle and found his hand grasping a willow branch and brandishing it. He had felt rage and he had not known where it came from.

He had dropped the willow switch, apologized to his stunned siblings and walked away. And from that day forward he had done the work his uncle expected of him but refused to oversee the work of the others. He had also broken off his courtship of a neighboring farmer's daughter, a girl his uncle had thought far too flighty for him, winning him the older man's approval for once. And he had waited for the day when his younger brother was ready to take over as head of the family so that Jeremiah might leave the farm for good and make a life for himself.

And here he was. He had found his life's work, not as a farmer like his uncle and father, but as a businessman. Everything had fallen into place. His deal with the Palmer brothers had secured his future with his employers, for they were delighted to have him bring them back the business they had lost when the Amish farmers balked at dealing directly with an outsider. The ice cream shop was doing all right as well. He had found a home and a community that had taken him in, welcomed him without reservation. He had friends in the Harnishers and Hadwells and others in the community. He even had family here with John and Mildred. And yet...

Jeremiah lay back on his single bed and stared out the open window at a sky filled with stars. On that night so very long ago there had been a single brilliant star, guiding the wise men to the stable. He could use a guiding star. He closed his eyes and silently prayed for the wisdom to see the path that God wanted him to follow and the courage to follow it.

The year following Merle's death, Pleasant and the children had spent Christmas Day at her father's house. There they had followed the traditions of her childhood. Focusing on the celebration of the birth of Jesus, the day was spent in quiet reflection. At sunrise they took the buggy to the beach and walked together in silence as the gentle gulf waves swirled around their bare feet. Then back home Gunther read the Scriptures aloud, Pleasant told the older children stories while Lydia sat with the twins letting them draw pictures of their idea of the Christmas story. Like many families, they fasted for most of the day, reminding themselves of those who were not nearly so blessed.

"I don't like being hungry," Henry told Pleasant as she and the children walked home at the end of the long day.

"Me, neither," Will chorused.

"And yet there are many people right here in this very country who do not have enough to eat," she reminded them.

"I know this girl in my class at school," Bettina said, "and I don't think she and her brother have enough to eat, Mama. They hardly have anything in their lunch buckets."

Pleasant knew the family. The man had married outside the faith and been shunned for it. He had a run-down house closer to the bay and he eked out a living finding work on commercial fishing boats when he could. He had continued to send his children to the Amish school and dress them in traditional clothing and the general feeling in the community had been to let them come.

"We have so much," Bettina continued. "Do you think we could take them something tomorrow, Mama?"

Pleasant considered the ramifications of such an act—for her children and even for her father's business if someone in the congregation found fault. Any act punishable by shunning was a serious offense and the power of the punishment lay in everyone in the community upholding the ban. "We'll see," she said and knew that the children saw her noncommittal as a way of saying "no."

But Bettina was not one to give up easily. "We could fill up a basket and then just leave it at their door," she suggested. "No one would have to know it was us."

Pleasant looked down at her children, their faces raised to hers, their expressions hopeful. They wanted to do something good, something so in keeping with the way that Jesus had lived his life. Surely it would be the right thing to do. "We'd have to get up very early," Pleasant warned.

"But it's Second Christmas and we'll be so excited that we probably won't sleep at all," Bettina said as all four children pressed closer to Pleasant, waiting for her to agree to Bettina's plan.

"I do have a basket I'm not using," she mused. "But what to fill it with?"

"Oh, Mama, we have cans and jars of fruits and vegetables to spare," Bettina exclaimed.

"But we shouldn't just fill it with food," Pleasant continued. "If we are going to do this then I expect each of you to give something special." She could see each child starting to consider what might be the right thing.

"I'll be right back," Rolf muttered and took off at a run toward the bakery.

"Bring back the rest of the bread and rolls left from yesterday," Bettina called after him. "I have a doll and a book," she said then turned her attention to the twins,

"And what about the puzzle Frau Yoder gave you—the one with too many pieces?"

Henry and Will nodded. "It's too hard for us," they agreed.

And as Rolf ran in one direction, the other three children hurried on to the house chattering away about what might be best to include in the basket. Pleasant had never been more proud of the children. She was well aware that Merle would have been horrified at the very idea that she might countenance any interaction with a family that had been shunned. Still, she couldn't help but think that he would have been proud as well. These were his children—loving, caring and good.

She had gotten the twins settled for the night and found a basket that she was filling with an assortment of jams and canned fruit and vegetables, when she heard footsteps and the low murmur of male voices through the open back door.

"Mama, Herr Troyer is going to help," Rolf announced breathlessly as he pulled Jeremiah into the kitchen. "I thought we could give them a special treat—ice cream—but I didn't think about how it would stay cold. But then I thought that we could put the basket on the porch and knock on the door and then hide until someone came out to get it and…" He gulped in air and glanced up at Jeremiah.

"I can pack the ice cream in ice and it should be fine," Jeremiah told her.

"But then they'll think the gift is from you," Bettina said as she laid her doll and a book and the twins' puzzle on the table next to the canned goods.

"It's not important who they think brought the gift,"

Pleasant reminded her. "Besides, they'll have the bread and rolls from the bakery and the ice cream from Herr Troyer…."

"And we can put in one of those dish towels from Yoder's store and a pencil from the hardware that has their name on it," Rolf added. "They won't be able to figure out who brought it."

Pleasant could see that Bettina was about to protest. "And that's the point, Bettina," she said softly. "The best gifts are those given without expectation of receiving anything in return—even acknowledgment of your good deed."

Bettina blushed. "I'm sorry. I just…"

"It's a wonderful thing you're doing," Jeremiah said. "Thank you for letting me be a part of it."

Satisfied, Bettina went back to planning the logistics of the delivery. "Rolf, you'll have to hitch up the wagon really early. I'll take care of getting the twins up and keeping them quiet so they won't spoil the surprise and…"

"Why don't I call for all of you just before dawn and we'll take a ride out there together," Jeremiah suggested. "I'll have the ice cream all packed in ice."

"That would be wonderful," Bettina exclaimed and for a moment, Pleasant could see the charmer that her daughter would one day become.

"Well, now that we've settled on a plan," she told the children, "I would suggest you get to bed. Dawn is going to come sooner than you may imagine."

She could hear the excited whispers of her two older children as they hurried down the hall and up to their rooms, leaving her alone with Jeremiah.

"Rolf forgot the bread and rolls," she said as she busied herself arranging things in the basket. "That's what he went to get...at the bakery."

"I can bring them in the morning. After all, the door is never locked, right?"

"Right," she murmured, still focusing on the basket. "You don't have to do this. I can explain to the children."

"Why wouldn't I want to be a part of something so perfectly tied to the season?"

"Well, not everyone would approve. The family has been shunned, after all. I don't even know if Bishop Troyer would approve and he's your family. Besides, you have a business to run and customers to please and if they knew you..."

He placed his hand on hers, stilling it from fussing further with the basket and forcing her to glance up at him.

"Pleasant," he said but stopped as their eyes met. He touched the tie of her prayer *kapp,* wrapping it loosely around his finger as he gazed down at her. He swallowed once and then again and she had to fight to keep from touching his cheek, burnished a golden brown after weeks of living in Florida.

Sun kissed, she thought, and felt the color rise to her cheeks as she realized that the kiss she was thinking of had nothing to do with the sun. She retreated a step so that she was free of his touch and forced a smile. "You should go," she said primly. "As I told the children, dawn will be here before we know it."

He nodded and turned to leave. And just before he went out the door he said, "By the way, just so we're clear on this, I have no interest in courting Lydia Good-loe."

"She's a good woman," Pleasant shot back, stopping him in his tracks.

He sighed heavily and turned to look at her through the screened door. "There are at least half a dozen good and eligible women in Celery Fields, Pleasant—including you. Should the time come when I'm so inclined, I prefer to do my own choosing."

And before she could even begin to come up with a response to that, he was gone.

Jeremiah was hardly surprised when the following morning Pleasant begged off going with the children and him to make their special delivery. "I still have pies to bake and bread rising," she protested as she stood in the yard while the children clamored aboard Jeremiah's wagon.

He knew he should be relieved. After all, he had just spent a mostly sleepless night imagining her shoulder brushing his as the wagon rumbled along the rutted road. And then after finally falling asleep he had been jolted awake with the thought that if they were seen together tongues would be wagging for weeks. Not so much about their errand to provide Christmas cheer to a shunned family. No, the very fact that Pleasant had been seen out riding with Jeremiah would be enough. Not even the buffer of the children could set the gossips to rest.

And as he hitched up the team of horses and drove through the darkness to Pleasant's house, he tried to come up with some reason why he couldn't go or she shouldn't go. But the truth was that he was so looking forward to having her next to him that his mind was a blank slate.

She, of course, had been the wiser of them, no doubt having considered the same hazards involved in the morning's adventure. She was risking enough allowing the children to go. Bettina and Rolf might be trusted to keep the secret but the twins had already revealed the name they had drawn and the gift they planned to give that person. The idea that those two would be able to keep quiet about something like this was simply ludicrous. And for that reason he decided that as soon as they had made the delivery and he had taken the children home, he would go immediately to his great-uncle's and tell him what they had done.

His great-uncle was just finishing his breakfast when Jeremiah arrived. His great-aunt insisted on frying him some patties of cornmeal mush while he explained what he and the children had just done.

"And you say it was Bettina's idea," John said as he sipped his morning coffee and Mildred refilled Jeremiah's cup.

"Yes, but…"

"Stop worrying, Jeremiah. You must learn that things here in Florida tend to be a bit less…strict. You and the children did a good thing today. You shared your bounty with a family less fortunate. How can that be considered a wrong?"

"But he has been shunned."

John lifted a shoulder in a gesture of dismissal. "And yet there are the children to be considered. You have said that Pleasant's children each gave up a toy for the other family?"

"More than one from what I could see," Jeremiah said.

"Well, it's not something we can condone on a regular basis but the children are innocents in their parents' decision to marry. I see no reason why they should be punished."

And that was the end of the discussion. As if knowing that having made up his mind her husband was ready to move to other matters, Mildred handed Jeremiah a package wrapped in brown paper. "From your great-uncle and me," she said.

Jeremiah grinned and ripped open the paper. Inside the cardboard box was an ice cream scoop he'd admired when he and John had gone into Sarasota to see what the competition might be. "It's perfect," he announced, mimicking the scooping of ice cream with it. "Your turn," he added, setting the scoop on the table while he went out to his wagon and returned with gifts.

For John there was a new fishing rod and for Mildred a box of beeswax candles. And as the three of them sat around the table finishing their breakfast and discussing when John might try out his new fishing pole, Jeremiah was overcome with a sense of peace and contentment. The only label he could put to it was that he had finally come home. For this was how life had been when his father was alive—serene and amiable.

"Are you coming with us to Pleasant's for Christmas dinner?" Mildred asked and just like that Jeremiah was brought face-to-face with the turmoil he'd awakened with that morning, namely how best to limit contact with the widow Obermeier in the future. After all, he had come within a hair's breadth of kissing her the night before. For a man determined to remain a bachelor, that would not do.

"Of course he's coming," John boomed, pushing his chair back from the table. "There isn't a person in this community who would miss the opportunity to have one of Pleasant's meals. We are blessed to be invited."

Jeremiah wasn't at all sure that Pleasant would agree—not the way she had avoided meeting his eyes when he'd dropped the children off after their delivery. So when he pulled the bishop's buggy up to her house to let his great-uncle and aunt off later that afternoon, he spent more time than was really required stabling the horse in her barn. Rolf was there to help and Jeremiah used the opportunity to pass the time with the boy, recalling the joy they had both witnessed earlier that morning when the fisherman came out and found the basket and gifts.

"I thought they would see us for sure," Rolf said, his voice carrying more excitement than Jeremiah had ever heard him express.

Jeremiah was sure that the fisherman had seen them for he had stood in the open doorway of the wooden shack for several minutes after calling his wife and children to see the gifts. And when the rest of his family had gone back inside, he had stepped out into the dirt-packed yard, turned to face the direction where they were waiting and tipped his hat.

"Mama said Papa would have been real proud of us for what we did," Rolf said.

"You miss you father a lot, don't you?"

Rolf shrugged. "I think about him sometimes and wish there was some way he could know that I'm working hard and stuff."

"You honor his memory by doing well in your studies and being such a hard worker," Jeremiah told him.

Rolf went quiet and studied his bare feet. "Did your papa ever whip you?" he asked, his voice so soft that Jeremiah was unsure if he had heard him correctly.

"You mean a paddling?"

Rolf nodded.

"Not my father," he replied. "But my uncle sometimes…"

"Papa used to get so mad at me and I never could figure out how to make him proud," Rolf admitted.

Jeremiah wrapped his arm around the boy's thin shoulders. "He would be proud of you today, Rolf. Really proud to call you his son."

He let the boy swipe away tears and then added, "Now we'd best get up to the house before they send out a search party looking for us."

Rolf laughed and backhanded one last tear as he fell into step with Jeremiah. "I think you might be right," he said as they crossed the yard together. "I think maybe if he'd lived long enough Papa would have liked me all right."

"I'm sure of it," Jeremiah said. But he wasn't—not really. From everything he'd heard about Merle Obermeier, he had been a hard and bitter man—a man who reminded Jeremiah a lot of his uncle. He wondered how many times Rolf had suffered the man's "whippings" and when he thought about the blows he had endured from his uncle being visited on Rolf, he felt his fists clench in rage. The kind of rage that he had fought to control all the time he had lived under his uncle's roof. The kind of rage that terrified him when it came over him and was at the very foundation of his determination never to marry and risk becoming what his uncle had been.

Chapter Twelve

Pleasant looked down the length of the long table laden with a feast that was the product of not only her hand, but those of her half sisters, Lydia and Greta, as well as Mildred Troyer. Later, she knew that they could anticipate visits from Hannah and her family as well as Hilda and Moses Yoder and their brood of seven. It would be a day filled with food, family and friends and, in her estimation, there could be no more precious gift than that.

She closed her eyes as everyone linked hands and bowed their heads in silent prayer. She had purposely seated Jeremiah at the far end of the table to the right of his great-uncle who held the place of honor at the head of the table where Merle would have sat. Of course, Merle would never have tolerated inviting so many extra people to share their holiday meal.

"We have six mouths of our own to feed without adding others," he had told her that first Christmas after they were married when she had suggested inviting her father and half sisters to share their dinner. "You've baked a pie to take when we go calling there later in the day. That will suffice."

Bishop Troyer's murmured "Amen" brought Pleasant back to the present with a jolt as all around her the room came suddenly alive with conversation, the clink of dishes being passed and food being served and the laughter of the children.

Pleasant was well aware that the year to come would be a challenging one but for now she was surrounded by loved ones and she felt a sense of peace and contentment such as she had not known for some time.

"No Brussels sprouts today, Frau Obermeier?" Jeremiah asked as Lydia passed him the bowl of green beans.

There were chuckles and smiles up and down the table, the tale of Jeremiah and the sprouts having been told in all three households at least once.

"Oh, you never know what might come with the next course, Herr Troyer," Pleasant replied, and encouraged by Jeremiah's look of surprise at her teasing, she continued, "I've been working on a special recipe for Brussels sprouts cones to serve your ice cream."

The twins made horrified faces and everyone laughed. "She's not serious," Bettina explained.

"On the other hand," Jeremiah said, "perhaps using that vegetable in ice cream might be something to try. I had a man call the other day who makes a soft drink with celery that he wanted me to serve in the shop."

"Celo," Gunther said, nodding.

The conversation turned then to the general state of business in Celery Fields as well as throughout the region as a whole. That led to a discussion of the prospects for rain and the possibility that the cooperative would be able to get the winter crops planted before the New Year.

"Enough talk of business," Mildred said after the men had dominated the conversation for most of the meal. "It's Christmas." She turned her attention to the children and added, "When I was a girl, long long ago, I lived in a place where it snowed and we would spend Second Christmas ice skating on the pond outside our back door."

"Was there a lot of snow?" Bettina asked, her eyes wide with the wonder of something she had never seen.

"There was," Mildred assured her. "Piles of it. Jeremiah, you must have had snow in Ohio at this time of year," she added.

"Piles and piles of it," he confirmed. "And yes, we went ice skating and sledding as well."

"What's 'sledding?'" Henry asked.

"You sit on a kind of wooden platform that's been fitted out with metal runners and slide down a hill on it," Jeremiah explained.

"And if you don't have a real sled," John said, "a piece of heavy cardboard will do—at least until it gets soaked through." He chuckled at the memory.

"Did you ever see snow, Mama?" Rolf asked.

"We had snow here once," she told them and then smiled. "Well, a few flakes. Remember, Papa, how Mama and I ran out to catch the flakes on our tongues?"

Gunther chuckled. "I remember that you were quite upset when they melted instantly—and your mother as well. I never saw anyone more frustrated than the two of you were." He shook his head at the memory. "Good times," he murmured, then he seemed to shake off the memory as he looked around the table and announced, "Well, are there any gifts to be opened or is this it?"

That set the children into immediate action as they scampered away from the table and claimed their spot on the braided rug in the front room and waited impatiently for the adults to follow their lead.

"Leave them," Pleasant told Mildred when the bishop's wife started clearing the table. "I don't think the children can contain their excitement much longer."

Mildred set down the plates she had gathered and followed Pleasant to the front room that had been decorated with potted poinsettias and cypress boughs. Several packages wrapped in brown paper that the children had illustrated with drawings added to the festive aura of the room. "Rolf, why don't you begin?" Pleasant suggested.

Rolf picked up a small package, crudely wrapped and tied with twine. He handed the package to Will. "I made it myself," he announced. "It's for your farm set."

Will tore off the paper, uncovering a wooden block that had been fashioned into a replica of a barn and painted a bright red. Pleasant saw the care with which Rolf had added details using black ink to mark the doors and window openings and pieces of sandpaper cut to simulate shingles for the roof.

"Thanks," Will murmured as he examined the piece.

"My turn," Bettina announced and handed Rolf a box covered in seashells. He opened the top to find nothing inside and looked at his sister with disappointment. "The box is the gift," she huffed with exasperation. "It's a place for you to keep your savings. Rolf is saving his earnings—the part he gets to keep—so that one day he can buy his own horse and buggy," she announced.

Rolf blushed. "Thank you, Bettina," he said softly and carefully replaced the lid on the box, running his fingers over the small white clam shells that everyone now could see had been glued in the shape of a buggy's wheel.

"I got Mama's name," Henry announced importantly and he pulled a small flat box from behind his back and presented it to Pleasant.

"What could it be?" she asked as she untied the ribbon.

"It's a new handkerchief," Henry said before she could fully open the box. "I did a whole bunch of chores for Frau Yoder and she let me pick it out."

"It's just what I needed," Pleasant assured him.

"Well, that's it," Gunther boomed, seeming to ignore the fact that Will was nearly in tears having not received a gift.

"What about Will?" Henry exclaimed and wrapped his arm around his twin.

"Oh, Will," Gunther exclaimed. "Did someone have Will's name?"

"Oh, Papa," Pleasant said, "stop teasing the boy." She handed Will his gift. "I had your name," she told him and her heart swelled when she saw the way he looked up at her, his eyes wide with surprise.

"What is it?" Henry asked, crowding close as Will unwrapped the box with great care. "Just rip it," Henry urged impatiently.

"It's a book," Will said, holding it up for everyone to see. "One I can read," he added as he thumbed through the pages. "I know this word," he pointed to a page. "See."

"I see it but what does it say?" Henry asked.

"See," Will repeated, tapping the word on the page.

Henry rolled his eyes. "Okay, but…"

"The word is 'see,'" Bettina told her younger brother.

Jeremiah leaned in closer to the twins from his position on a chair behind them. "Do you know that word?" he asked.

"Look?" Will guessed.

"That's right. And this one?"

Both twins studied the word for a long moment.

"What is the dog in the picture doing?" Jeremiah asked.

"Running," Henry said. "The word is running?"

"Shorter," Jeremiah coached.

"Run," the twins announced together and everyone applauded.

Watching Jeremiah teaching the boys, Pleasant felt her heart quicken. In the scene before her, she saw the only gift she had always truly longed for—a family—father, mother, children. Jeremiah would make such a good and patient father, she thought. Look how Rolf had blossomed under his tutelage. And Bettina had gotten in the habit of stopping by the ice cream shop after her chores at the bakery were done to tell Jeremiah her latest idea for some new ice cream flavor.

"Well," she said, her voice husky with emotion, "did anyone save room for dessert?"

"I did," the twins chorused, the book momentarily forgotten.

"Well then, I'm going to need some help clearing

away the table," Pleasant said, leading the way back to the dining room.

It was later that evening, after the children had finally gone to sleep and the last of her company had gone home, that Pleasant was putting away the last of the dishes and savoring the memory of the day just past. Hannah and her family had arrived just in time for dessert and then stayed to visit. Then the Yoders had arrived and all the children had gone outside to play hide-and-seek while the men sat on the front porch discussing business and other news and the women gathered in the kitchen to put away the leftover food and wash and dry the dishes. And through it all, Pleasant could not seem to avoid thinking of Jeremiah. She heard the sound of his laughter as he joined in the game with the children and was touched by the way he leaned forward attentively listening to the talk of Gunther and John. It was almost as if he was as eager to learn from them as he had been to teach the twins earlier. But most of all she was all too aware of how often he had glanced her way, watching her as she moved through the rituals of the day and smiling as if they shared a secret when she worked up the nerve to meet his look directly.

She placed the last cup on its hook and then wrapped her hands around her sides, stretching her back. It had been a long day, but one filled with such joy that as tired as she was, she was reluctant to see it end. She needed sleep because she had been up before dawn and would be the following day as well. She unpinned her prayer *kapp* as she started down the hall toward the stairs. But then a light warm breeze fluttered through the open front door, drawing her outside for one more look, so she set her *kapp* on the small side table and stepped out onto the porch.

The street was deserted and most houses were completely dark but the sky was filled with stars and a sliver of a new moon. She closed her eyes and let the peace and silence surround her. When she heard the front gate open and close, she opened her eyes and moved from the shadows into the pool of light cast by the kerosene lamp inside her front door. "Who's there?" she asked, but felt no alarm, only concern that anyone out at this hour must be someone in need.

"It's me," Jeremiah said. "I didn't mean to disturb you," he added as he came up the path. "I thought that you and the children—I mean everyone seems to be sleeping and..."

She took a step closer, trying to see him in the dark. "Is something wrong, Jeremiah?"

"Not at all," he said. "I just..."

He was standing on the steps now, holding something in his hands. "I brought you this," he said and presented her with an orchid plant, its long tendril roots trailing over her hands even as she caught a whiff of the delicate flower's subtle perfume.

"It's beautiful but..." But what? Was she going to remind him that giving her a gift was inappropriate in their culture?

"It was growing out behind the shop in a thicket of pepper trees back there. I was going to give it to you to thank you for all the work you did to help make the ice cream shop's opening such a success, but that didn't seem like a good idea. I mean people might get the wrong idea and all."

As they would now, she thought, resisting the urge to take a quick look around to be sure no one was peering out a window or coming along the street. "Then why now?" she asked.

He glanced away and chuckled in that way that she had come to realize marked the evidence of his discomfort and shyness. "I'm not sure. It just seemed the right time. Today was very special for me, Pleasant. It's been a very long time since I felt so much a part of things— of a family. Thank you."

"You're welcome, but Jeremiah, surely you know by now that the entire community has come to respect you and see you as one of our own. Just in the short time you've been here you have somehow made yourself a part of us."

He stepped onto the porch and joined her in the pool of golden lamplight. "Could we sit a minute?" he asked, indicating the porch swing. "I have something I want to explain to you."

She should refuse. She should thank him again for the orchid and go back inside.

Instead she sat on the swing and waited for him to join her.

"After my father died," he began, then cleared his throat and started again. "Living with my uncle changed me."

"In what way?"

He was quiet for a long moment. "My uncle was a man who…" He shook his head and leaned forward, resting his elbows on his knees.

Although every instinct made her want to offer him some comfort, she resisted the urge to place her hand on his broad back. "Did you come to bring the orchid or perhaps there was something more, Jeremiah?"

He sighed. "That's just it. I did come to place that orchid in your tree so that you might discover it and not know that it came from me. I didn't want to cause you any concern about what others might think, Pleasant. But then you were here—it was almost like you were waiting for me, and all of a sudden I thought I must have come because I needed to tell you why I can never allow myself to have feelings for you."

Of all the things she might have imagined him saying, this was surely the very last. Had he read her thoughts? Known that she had observed him, especially on the day just passed, and thought what a good father he might make? Had she revealed far too much of her own longing that it might still be possible for a man like him—handsome and gentle and kind—to love her?

She twisted her fingers together nervously. "You hardly owe me any explanation, Jeremiah," she said primly. "If this is about my comments regarding Lydia…"

To her shock he grasped her hands stilling them. "This is not about Lydia, Pleasant. It is you that I…" He shook his head miserably and released her hands.

"My uncle was a bitter man, Pleasant—a man who at a young age took on a great deal of responsibility. I can understand that now. He wasn't always so hard but in the time that we lived with him, the need to care for his own eight children and our family of seven—it was a lot to ask. Earlier today, Rolf asked me if my father had ever whipped me—his word—and admitted to me that your late husband had punished him on more than one occasion."

"You're not making any sense," Pleasant said, her heart racing with the unspoken fear that something was about to change for her, something that would spoil all of the peaceful contentment she had been feeling just minutes earlier.

"I don't want to become like my uncle—or like Merle, if I have understood Rolf correctly."

Pleasant was torn between the loyalty she felt she should have to her late husband and the realization that Rolf had turned to Jeremiah instead of her to admit how much his father had hurt him emotionally as well as physically. "Why would you think that might happen?"

"I have a temper—all the men in my family do. And sometimes that temper has been hard to manage and sometimes that temper has nearly brought me to strike out at others—my younger brothers, for example."

Pleasant was overcome with confusion. Why was he saying these things? Why tonight of all nights? Why was he determined to spoil this perfect day for her? She stood up. "I think you should go," she said stiffly. "Thank you for the orchid. I'll place it in the banyan tree early tomorrow. The children will be delighted." She took a step toward the door. "Good night, Jeremiah."

He caught her hand and spun her so that they were no more than inches apart. "I am trying to tell you that I care for you, Pleasant, but…"

"You have been kind to the children and to me, Jeremiah. Please don't concern yourself that I have taken that kindness for anything more than…"

He cupped her face in his hands and kissed her, and her instinct to protest was lost in the gentle pressure of his lips meeting hers. She closed her eyes and allowed herself this one moment of pure bliss, and she was still reeling from the tenderness of that kiss when he let her go and walked away.

Jeremiah's residence was dark when Pleasant went to the bakery the following morning. Clearly, he had left early for his shift at the ice plant. Business would be slower than usual as people recovered from the festivities of the holiday and she wondered whether or not she should prepare the full weekly order of ice cream cones or if Jeremiah might decide to close the shop for a few days.

"Have you seen Jeremiah this morning?" she asked her father when he came to work on the accounts later that morning.

"He said something about having the early shift this week—said he needed to get his wagon loaded early for the delivery out to the co-op."

Vaguely, Pleasant recalled some conversation the day before about Jeremiah providing the ice necessary to properly preserve the winter celery crop that was almost ready to be harvested.

"He'll be back then," Pleasant murmured more to reassure herself than to respond to her father.

But Gunther laid down the paper he was studying and turned his attention to her. "I expect he will," he said. "Did you need something, Pleasant?"

She felt her cheeks growing red with embarrassment and moved closer to the hot ovens so her father might assign her rosy cheeks to the heat. "I just wondered about this week's order for cones."

"Good point. I can't imagine that he'll be wanting the full order. With the holiday and all we're already nearly half through the week." He scribbled a note on a piece of scrap paper and taped it to the top of his roll-top desk.

Pleasant smiled. This was her father's unique filing system—scraps of paper posted here and there plus stacks of files that littered the floor around him. But he knew where everything was and woe be it to anyone who tried to put his mess into some sort of logical order.

"I'll make half an order today and if he wants the rest I'll have time tomorrow," she announced as she began gathering the supplies she would need to make the cones.

"How are you doing, child?" Gunther asked after a moment, and Pleasant realized that he had not gone back to his work but had been watching her instead. "That was quite a spread you and the children put out for everyone yesterday. Are you sure that you didn't overdo?"

"The one thing the children and I do not lack for is food, Papa," she said as she cut lard into sugar. "At our weekly frolics, all the women have put up jars of fruit and canned vegetables to last everyone in the community for some time. And we still have the chickens for eggs and the cows to give us milk and…"

"The house needs work," Gunther reminded her.

"It's needed work for over a year now. We'll get to it."

"I imagine that the money that Jeremiah pays Rolf is a help."

"I put that money away for the children," Pleasant admitted. "For their future." She heard a horse snort and then the soft plodding of Jeremiah's team of Belgians entering the yard behind his shop. *He's back,* she thought and had to bear down on her mixing to restrain herself from going out to meet him.

"Looks like you can clear up the cone order for yourself," Gunther said as he reached up and ripped down the note he'd written himself and threw it in the wastebasket. "He's coming this way." And when Gunther pushed away from his desk and went to meet Jeremiah, it was all Pleasant could do not to collapse in the chair he had vacated, for suddenly her knees seemed to have turned to water.

Jeremiah had come to a decision. Living and working next door to Pleasant Obermeier was a bad idea. Going to her house for any reason was even worse. And worst—yet best—of all had been his impulsive act of kissing her. It had been all he could do to walk away from her after that. Every fiber of his being had screamed for him to stay, to touch the soft thick hair that swept back from her forehead and was always covered by her *kapp.* And after touching her face, his palms cradling the soft smoothness of her skin, he had had to drag his hands away and the clenched fists at his sides as he strode back down the street had not been clenched in anger, but rather in a need to maintain control, to keep himself from turning around and running back to her.

The kiss—her breath shallow and warm against his lips, the instant of resistance that turned quickly to surrender. He had acted out of frustration, hardly knowing what he was about to do before he had done it, and then it had been too late. He was lost. He had permitted the one thing he had promised himself he would never allow—he had opened his heart to the possibility of love.

"How did it go?" Gunther's booming voice jolted Jeremiah out of his reverie.

"Fine. Good. Is Pleasant here?"

"*Ja.* She has a question about the cones."

"The cones?" Of all the things Jeremiah had imagined that he and Pleasant might say to each other this morning, discussing ice cream cones was not even on the list.

"*Ja.* With Christmas and all, do you need the week's full order? She's started with half, but…"

So that was the way she had decided to handle things. Business as usual. It was probably best, but Jeremiah couldn't help but feel a little disappointed. "Half is good," he muttered. *Well, she's just being practical,* he told himself. After all he was the one who had told her he would never marry. Evidently, she had thought through his impulsive act and decided not to read anything into it. He turned back toward the wagon where the horses were pawing the ground, impatient to be free of their harness.

"I thought you wanted to see Pleasant about something," Gunther called after him.

"It'll keep until I get back," he said without breaking stride.

"You're going away?"

Jeremiah had reached his team of horses and began unhitching the wagon. "I want to go and see my family back in Ohio." *I need to remind myself why I resolved to remain single and why I left there in the first place.*

"What about the shop and your job?" Gunther had followed him and was helping him unhitch and stable the team.

"The shop can be closed until after the first of the year and I've asked for the time off. After all, harvesting won't get started in earnest until January."

Gunther nodded but he was looking at Jeremiah with concern. "Are you all right, Jeremiah?"

"Just need to see my family," Jeremiah replied. "Tell Pleasant not to worry. I'll leave a list of chores for Rolf to handle so he won't lose any of his weekly pay." He could see that Pleasant had come to the door of the bakery's kitchen and was watching them. "And that goes for paying you what we agreed as well, Gunther."

"You're leaving right away then?"

"There's a train I can take this afternoon."

"And the half order of cones Pleasant is making?"

Jeremiah had forgotten all about that. "Box them up and I'll take them with me. My former employer, Peter Osgood, will enjoy tasting what we came up with and he can use the rest for serving his ice cream."

Gunther was shaking his head as if to say none of this made any sense but he would not insult Jeremiah by questioning him further. "I'll let Pleasant know," he said, patting the rump of one of the horses as he headed back to the bakery.

"And tell her..." *Tell her what? That you don't*

regret the kiss? That it doesn't change anything? That it changes everything and that's why you're running away? "Thank her for yesterday," he finished lamely.

"Wouldn't hurt to do that yourself," he heard Gunther grumble as he walked away.

"Yeah, it would," he murmured as he watched Pleasant open the screen door to receive her father. "Just being in the same room with her right now would hurt more than you could possibly imagine."

Chapter Thirteen

Jeremiah had been gone a week when reports of the first cases of influenza were reported in South Carolina. Pleasant was immediately transported back to the virulent 1918 epidemic when her mother had been stricken down and eventually died of the virus. Now news of the deaths of a young mother and two school-children in Georgia spread quickly and in spite of official assurances that this was nothing like the 1918 epidemic, Pleasant and other parents in Celery Fields considered how best to protect their loved ones—especially the children—from harm.

"We're taking the twins and Caleb and going to Wisconsin until this passes," Hannah told Pleasant one day. "We could take your children with us, Pleasant."

"I couldn't ask that of you," Pleasant exclaimed. "You have enough to worry about with your own three and then a new baby on the way."

"That's the main reason Levi insists on going," Hannah admitted as she eased herself onto Gunther's desk chair and let out a sigh of exhaustion. "I told him that he's being overly cautious, but you know Levi."

Pleasant saw the dreamy-eyed look her friend always got whenever she talked about her husband. "You should go," she said. "Levi's right and if his brother has room…"

When Caleb had run away with Levi's circus, Pleasant, Hannah and Gunther had spent several days staying with Levi's brother, Matthew, until arrangements could be made for them to return to Florida.

"Oh, Matthew and Mae have more than enough room and there's also Levi's old house on the circus grounds that's not being used. Plenty of room for your four—and you as well."

"I couldn't leave Papa, and who would mind the business? I mean these days it's all we have," she reminded her friend.

"Then let me take the children," Hannah pressed. "That will relieve you of some responsibility at a time when you need to mind your strength. If you get too run down then you're at risk as well and then what would the children do?"

It made perfect sense.

"Jake has given us the use of Levi's old private railway car for the trip. It will be an adventure for the children and once they reach Wisconsin they'll have the opportunity to see snow and go ice-skating." When Levi had decided to return to his Amish roots, he had sold his company to his business manager and long-time friend, Jake Jenkins. The two had remained close, spending time together during the months that the circus—and Jake—resided in nearby Sarasota.

"You make it sound so exciting," Pleasant said, wavering in spite of her doubts.

Hannah grinned. "Don't you remember what fun we had when we were there—and the journey itself?"

"You were a wreck worrying about Caleb for most of the time," Pleasant said with a grin.

"Well, that aside, we had some good times." She pushed herself to her feet. "Think about it. We're leaving on Friday." She pressed Pleasant's arm on her way to the door. "It's no bother, Pleasant, and I'd really like to do this for you. Levi and I both would. In fact, he was the one who suggested it."

Pleasant swallowed around the lump that had formed in her throat. *"Danke,"* she whispered, surprised to find herself near tears.

After Hannah left, Pleasant thought about the possibility. It was true that ever since she had learned of the disease and how it had already claimed three lives, she had laid awake nights worrying over the children and how best to keep them safe. The idea that she might be the one to fall ill had never occurred to her. What would the children do then? Who would care for them? Hilda Yoder had already taken her seven and gone to stay with her sister in Pennsylvania. Others had followed until the schoolhouse was practically empty and Bishop Troyer had told Lydia that the elders had decided to close the school for the time being.

Of course, no school meant no teacher's stipend and that meant that the financial situation for Pleasant and her extended family was even more dire. The picture was further complicated by the fact that with several families leaving to stay with out-of-town relatives, business at the bakery was practically nonexistent. Jeremiah had closed down the ice cream business when he left to visit his family and Pleasant really doubted that he would reopen once he returned—at least not until life got back to normal for the community.

What if he didn't return? What if he decided to stay in Ohio with his family? What if he decided that he'd made a mistake leaving them and now with the threat of another flu epidemic he'd be better off not coming back at all?

But surely his contract with the Palmer cooperative would be hard to abandon. After all, by all reports it—along with his job at the ice plant—would assure him of a steady income. As he had promised he had left work for Rolf and paid him in advance. But if he decided to permanently close the ice cream shop, Rolf would be devastated. She thought about how hard the boy had worked to live up to Jeremiah's expectations—or more likely the expectations he demanded of himself in order to be able to impress Jeremiah when his employer returned. That reflected the years when Rolf had tried everything he could think of to earn his father's approval—and failed.

Until the news of the spread of a new influenza, Pleasant had been able to think of little else than the night when she and Jeremiah had shared their first—and only—kiss and he had told her the story of his uncle. She understood that it was his fear that he might one day follow in the man's path that had driven him to leave town so suddenly and kept him away for over a week now. He had admitted to having feelings for her—and the children—feelings that he thought were not in their best interests. And she had responded to his absence by denying her own feelings for him, by assuring herself that she did not think of him as more than a good friend and neighbor. But every night when she said her prayers she prayed for forgiveness for the lie she told herself each day. For in spite of her determination to never again permit herself to surrender to romantic foolishness, the truth was that she had fallen deeply and irrevocably in love with Jeremiah Troyer.

It was impossible, of course. By his own report, he was determined never to marry and it was the height of arrogance to believe for one minute that he would choose her should he ever decide to change his mind. Under those circumstances she examined the kiss. What could he have possibly been thinking to act so impulsively? For she had no doubt that it had been impulsive—and that he had regretted his folly.

And yet the way he had cupped her cheeks with his palms had been so incredibly tender and surely a kiss delivered as an act of impulse would have been far more forceful. His lips pressed to hers had been soft and warm and ever so gentle. *Oh, stop being such a fool,* she chastised herself and headed for the bakery even though there was little for her to do there.

The bell over the door jangled as she opened and closed the bakery door. "Papa?" she called. "It's just me," she added as she headed for the kitchen.

She soaked a rag in hot water and started to wipe down the long worktable as she told her father about Hannah's offer. But when he didn't reply, she turned to see what had distracted him and found him hunched over his desk, his breathing shallow.

"Papa!" She knelt next to him and felt his forehead

with the back of her hand. He didn't seem to be feverish, but he was very pale. "Papa, what is it?"

"Nothing," he replied weakly. "Just a little…" His eyes rolled back as he slid from the chair to the floor.

"Papa!" Pleasant ran to the front door and cried out for help, then returned to her father's side. He was grimacing in pain and moaning when Moses Yoder and Roger Hadwell came running.

"He needs a doctor," Moses announced.

"I'll go," Roger volunteered and Pleasant knew that he was on his way to the nearest house occupied by an *Englisch* family where they would have a telephone.

"Hurry," she called, then knelt beside her father pulling the cushion from his desk chair to place under his head. "The doctor's coming," she assured him. "It will be all right, Papa." She fought back tears and tried to smile so that he would not see how frightened she was. "I'll stay with you," she promised as she grasped her father's hand between both of hers.

"Do you want me to go get Lydia and Greta?" Moses asked, his voice somber.

At first the question irritated Pleasant. Gunther would be fine as soon as the doctor could tend to him and they could get him moved to the house. Then Lydia and Greta could be of some help but for now…

But then she glanced up at Moses and in his face she saw the truth. Her father might be dying. "Yes," she said and as she felt her father's hand go slack, she murmured, "Hurry, please."

"Oh, Papa," she whispered as soon as they were alone, "please don't leave us. We need you so." Like her father and every Amish person she had ever known,

Pleasant did not believe in praying for personal favors, but seeing her strong, good and gentle father so helpless, she was sorely tempted to beg for his life.

"Pleasant?"

"Right here, Papa," she assured him.

"Send the children with Hannah."

So he had heard her. Through all his pain and discomfort as the force that might well end his life had struck, he had heard her say that Hannah and Levi were offering to take the children north until the danger of the influenza could pass. "Yes," she agreed clutching his hand.

"And the girls as well—they can look after the little ones." *The girls* had always been his way of referring to Lydia and Greta. He swallowed with great difficulty. "You go, too."

"No. There's too much to be done. We have the bakery and…"

He attempted a laugh that sounded more like a gurgle, then gathered his strength. "You'll need to start over, Pleasant—you and the girls and Merle's children. Go see the Palmers and see if you can sell them everything. Take Jeremiah with you so he can make a good deal for you. He knows them and…"

"Stop talking such foolishness," Pleasant chided as she wiped his brow and noticed how very white and thin his hair had grown. "We'll be all right. You'll be all right," she said, her voice choking on the words as she faced the reality that the doctor was not likely to make it in time.

"Do as I say," he countered and then opened his rheumy blue eyes and looked at her. "You're a good

woman, Pleasant. Always caring for others. I wish…"
He closed his eyes and drew in a long shuddering
breath.

"Papa?" Pleasant leaned close to catch the words that
came next.

"I wish," he whispered, "you to be happy."

"I am happy, Papa," she assured him, making no at-
tempt now to hide her tears. "I have been so blessed
and…"

The thunder of running feet came from two direc-
tions. At the same time that Moses, Lydia and Greta
set the bell to jangling over the front door, Roger
Hadwell came through the back door of the bakery
with the doctor. Greta was nearly hysterical, clinging
to her sister as the two of them stood aside to allow
the doctor to examine their father. Knowing that she
needed to give the doctor room, Pleasant reluctantly let
go of Gunther's hand and went to stand with her half
sisters. And as the three of them held on to each other,
the doctor turned to them and shook his head. "I'm
very sorry for your loss," he murmured before turning to speak quietly to Moses and Roger. The two men
nodded and patted the doctor on his back and thanked
him for coming as they walked him to the door. And
as Pleasant looked at her grieving sisters, she realized
that once again she was the one everyone would look
to for answers to the question of what to do now. The
problem was that she had no answers.

When Jeremiah stepped off the train after spending
over two weeks with his mother and siblings in Ohio,
he felt none of the optimism he had felt that first time

he'd arrived at the station. This time no one was there to meet him since he hadn't let anyone know he was on his way back. The extreme change in temperature from the icy January winds that he'd left behind in Ohio to the balmy warmth of Florida took some getting used to as he carried his single valise up Main Street and headed east and north to Celery Fields.

He saw that there had been little or no rain to relieve the drought the area had suffered for months now. His throat felt choked and his eyes itched with the sandy dust that blew around him as he slowly made his way back home. For he had no doubt that Florida was his home now. There had been nothing left for him in Ohio. There among his own friends and family he had felt always like a visitor, an outsider observing people and places that should have seemed poignantly familiar, but that in truth only felt strange, even foreign.

Wiping sweat from his brow, he saw the cluster of buildings that formed the community of Celery Fields in the distance, took a firmer hold on his suitcase and quickened his step. But the closer he came, the more aware he became that the place seemed almost deserted. His pulse quickened. Had something happened in his absence? Had others closed up shop and gone back to their families in the Midwest?

Pleasant.

Now he found that he was running, stumbling a little as the suitcase knocked against his side. He dropped his suitcase next to the back door of the ice cream shop and hurried around to the front. The street was deserted, but at the far end he saw a line of people filing slowly out of Gunther's house, following a buggy used only for one reason—to carry the dead to their final resting place. When he saw Pleasant and her half sisters walking behind the buggy, he felt as if he'd been kicked by a horse. The body inside that coffin had to be Gunther's—a man he had known for too short a time and one who would be sorely missed by everyone in the community.

He fell into step with the last of the mourners thankful that he had worn his good suit for traveling and so was appropriately and respectfully attired to pay his last respects to Gunther. At the small cemetery, his great-uncle offered a few words of consolation and called for a final silent prayer. Jeremiah kept his eyes on Pleasant who was fully occupied tending to her youngest half sister. Greta seemed inconsolable and clung to Pleasant who stood next to her father's grave as the coffin was slowly lowered by ropes into the ground. As soon as the graveside part of the service was finished, the mourners slowly made their way back to Gunther's modest house. There would be a meal for everyone to share and then the people of Celery Fields would return to their regular routines. Death was just one more piece of God's overall plan for life on earth. The goal for the Amish was to live each day in such a way as to guarantee eternal happiness in Heaven. Certainly Gunther had achieved that.

"Good to have you back," Levi Harnisher said as he came alongside Jeremiah.

"I didn't know," Jeremiah said.

"It was sudden. Heart attack."

They walked on toward Gunther's house and Jeremiah became aware that several people he would have expected to see were not among the small gathering. "Where is Frau Yoder and…"

"There have been reports of a flu epidemic north of here—moving this way. Several of the women have taken their children and gone to stay with relatives up north until we know for sure that it's not like it was in 1918. Hannah is taking our children and Pleasant's to Wisconsin tomorrow."

"And Pleasant?"

"No. She'll stay here. Lydia and Greta have offered to go and care for the children. My former business partner is providing his private railroad car to take them to my brother's farm in Wisconsin."

"But she should go as well."

Levi shook his head as if this was an argument he and others had made and lost. "She's determined to stay. Says there's no one else to take charge of the bakery or manage two houses or…"

Jeremiah picked up the pace, determined to have a word with Pleasant and convince her to go with the children and other women. "There's no reason for her to stay," he said. "I can easily…."

Levi grasped his arm. "Give her some time," he advised. "Gunther's death was a shock for everyone and I expect for Pleasant it was especially unexpected. She relied on him as much as he relied on her."

It was sound advice and counsel he knew he should heed. So it was hard to explain why after finally seeing her alone for the moment and expressing his sympathies for her loss, the first words that Jeremiah said to her were, "You should go to Wisconsin."

"There is work to be done here." She looked and

sounded exhausted and all Jeremiah could think about was that in her present condition, she was as likely as anyone to contract the virus should it make its way to Celery Fields.

"I can do that," he said.

She looked directly at him for the first time and gave him a wan smile. "Indeed? You will collect the eggs, feed the livestock, milk the cows, bake the breads and other wares and…"

"Stop it," he said softly. "You know what I mean."

"No, I don't, Jeremiah. You've been gone. Things here are not the same. Not the same at all."

The look she gave him made him wonder if they were still discussing her father's death and the threat of a flu epidemic. "I am here for you, Pleasant. We all are."

Again, she managed the weak smile that seemed to take more of an effort than she needed at the moment. "I know that and I appreciate it. Now please excuse me. I need to see about the children." She moved away from him. He watched as she paused to thank Hannah and the other women for all that they had done for her and realized that her response to him had been no different than her response to all the others who had gathered in Gunther's house to prepare the meals and care for the children.

He felt a wave of mild irritation at her unwillingness to accept help—no, to accept *his* help. But then he noticed that she was thinner than he remembered and her skin was so very pale, and the light that had glowed in her eyes was no longer there, and he wanted only to go to her, hold her and tell her everything was going to be all right.

"Herr Troyer?"

Jeremiah looked down at Rolf. The boy was wearing his Sunday clothes and clutching a piece of paper that Jeremiah recognized as the list of chores he'd left for the boy to take care of while he was gone. "Hello, Rolf."

"I have to go to Wisconsin tomorrow so I won't be able to work for you anymore."

"Until you come back," Jeremiah said.

Rolf shrugged and looked down at his shoes. Then he released a sigh worthy of a man three times his age. "What if we never come back?"

Jeremiah knelt so that he was eye to eye with the boy. "You'll be back. Your mother will see to that."

"She's not really our mother."

"Yes, she is—in every way that really counts," Jeremiah assured him.

Rolf eyed him suspiciously for a long moment.

"You can depend on her," Jeremiah stressed. "She loves you and your sister and the twins as if you were her own children."

Rolf nodded. "Then why isn't she coming with us?"

Jeremiah had no answer for the boy. "She has her reasons. Remember what it was like when your father died?

"Well, her father just died and she's sad and she needs all of us to understand that and do whatever we can to make her feel better."

"I don't see how sending us away will make her feel better. Seems to me she's going to miss us a lot."

"You're right about one thing—she will miss you very much. But the other side of that is that she's doing this to make sure you and the others are safe from the virus that's been spreading this way."

"They closed the school down."

"Well, there you go. They would never close the school unless things were serious. Your mother just wants to do everything she can to protect you."

Jeremiah saw understanding dawn in the eyes of the boy. "She's taking care of us just like she promised," Rolf said. "Even though it makes her sad to see us go so far away."

"That's right, so you must promise to write to her and tell her all about Wisconsin. You're going to see snow and go ice skating and sledding...."

Rolf grinned. "I never thought about that. Real snow?"

Jeremiah stood up and ruffled the boy's hair. "The real stuff. There was a foot or more on the ground when I left Ohio a few days ago."

"I have to tell Bettina," Rolf said as he headed across the room to where Bettina was standing with Pleasant.

Jeremiah saw Pleasant look at Rolf, first with alarm and then with relief as he breathlessly reported his news and then took off again, this time with Bettina and no doubt to find the twins. Pleasant smiled a genuine smile as she watched them go and then turned to look back at him. "Thank you," she mouthed.

Jeremiah nodded but he was thinking that there was no need to thank him. *It's the kind of thing you do when you care deeply about someone,* he thought. *The way I care about you.*

Chapter Fourteen

Pleasant had never imagined that a person could endure such unrelenting loneliness. Each day that passed seemed more like a month. She missed her father's hearty laughter, his mumbling to himself as she baked while he sat at his desk going over the accounts, and most of all she missed knowing that she could come to him with anything that might be troubling her. The absence of the children was by far the hardest to bear. The long silent days at the bakery followed by endless nights alone in the big empty house only accented her isolation. The whole community seemed deserted with so many of the women and children absent and the men trying to manage alone.

Jeremiah was barely around. She had thought that he might stop by or come to see the children and Hannah and her family off at the train station, but other than their brief encounter at her father's funeral, she had caught sight of him only now and then. He was gone all day and into the evening, the extra work he had taken on with the cooperative now demanding even more of his time. What time he wasn't working at the cooperative or at the ice plant, he spent making deliveries to his regular customers. He had posted a large sign in the window of the ice cream shop announcing that the creamery would reopen in spring and every Friday without fail, Pleasant found an envelope slipped through the bakery's mail slot with payment for the standing order of ice cream cones—cones she no longer made.

She had tried returning the money, taking it to his residence after closing the bakery for the day and after finding no one home, leaving the envelope with a note under his door. But the envelope and money had been back the following day. She was not in the mood to play his game so she started putting the money aside in a special tin box she kept in the bottom drawer of her father's desk. One day she would personally present him that box and its contents and if he refused it she would hand it over to the bishop as a donation for the congregation. Satisfied that she had solved the problem, she resolved not to give one more minute's thought to Jeremiah Troyer—and failed miserably.

For with her father's passing and Hannah leaving for Wisconsin, Pleasant realized that the two people she had relied on the most for conversation and counsel had been removed from her life. She even missed Hilda Yoder. That thought made her smile. After all the times she had wished Hilda would simply leave her alone and let her tend to her business and the children in her way, it was ironic that at this time she would have welcomed her sister-in-law's unannounced arrival and unsolicited guidance.

The truth was that without Gunther, Hannah or Hilda

and the distraction of the children and their needs, she
found she focused all of her thoughts on Jeremiah. She
was far too aware of his comings and goings—even
those that she did not witness. Shortly after she arrived
at the bakery each morning she heard him hitch up his
wagon. She strained to follow the laborious creaking
of the wagon wheels as he drove away and counted it
an especially good morning if she caught the sound of
him clicking his tongue to urge the team of Belgians
onward or a glimpse of him through the open door of
the bakery.

By the time she closed the bakery for the day, he
had not returned and she knew that after working his
shift and making his deliveries, he would have spent
long hours at the cooperative making sure the harvested
crops were properly chilled and prepared for shipment.
Sometimes when she sat alone on the front porch of
Merle's house after dark, she saw a dim light in the ice
cream shop at the opposite end of the street. She imagined him working on his accounts or perhaps he was
relaxing from the day's backbreaking work by creating
some new ice cream concoction to offer come spring.

They saw each other at the biweekly church services, but with so many of the women gone, Pleasant
joined those women who were still in residence in the
kitchen. In those homes where the woman of the house
was absent and the male members of the family had not
kept up with the housekeeping, Pleasant and the other
women were well aware that in such a case, they would
need to arrive early to make sure the womanless house
was clean and ready for services. They would also need
to stay late washing dishes and scrubbing pots and pans

used for the meal served following services. She was
relieved that on this particular Sunday services were
to be held in Grace Hadwell's house and Grace along
with Mildred Troyer worked side by side with Pleasant
in the kitchen.

During services, Pleasant sat between Mildred and
Grace and tried to find solace in the words of Bishop
Troyer for her grief over the loss of her father and her
abject loneliness without the chatter of her children
around. But her mind wandered to other matters—the
bakery and what to do with it. And what about her father's house? Would it be best to have Lydia and Greta
move in with her or should they stay where they were?

Her eyes as well as her mind wandered until her gaze
came to rest on Jeremiah. She was cognizant of his
every twitch, the way his shoulders and back usually
so ramrod straight seemed somehow to have folded in
on him, and the way he stared at the floor rather than
at the preacher who droned on about wandering in the
wilderness. She supposed the lesson was about Moses
and the chosen ones but the truth was that it seemed
to be more immediate than that. She felt as if she were
the wanderer, the lost one, for what was she going to
do now?

Business at the bakery had fallen off even more with
the absence of so many of the women and children, and
with the school closed there was very little income for
Lydia and Greta to live on once they returned. Then
there was her house and the farm. She had to face the
fact that for all intents and purposes she was now the
head of Gunther's household as well as Merle's. She

felt abandoned and bereft and she was so very tired of being the strong one.

Not that other members of the community hadn't rallied to her needs. Roger Hadwell had shown up one Saturday morning with a crew of neighbors to make much needed repairs to Merle's house and Josef Bontrager showed up every morning to feed and milk the cows, feed the chickens, clean out the chicken coop and barn and deliver the milk and eggs she would use for the day's baking. It was the way of her people— neighbor helping neighbor—and she did not think of these kind and generous acts as charity. Certainly she repaid them in kind through her work on Sunday mornings when there were services and with the bread and baked goods she handed Josef after he made his daily delivery.

Bishop Troyer called for the final prayer and Pleasant bowed her head, closing her eyes tight as she chided herself for not giving herself over to God's work instead of dwelling on her own unhappiness. There had been no reports of cases of influenza in the area for nearly a week now and that meant that perhaps the danger had passed and the children—and Hannah and Lydia and Greta—would soon be able to come home. The thought brought her a sense of peace and when she opened her eyes she smiled at Mildred Troyer who was sitting next to her.

But Mildred met her smile with a worried frown.

"Mildred, is anything the matter?" Pleasant asked.

"It's Jeremiah," Mildred admitted, casting a glance toward her great-nephew who was already making his way across the yard to his buggy. "I'm worried about his health. He's lost weight since coming back and he has this cough and he's working so very hard. John and I barely see him and frankly when he did show up this morning, I could not believe the difference in him."

Pleasant studied Jeremiah for a long moment and almost as if he felt her gaze he glanced her way, hesitated for a moment and then immediately continued on his way. "He does look tired," she admitted and did not add that she'd observed a brightness of his eyes that did not seem to come from any kind of pleasure at seeing her but rather appeared to be the glimmer of fever such as she had seen when the children had been ill with colds. "Perhaps Bishop Troyer could persuade him to see a doctor."

"You agree then?"

"I agree that he doesn't look well," Pleasant said.

"I'm so afraid that perhaps in his travels he contracted the virus," Mildred said and this time she covered her lips with her clenched fist and her voice was a whisper.

Alarm flooded through Pleasant like a sudden downpour. If Jeremiah were ill with the virus then there was no chance that the children would be able to return. More to the point if he were ill, he could be in serious danger. In addition to the early deaths reported in Georgia, there had been rumors of at least half a dozen additional deaths. The numbers were nowhere near as many as during the epidemic but even one death was enough to warrant concern. Her panic at the very idea that after everything else she might lose Jeremiah surprised her. Lose him? What did that mean? It wasn't as if they had any real connection. "He should be quarantined immediately until the doctor can examine him."

Mildred sighed. "Try and tell him that. He assures me that he's just tired from working such long hours—makes a joke about being soft." She hesitated a moment. "He has great respect for you, Pleasant. Perhaps you could speak with him?"

"I..."

"Please try to make him understand that he does himself no favors by working so hard that he becomes ill. His uncle is no longer alive to know of his successes and..."

"I don't understand."

Mildred sighed. "Oh, Pleasant, you, of all people understand. Jeremiah's uncle was a lot like Merle. There was no pleasing the man although certainly Jeremiah spent most of his youth trying—just as Rolf did with Merle."

Pleasant felt that she should defend her late husband's memory but this was the bishop's wife and certainly she had known Merle as well as anyone had. "All right," she agreed and Mildred's smile reflected her relief. "But I can't imagine that..."

"Just talk to him," Mildred urged.

Through the long afternoon after leaving services and returning to her house, Pleasant thought of little other than how best to approach Jeremiah with Mildred's concerns. He did not strike her as a man who would take kindly to meddling and certainly she would be meddling. Besides, it was the Sabbath, so there was no possibility that she could go to the bakery and hope to see him out in the yard or sitting on the stoop out-

side the ice cream shop. On the other hand, she needed
to take care of some things at her father's house—a
dwelling that sat not twenty yards to the other side of
Jeremiah's shop and residence. Perhaps she would see
him after all and it would be rude not to stop and exchange pleasantries.

Having settled on a plan, the outcome lay in God's
hands, for unless Jeremiah made his presence known
to her, there was little she could do to draw him out.
It would certainly be totally inappropriate for her to
knock at his door.

But knocking at his door was exactly what she found
herself doing not twenty minutes later after she had
entered Gunther's dim and shadowy house and found
a large black snake coiled in a corner of the kitchen.
There wasn't much that Pleasant feared in this world
but she drew the line at snakes, even harmless ones as
she suspected this one was.

"Pleasant?"

Jeremiah seemed confused when he opened the door,
as if he had not quite awakened and yet before knocking she had heard him coughing and moving around his
small kitchen. "I'm sorry to bother you, Jeremiah, but
I was at my father's—I wanted to…. Well, it doesn't
really matter why."

Jeremiah shook his head as if to clear it and in the
afternoon light she saw that she had been right about
his feverish eyes. "What's happened?" he asked, glancing toward Gunther's house as if expecting to see some
catastrophe.

"There's a snake in the kitchen—a large one. Harmless probably but…"

Jeremiah smiled. "Well, well, well. I must say I never saw the day that you would be afraid of anything, Pleasant."

"I'm not afraid of the thing," she protested. "I simply don't like snakes." She tried to disguise an involuntary shudder and failed.

His grin broadened. "Give me a minute." He disappeared inside and returned a moment later with a large basket and a walking stick. "Are you coming or do you want to wait here?" he asked as he stepped past her and walked toward Gunther's open back door. "Chances are the thing has already vacated the premises since you left the door open."

Pleasant trudged along behind him, torn between hoping he was right and the fact that if the snake had simply disappeared how she would know for sure the thing wasn't lurking elsewhere in the house.

"Nope," Jeremiah called as soon as he stepped inside Gunther's kitchen. "Still here."

Pleasant edged closer, her hands and forearms wrapped in her apron as she tried to see what was happening. Then she heard a ruckus as if Jeremiah and the snake were engaged in combat and she shrieked. Just then Jeremiah emerged holding the basket in one hand and pushing the snake back inside it with the walking stick. "One snake removed," he announced but he made no further effort to dispose of the thing.

"Well, now what?" Pleasant asked.

Jeremiah picked up a flour sack from a stack on Gunther's back porch and after some effort he guided the snake into the bag and secured the top. "I could kill it," he offered.

Pleasant was horrified. "You wouldn't. That's one of God's own creatures and it's the Sabbath."

"I don't understand. Are you saying you want me to wait until it's no longer the Sabbath and then kill it?"

"I don't want you to kill it at all," she fumed. "Just…" She glanced around at the fields that stretched out beyond his shop and Gunther's house. "Just take it out there and let it go far away from the house and the school and anywhere else it might decide to nest."

"Yes, ma'am. But you'll have to come along."

"Why?"

"Because I want you to see that it's truly gone. I won't be the cause of you not getting your rest because you're imagining some snake crawling around."

"Very well," she huffed and started off through the nearest field. Behind her she heard him chuckle and then he started to cough.

She turned to see him doubled over as the coughing racked his entire body. He dropped the flour sack and the tie loosened and she was aware that the snake was slithering off into the field but snake or no snake, she ran to Jeremiah. Supporting him with her arm around his waist she waited for the bout of coughing to end. She was aware that he was gasping for air and she looked around in a panic hoping to see some neighbor that she might call upon to help her get Jeremiah to a place where he could sit down and regain some of the strength that the deep racking cough had sapped.

But there was no one in sight. "All right," she said calmly. "You'll be all right." She might have been speaking to one of her own children. "Lean on me and let's get you back to the house."

He did as she instructed, leaning heavily against her as together they stumbled over the uneven ground to his rooms behind the ice cream shop. Every step of the way she scanned her surroundings for any sign of someone out and about who might help her get him safely home and then go for help. But the lanes leading off the main street of Celery Fields were even more deserted than usual. She tightened her grip on him and saw that her father's house was much closer than his place was. "Come on," she encouraged him. "Just a few more steps."

Thankfully, the back door to Gunther's house required only one small step up to reach. Once inside the kitchen she considered her next move and headed for her father's room just off the hall that led to the front of the house. There she moved as close as possible to the narrow bed and released her hold on Jeremiah, guiding his fall so that he landed on the bed. Somewhere along the way she realized that his hat had come off and she could see that his hair was soaked with perspiration as was his shirt.

"I'll get you some water," she said as she lifted his feet onto the bed, not caring that his shoes were caked with dirt from the fields. He rolled to his back and threw his forearm over his face to shut out the light which seemed to cause him actual pain. "Water," she murmured and hurried back to the kitchen.

She pumped water into a white enameled pan and threw a couple of dish towels over one shoulder. Next she filled a pitcher with water and set it and a glass in the pan of water so she could carry everything at once.

Hurrying back down the hall she thought she heard Jeremiah call out. "Coming," she called back.

But when she reached the room he was lying flat on his back, his arm still covering his face and his breathing came in short bursts as if the air could not find its way through his lungs. She set the basin of water on the floor near the head of the bed and pulled a wooden armless rocker that Gunther had made for her mother, closer. Setting the pitcher and drinking glass aside for the moment, she soaked one towel and squeezed the excess water from it before gently swabbing his lips that she now realized were chapped and cracked. He sucked at the moisture as a man who had wandered for days in the desert might.

"Let me wipe your brow," she murmured as she gently pulled the towel free of his mouth and refolded it so that she could dab sweat from his cheeks and forehead. His arm fell heavily to his side but he kept his eyes closed and moaned when she laid the cool towel over them. "Jeremiah, you are very ill and I must go for help."

He rolled his head from side to side.

"I have some water here," she continued. "See if you can sip a little." She cradled the back of his neck with one arm while she maneuvered the glass to his lips with the other. A little water made it into his mouth while more of it trickled down his neck and as soon as he tried to swallow he started to cough. Pushing her hand away he curled onto his side and let the coughing spell have its way with him. When finally it passed he rolled to his back, gasping for breath once again.

Pleasant brushed his hair back from his forehead

and in so doing realized that he was burning up. At the same time he was taken by such a chill that his entire body arched and his teeth chattered uncontrollably.

"Blankets," she instructed herself and spread the quilt that had been folded at the end of Gunther's bed over Jeremiah. Instinctively, he reached for it and pulled it closer. Pleasant raced to the bedroom her half sisters shared and grabbed the quilts from both beds. She spread them over Jeremiah, wiped his face and then laid a cool towel over his forehead and eyes.

"I have to go," she whispered, appreciating for perhaps the first time in her life the value of conveniences such as telephones that the *Englisch* world took for granted. "I'll be back," she promised and realized that Jeremiah's breathing had quieted and he was lying very still. "Don't you dare die on me, Jeremiah," she said in her normal voice, and as she ran from Gunther's house all the way to the bishop's home three streets away she was certain that she had only imagined the twitch of a smile that had seemed to relax Jeremiah's features.

Jeremiah was only dimly aware of the activity that surrounded him. He was having some trouble distinguishing reality from fantasy. Had he dreamed that Pleasant had shown up at his door? Certainly he had dreamed that many times before, wishing for it to be so. And what about the snake? No, surely that had been real for he had never been more aware of how the fever he'd been fighting for a week now had sapped his strength as he was when trying to wrestle that snake into the basket.

But everything after that was a blur. The light hurt

his eyes. Surely that was not a good sign. And he felt
as if he had been soaked in a hot shower, but then he
had thought himself cast out into the snow without his
coat. He was freezing. There was a woman's gentle
voice speaking to him as his mother once had. But then
he had heard Pleasant's unmistakable order that he was
not to die on her. The statement had made him smile,
for only Pleasant would take his dying so personally.
And then everything went quiet and he stopped trying
to make sense of things and gave in to sleep.

He was awakened by the low murmur of voices—
John speaking in English to another man who was
making little effort to monitor the volume of his voice.
"Pneumonia," he boomed. "No, not the influenza at
all. We haven't seen a case of that in at least a couple
of weeks now and none have been reported anywhere
near here. Your nephew is not contagious, sir, just a
very very sick man."

I can't be sick, Jeremiah mentally argued with the
man.

"Prolonged rest is the key," the man that Jeremiah
had to assume was the doctor announced. "I'll stop
back tomorrow."

Footsteps on the planked floors, a screen door opening and closing with a click, the start-up of a car engine
and the sound of the doctor's automobile driving away.
Jeremiah waited to be sure the doctor was gone and
then rolled to his side and pushed himself into a sitting position. Instantly, everything around him started
to spin and shutting his eyes seemed the only recourse
for making it stop.

"What do you think you're doing?" Pleasant asked,

her tone that of a schoolteacher reprimanding an errant child. "Lie back down in that bed right now."

"I have work to do," Jeremiah said, opening his eyes and gripping the side of the bed just in case. He cleared his throat, trying to rid himself of the huskiness in his voice, and looked around for his shoes. He located them standing in a corner of the room underneath a hook that held his hat. "Where am I?"

"My father's house and if you don't even know where you are then it is beyond me how you think you might be able to concentrate on your work. Besides, it is the Sabbath. Now see if you can swallow a little of this chicken broth that your Aunt Mildred made for you."

He accepted the mug and sipped the hot broth while he watched her bustling around the room stacking towels and fresh linens on a small side table. "I thought I heard Uncle John speaking with the doctor."

"You did. The doctor will return tomorrow. Bishop Troyer has gone home to gather some things he will need while he stays the night with you. Tomorrow the doctor says you can be moved to the bishop's house for the duration."

"And what is the duration?"

She shrugged. "Whatever time it takes for you to heal. It could be a month or…"

"I don't have a month," Jeremiah protested and that set off a coughing spell that racked his chest with indescribable pain and made breathing seem suddenly impossible. He gripped the mattress harder and waited for the coughing to pass, then gulped in air and fought for his next breath.

Pleasant removed the cup of broth from his hand

and knelt next to him. "Slowly," she coached. "The doctor says that it's the panic that can make it worse." She drew in a deep breath of her own and slowly blew it out through pursed lips. And because that reminded him of the kiss they had shared and of his vow not to permit himself to think about that—or her—or the idea that there might be a future for them, he turned away from her.

"How did I get here—to Gunther's?" His voice was weak, barely more than a whisper now.

"There was a snake in the kitchen earlier when I came to check on the house and I came to your house—because it was the closest," she added defensively.

Jeremiah smiled. So the snake had been real as had her fear of it. "Thank you," he said.

Once again she was on her feet and moving around the room, adjusting a lamp shade, refolding a towel. "There's hardly any reason to thank me," she protested. "Had I not gotten you to take care of the snake, you probably would not have overexerted yourself and…"

"Or I might have laid there in my rooms and been unable to catch my breath and…"

"You are not going to die, Jeremiah Troyer. At least not in the near term unless, of course, you refuse to follow doctor's orders and insist on driving yourself too hard and making yourself even sicker in the bargain." Seemingly satisfied that she had properly stocked the sickroom, Pleasant sat down in the lone chair—a small rocking chair and picked up some mending.

"Are you staying as well?"

"I am waiting for the bishop to return. You are too weak to be left alone." She bent to her work, slowly removing the thread from the hem of a pair of boys' trousers.

With little strength and no other real choice, Jeremiah lay back on the bed and watched her. "You make a good nurse," he said.

"I know nothing about that profession," she replied around a half dozen straight pins that she had placed between her lips and was using to set the new hem. "Anyone would have done exactly as I did under the circumstances."

"I can't figure out how you managed to drag me back here. We were in the fields, weren't we?"

"Disposing of the snake—yes."

He had a sudden memory of her arm around his waist, her fingers gripping his side as she urged him to lean on her. "We must have looked like participants in a sack race coming across that field," he said with a chuckle.

"God was with us," she murmured, ducking her head to hide her smile.

He closed his eyes and pulled the quilt that he'd cast aside when he tried to sit up around his shoulders. Instantly, she was at his side. "Are you chilled?" She did not wait for an answer but spread the covers over him and then felt his forehead with the back of her hand.

Her skin was soft and smooth and so wonderfully cool against his brow that it calmed him. "Tired," he muttered. "So very tired."

"Then rest," she replied and readjusted the covers.

"Don't go," he said.

"I'm right here," she replied and he heard the creak

of the cane seat of the rocking chair as she sat down next to him.

"Gut," he murmured. Pleasant was there. She would make sure he was all right. She would take care of everything—his job, his business…and him.

Chapter Fifteen

To Pleasant's surprise, Jeremiah turned out to be a very good patient. He took his medicine, followed the doctor's instructions to get plenty of rest and seemed content to allow his Aunt Mildred to mother him. He spent a week at Mildred and John's house and then moved back to his rooms behind the ice cream shop. Levi had organized the men of Celery Fields to cover Jeremiah's work from his shifts at the ice plant to the delivery of ice to homes in the area to the delivery of ice to the cooperative. All of this Pleasant learned from Mildred when the older woman stopped by the bakery after checking on Jeremiah.

For her part she kept her distance, taking comfort in the news of his recovery but stopping short of visiting him herself. She told herself that she was only doing what was proper, but in truth she knew that she had allowed herself to become too involved in his life— she had allowed herself to care for him in ways that were not appropriate and certainly not something that he would welcome given his determination never to marry.

So when the train carrying Hannah and the children along with Lydia and Greta returned a week after Jeremiah had moved back to his place behind the ice cream shop, Pleasant was both ecstatic at having her children and dear friend home again and relieved that surely now her days would once again be so full that she would not have time to think about Jeremiah so much.

Hilda Yoder and her children had been back for three days now and Pleasant was anxious to have her own family home again. But she had not realized how very much she had missed the children until she saw them coming toward her at the station. Rolf looked as if he had grown another two inches in just the two weeks they had been away. And Bettina walked with a quiet grace that was new for her and reminded Pleasant of Levi's sister-in-law, Mae. The twins, however, did not seem to have changed at all. They ran pell-mell to her open arms, competing to be the first to report all of the new experiences they had shared.

Hannah and Lydia and Greta stood off to one side waiting their turn to be welcomed home while Caleb and Levi took charge of loading their luggage onto the buggy.

"Thank you so much," Pleasant said to Hannah after the twins had run off to tell Levi of their adventures.

"How are things here?" Hannah asked. "I understand that Jeremiah Troyer has fallen ill?"

Pleasant nodded. "Pneumonia. God has blessed him and the medicine—penicillin—that the doctor gave him seems to have brought him through the worst of it. He's doing much better but he's been left weak as a newborn kitten." She did not add that in spite of the efforts of

Levi and the other men in the community to keep Jeremiah's agreement with the Palmer brothers, she had noticed the truck of a competing ice delivery service parked outside the offices of the cooperative as she followed Levi in her own buggy on their way to meet the train.

"He can't work then?"

"Not yet. But Levi and the others have helped out."

"And how is business at the bakery?"

Pleasant smiled. "Better since the threat of the flu passed. We're even getting orders again from merchants in Sarasota. Apparently, business there has started to improve with the arrival of the winter visitors. Not so many as in the past but some."

"So, once again God has blessed our community," Hannah said with a sigh of relief. "And I am more than a little anxious to get home and see how Levi has fared these last two weeks."

Pleasant smiled. "Your house is spotless."

"I doubt that but whatever its state it will be good to be home again." She smiled at her husband who helped her into the front seat of their buggy while Caleb took his place with his younger siblings in back. Once seated, Hannah's pregnancy became more obvious as she folded her hands over her stomach pressing the fullness of her skirt around it.

Pleasant waved to them as they drove away and then turned to her own family—grown now to include her two half sisters. It occurred to her that they had some decisions to make starting with whether or not Lydia and Greta would move in with her or stay in their father's house. Lydia was certainly of age to manage a household, but she also had the school to manage. Greta would no doubt marry Josef Bontrager as soon as that young man worked up his nerve to ask her and that would leave Lydia alone.

"Let's go home," Lydia said quietly as they watched the Harnisher family drive away. And as if she had been thinking the same thoughts as Pleasant, she added, "We can work out the details of where Greta and I will reside tomorrow. For today, I just want to be at home, all right?"

"Of course," Pleasant assured her and then orchestrated the loading of the four children and three adults into her small buggy. Greta rode in back with the twins cuddled in her lap and Rolf and Bettina crowded to either side of her while Lydia rode up front with Pleasant. The children continued to fill her in on everything they had seen and everyone they had met on their journey, but Pleasant saw that Jeremiah's competitor's truck was still at the cooperative as they passed and her thoughts wandered. "I need to make one stop," she said as she turned the buggy onto the sandy road that led to the low concrete building housing the offices of the cooperative.

Just as she pulled the buggy to a halt, a man exited the offices and got into the truck and drove away.

"I'll be right back," Pleasant said as she climbed down and walked stiffly toward the front door of the building. She had no idea what she was going to say or even who might be available to hear her out, but she would not stand by and let someone else take business away from Jeremiah.

"May I help you?" A young woman, her lips lined

with lipstick and her hair artificially curled glanced up
with surprise when Pleasant entered the small reception
area.

"I wonder if the manager is available."

"Sorry. Everyone has gone for the day. I was just
getting ready to close up myself and…"

"I saw a truck outside just now—a truck for the
Venice Ice Company?"

To Pleasant's surprise, the woman blushed scarlet
red and became more than a little agitated, wringing
her hands and glancing around as if expecting someone
to pop out of a closed doorway at any moment. "Please
don't say anything," she said, her voice barely above a
whisper. "Hank's my boyfriend and he just stopped by
to…if my bosses knew that I was entertaining…please,"
she pleaded.

Relief flooded Pleasant. "Oh, I see. Then that young
man was not here on business for…"

"No and there's the trouble, don't you see? He was
supposed to be finishing up his delivery route but then
he saw that the Palmers' car was gone and he…"

"Please don't feel you owe me any explanation,
Miss." Pleasant turned back to the door.

"Shall I tell my bosses that you wanted to see them?"

"No. That won't be necessary," Pleasant replied.
"Good day."

Outside, Pleasant ignored Lydia's curious glance as
she climbed back into the buggy and took the reins.

"Is everything all right?"

"Yes. Perfectly all right now that my family is safely
home again," Pleasant assured her; *and Jeremiah's
business is apparently safe as well.*

* * *

The better Jeremiah felt the more restless he became and yet it was clear that he did not yet have the strength to manage the heavy work of his job at the ice plant or making deliveries. Levi stopped by daily to give him reports about who would be making the deliveries that day and who would be going to the cooperative to handle things there. Business throughout the region was improving and everyone was relieved about that. And Jeremiah was most appreciative of the ways his neighbors in Celery Fields had stepped in to help him while managing their own farms and businesses, but he felt the need to repay them in some way and sooner rather than later.

A few days earlier the doctor had given permission for him to move back to his rooms behind the ice cream shop. Mildred and John came by several times a day on the excuse of bringing him food or the need to do his laundry or some other housekeeping chore. He was well aware that his great-aunt and -uncle were more interested in checking up on him to make sure he didn't overdo than they were in delivering food or taking care of household matters. Still, he was relieved to be back in his own place waking each morning to the smell of fresh bread baking next door and thoughts of Pleasant.

He lay back on his narrow bed with his arms crossed behind his head and savored the aroma of Pleasant's rye bread. Later in the morning she would bake up some pies and other sweets to fill the display case in the front of the shop. He felt a sudden hunger for one of her molasses cookies and driven by that hunger he got himself dressed and walked slowly across the yard that separated her business from his. He refused to admit to himself that it wasn't molasses cookies drawing him to the bakery. It was the fact that it had been days since he'd seen Pleasant, much less talked to her, and he missed her.

"Guten morgen," he said and realized that his voice was still raspy from the effects of his illness and from lack of use. Pleasant spun around.

"I...*ja...guten morgen.*" She seemed unusually flustered by his presence, wiping her hands on a towel and looking anywhere but directly at him. "Should you be out like this?" she asked.

"The doctor suggested a few short walks as a way to regain my strength. From my shop to yours would seem to fit the bill. I had hoped there might be one of your molasses cookies available to give me the strength to make it home again." He opened the screen door and entered the kitchen but he was aware that he needed to be cautious in his movements. For reasons he didn't fully understand, Pleasant was as skittish around him as a newborn colt.

"I was just about to bake a batch," she said nodding to the trays lined up on the worktable. "I could bring you some once they cool."

"I'll wait if that's all right." He glanced toward Gunther's desk, the chair pushed in so that it did not invite anyone to sit there. "How's business?" he asked leaning against the doorway.

"Better," she said and seemed to relax. "For everyone, I think. For the bakery it means that some of the customers we had from Sarasota—shops and restaurants that carried our goods—have come back to us.

And there are a surprising number of winter tourists in the area—some of them have found their way here. They come because they are curious to see how we live and then they stay to shop."

"I was thinking about reopening the ice cream shop," Jeremiah said.

Pleasant frowned. "That would be a great deal of work for you. Just churning the ice cream takes so much effort and…"

"I was thinking that maybe Rolf and Caleb Harnisher could do that part of it." He waited to see how she would react to this idea.

"That might work but still there's everything else and you've been so ill and…"

"But I am better now, Pleasant, and I will get a little stronger every day. Besides, I would like to find some way to express my gratitude for everything that's been done for me."

"You know that no one expects repayment or thanks, Jeremiah. In fact…"

He nodded. "I understand that I have to take care in how I offer my gratitude, but that's the very reason reopening the ice cream shop might just be the answer. Uncle John mentioned the idea of a community picnic the other day and I was thinking that I could donate the ice cream for that as a way of letting folks know the ice cream shop is back in business. The question is whether with all you have to do, can you make the cones?"

"Of course, and speaking of that…" She went to Gunther's desk and opened a drawer. From far in the back of it she removed a tin box and handed it to him.

"What's this? A present?" He grinned.

"If that's how you choose to think of it but be assured that it is a gift you have given yourself."

Intrigued, he opened the box and his eyes widened when he saw the stack of money it contained. "What is this?"

"My father would never have accepted payment for goods never delivered," she explained, "and neither will I. Since you refused to stop leaving the weekly payment for cones never delivered I have kept the money here. And now that you are prepared to go back into business and apparently hire extra help, it is money I'm sure you can put to good use."

He closed the box and set it on the desk. "You are one stubborn woman, Pleasant Obermeier."

She apparently chose to ignore this, turning her attention to the ovens where she checked on the progress of the cookies. She slid one tray out and set it with a clatter on the worktable. He reached for a cookie and she swatted his hand away. "You'll burn yourself. Let them cool first."

He caught her hand in his and held on. It was an act of pure impulse but one that he did not regret. "Did you love him—your husband?" he asked and was as stunned as she obviously was at the question.

She pulled her fingers free of his and focused on removing the cookies from the pan to a large glass plate. At first he thought that she would ignore his question as she had his comment about her being stubborn, but after a moment she said, "Merle was not a man who believed in the kind of romantic love that I think you may mean."

"But you do believe in it?"

She pressed her lips into a thin line and then looked up at him. "I am a widow with four children and two half sisters who depend on me," she replied. "I have no time to think about such foolishness."

"Why not?" he pressed. "You're still relatively young and you have much to offer."

She placed the last cookie on the plate and then rested her hands on the edge of the worktable, her head bowed and her fingers clutching the table as if she drew strength from it. "Why are you doing this?" she whispered.

Why, indeed?

"Because I think perhaps it would be good to see someone care for you the way you care for everyone around you, Pleasant. Because I would like to see you happy."

She swiped at her eyes with the back of her hand and he moved closer but she waved him away. "I have four beautiful children, Jeremiah. I have sisters that I have come to treasure and wonderful friends in a community that has sustained me through many difficult times. Why would you push me to want more?"

Because I have come to love you. The clarity of that admission was almost his undoing. Everything he had ever promised himself he would never allow was unraveled in those few words and yet the truth they held could not be denied. "Pleasant, we are two people walking through this life on parallel paths. Might we not see what would happen should we try walking the path together?"

Her eyes sparkled with unshed tears and disbelief as

she looked up at him. "I do not need your pity, Jeremiah Troyer."

"I am not offering pity, Pleasant. I am offering my love."

She was speechless and did what he had observed was her natural reaction to such loss of control of the situation. She focused on something else. Placing two cookies in front of him she picked up the glass plate and headed to the front of the bakery. "You have been ill," she said as she deliberately put distance between them. "And such a serious illness—especially after the loss of a good friend—for certainly you and Gunther had become…"

He caught up with her and waited for her to place the plate of cookies in the display case before touching her lightly on her arm. "I am not delusional, Pleasant, and I know exactly what I just said. I will admit that it came as a surprise to me as it apparently did to you but that in no way changes the fact of it. I have feelings for you that go well beyond that of a neighbor for a neighbor. I believe that you return at least a portion of those same feelings and I am suggesting that we recognize that perhaps this is why God has brought us to this place at this time."

"Yet on Second Christmas you told me…"

"I also kissed you, Pleasant, and you kissed me back."

The bell over the bakery door announced the arrival of a customer and both Jeremiah and Pleasant jumped as if they had been caught doing something they shouldn't be doing.

"Well, Jeremiah," Hilda Yoder said as she eyed the

two of them, "it would appear that you are indeed on the mend."

"Jeremiah was just…just…" Pleasant stuttered.

"I stopped by to see if Pleasant would have time to bake up an order of cones for my ice cream, Frau Yoder. I'm sure you've heard that the bishop has suggested a community picnic to celebrate the end to the threat of a flu epidemic and the return of the children and re-opening of the school. It is my intention to provide the ice cream for that event."

"I see," Hilda said, still eyeing them both suspiciously.

"And I was just saying that I could definitely bake the cones once the bishop decides on the date for the picnic," Pleasant added as she edged around Jeremiah and moved closer to her former sister-in-law.

"That's what I came to tell you. The bishop was just in the store and said that the picnic is to be a week from Saturday." Hilda turned her full attention to Jeremiah. "Are you sure you're up to the challenge of this, Jeremiah? Churning ice cream to serve the entire community could…"

"I plan to hire help," Jeremiah told her. "Pleasant's son Rolf and Caleb Harnisher…and what about your eldest son? He's a good strong boy."

"I suppose that would be all right," Hilda replied and Jeremiah could see that she was pleased to be asked.

"Then it's all settled," he said. "And now if you'll excuse me, I expect my Aunt Mildred has gone to my house to prepare my lunch and she'll worry when she discovers that I'm not there. I'll just go out the back," he said as he turned away from Hilda so that she would not see the pleading look he gave Pleasant. "Think about it," he mouthed and when she nodded, his heart felt as if it might actually pound its way right out of his chest.

Think about it? As if she could think of anything else. Not even Hilda's chatter distracted her as she tried to find some order in the events of the past few minutes. Several people in the community had commented on the fact that Jeremiah seemed to be a man prone to sudden decisions and even rash actions. The evidence of that lay in his decision to pull up stakes and leave a perfectly good farming business to start over in Florida. Further evidence lay in his sudden decision to head north after the holidays. Speculation had run rampant that he had realized the folly of his decision and decided to return to his family and possibly reclaim his place there. Pleasant doubted if anyone would be surprised at the way in which he had orchestrated a complete about-face from his earlier lifelong bachelor status to ask her permission to court her. For that was what he was asking, wasn't it?

"Are you listening, Pleasant?" Hilda demanded.

"I apologize. I have a great deal on my mind and now with the addition of Jeremiah's…"

"Precisely," Hilda huffed. "As I was saying, you have become the focal point for some village gossip, Pleasant, and it does you no good to continue your contact with this man."

"It's business," Pleasant protested and felt she did not need to add that it was business she could use.

"And yet, I have learned that you were alone with the man when he fell ill, that you got him to your father's

house and were in there for some time with him—
alone—before additional help could arrive."

"Would you have had me leave the poor man lying in
the fields?" Pleasant snapped. "I'm sorry, Hilda. That
was uncalled for. I assure you that the relationship between Herr Troyer and myself is strictly…"

"I saw his hand on your arm when I entered the
bakery, Pleasant."

Pleasant would not lie to cover the truth of Hilda's
accusation so she remained silent.

"My dear, nothing would make Moses and me happier than to see you find a good man. You deserve that
after everything Merle put you through."

Pleasant's eyes widened with shock, but Hilda waved
away her surprise.

"Oh, I know what my brother was, Pleasant. I had
hoped—we all had—that once he married you he might
change, but…" She shook her head. "I know that he
struck not only the children but you as well and I am
sorry for that. His temper had always been uncontrol-
lable. Even when we were children…"

"Oh, Hilda, are you saying that Merle struck you?"

Hilda nodded. "He always had to be in control and
whenever that control seemed threatened, he would lash
out, usually at the ones nearest and dearest to him."

"And yet, he did love the children—and their
mother," Pleasant reminded Hilda, feeling a duty to
defend her late husband. When Hilda said nothing,
Pleasant said, "I know you worry about me, Hilda, and
I am grateful for that, but Jeremiah…"

Hilda held up her hand to stop her from saying anything further. "Mark my words, Pleasant, you need to

watch yourself where that man is concerned. You have a reputation to maintain—a reputation that reflects on those children and now on your sisters as well."

Pleasant realized that Hilda was waiting for some kind of assurance that she had heard and would heed the warning so she chose her words with care. "I appreciate your advice as always, Hilda, but I assure you that you have nothing to be concerned about. It is business, nothing more."

"Suit yourself," Hilda said, "but a man puts his hand on you—well, it raises questions." And before Pleasant could say anything more, Hilda turned on her heel and left the bakery.

She was right, of course, Pleasant thought once she was alone again. Anyone could have walked in. Anyone could have glanced through the bakery windows and wondered why Jeremiah was standing behind the display case instead of in front of it and why he was standing there with her. And Hilda was right to remind Pleasant of her obligation to the children and to Lydia and Greta since she was now the head of both households.

Oh, but she was so very tired of the bonds that came with duty—the shoulds and could-nots. She loved her friends and family and certainly at her age she should know better than to indulge herself in some romantic fantasy. And yet the idea of being courted by a man as handsome and filled with joy as Jeremiah was—no! Not a man *like* Jeremiah, but Jeremiah himself. All her life she had lived by the traditions of her faith and she was not about to change now. And yet was there some possibility that Jeremiah had been right—that God had a plan for them? Surely there was no harm in getting to know each other a little better. If nothing else, he was good with the children and certainly Rolf needed the influence of a successful man in his life.

She put down the mixing bowl she'd been cradling in her arm while beating batter for a cake and smoothed her apron. Then she wrapped the cookies he'd left on the worktable in wax paper and stepped outside. To her relief, Jeremiah was outside as well for it would not do to call on him in his private residence without the buffer of either the children or another adult. He was standing outside the ice cream shop making notes on a folded piece of paper with a stub of a pencil.

"You forgot the cookies," she said and handed him the package.

"So I did. Thanks." He put down the paper and pencil and unwrapped the cookies. As he took a bite of one, he looked at her and a half smile skittered over his lips. "Best I ever had," he proclaimed, waving the half eaten cookie in her direction.

"I was wondering if you would be wanting the sample cones again? For the picnic?"

"What do you think?" He started on the second cookie.

"I wouldn't think so if the ice cream is for the picnic. I just thought perhaps for the reopening of the shop you might want to repeat…"

"The regular cones will be fine," he said, dusting off the crumbs of cookies that had stuck to his fingers.

"All right," she said and paused. Back in the bakery she had been so clear about what she wanted to say to him but standing here not a foot from him was a different matter altogether.

"Was there something else, Pleasant?"

Was it her overactive imagination playing tricks on her once again or was there a hint of hope in that question?

"I—uh—about what we were discussing before Hilda came in."

He released a ragged sigh and frowned. "Look, I…"

"If you're feeling up to it, I thought perhaps you and the bishop and your Aunt Mildred might come over for supper this evening. We could discuss the plans for the picnic."

This time she did not need to imagine the interpretation of his expression. Disappointment lined the corners of his mouth and eyes as plainly as a smile might have. "So, it's business as always with you, is it, Pleasant?"

"No. That is… Oh, Jeremiah, why must you make things so difficult?"

He laughed incredulously. "Me? What about you?"

She straightened her spine, preparing to speak her piece and then get away from him as quickly as possible. "Courting in the true sense is out of the question. However…"

"Why?"

"However," she stressed, "I have decided that it would be good for us to know each other better. We are neighbors after all and business associates and the children are fond of you."

"You have decided?"

She truly wished he would stop challenging her with

questions. *So leave.* But her feet remained rooted to the ground.

He took half a step closer. "And what if I have decided something entirely different, Pleasant?" He lowered his voice. "What if I have decided that one kiss simply will not do?"

She felt the blood rush to her cheeks at the very idea of repeating that kiss. "Stop it," she said but her voice failed her and the words came out on a whisper.

Jeremiah moved a step away from her. "I will come for supper."

"With the bishop," she amended.

"With the bishop," he agreed.

"Das ist gut," she said and forced herself to turn back toward the bakery.

"And afterward," he added when she was a good ten steps from him, "after the children are in bed and my uncle and aunt are safely home again, I will come back and you and I will start to tell one another our stories, Pleasant."

The idea of sitting with Jeremiah on her back porch after everyone else in the community was asleep and telling him all the things she had kept in her heart filled her with such a rush of joy that Pleasant found she could not speak. And so without looking back at him, she said only one word. *"Ja."*

Chapter Sixteen

Ever since Gunther's death, Pleasant had taken to closing the bakery on Mondays. She made use of that day to tend to household matters and she continued to participate in the weekly frolics the women of the community had established. On the Monday that followed a week of nightly visits from Jeremiah, she drove her buggy to the Harnisher farm, anxious to see Hannah even if she really couldn't talk to her friend about Jeremiah with the other women around.

She was so confused by him. As he had promised, he came to her back porch every night around nine and took a seat on the first step. He did not knock or otherwise make his presence known, just sat out there and waited for her to join him. "And what if I didn't come out here?" she'd asked him on the third night.

"Then I would assume you had something else to do and leave, but I would be back the next night and the one after that," he told her. "You don't have to worry, Pleasant. We're just going to talk—for now."

And the implied promise that somewhere down the road they might do more than talk—that there might be a repeat of that sweet kiss they had shared on Christmas, was the last thought Pleasant had as she drifted off to sleep each night and the first that she awoke to each morning.

After a week of his visits, she knew more about him than she had ever known about Merle and she had shared things with him that she had never told anyone else—not even her best friend, Hannah. But the fact was that she was falling deeply in love with Jeremiah and before she would risk disappointment in romance for a third time in her life, she needed the advice of someone who had known true love. How did a person know for certain?

As if Hannah had understood Pleasant's need to talk, she suggested that the other women take charge of the housecleaning while she and Pleasant worked in the garden. "That way we can make short work of both tasks and have time for some quilting and conversation before everyone needs to get home."

Only Hilda seemed about to object but seeing that she was alone in that, she bit her lip and took charge of organizing the other women while Hannah and Pleasant escaped to the large kitchen garden that Hannah had planted close to the house.

"All right," Hannah said as Pleasant knelt along the border of the garden and started pulling weeds. "Talk to me. Levi tells me that Jeremiah is courting you."

Pleasant sucked in her breath. "He said that?"

"The women aren't the only ones who talk, Pleasant. Besides, Levi and Jeremiah have become good friends." She set down a bucket of water for Pleasant to use in softening the hard ground. "So?"

"Courting is too strong a word. We are getting better acquainted. The children admire him—especially Rolf—and I need to make certain that..."

"Stop that," Hannah said with more irritation than Pleasant had ever heard from her. "You have waited your whole life for a man like Jeremiah—a good man—a man who will be good to you."

"How can you know that?"

"I know that he is not at all like Merle. I know from what you have told me and what he has told Levi that he has tried hard to be honest with you about his intentions."

"Oh, I don't know," Pleasant said. "At first he made it very clear that he was not going to marry—ever."

"And now?"

"Now he...he professes to love me," she said, her voice fading away with the wonder of saying those words aloud instead of savoring them in her heart when she was alone.

"And do you love him?"

There was no sense beating around the bush with Hannah. She seemed to be able to see through Pleasant's protests and excuses better than anyone Pleasant had ever known. "I love him," she admitted.

To her surprise, Hannah laughed. "Well, you don't have to make it sound like the worst thing that has ever happened to you. This is a good thing—he loves you and you love him." She dusted dirt off her hands and stood up. "So call it what you like—getting better acquainted or whatever suits you. He's courting you and you are permitting that courtship."

"Leading to what?" Pleasant asked the single question that had plagued her every night after Jeremiah returned to his house.

"Marriage, a father for those children, a companion for you to share the rest of your days with, a…"

"He has changed his mind once," Pleasant told her friend. "There is nothing to say that he won't realize his mistake and change it back to his decision never to marry."

"Oh, Pleasant, you are a woman of great faith. Surely you have prayed on this matter."

"Well, of course. I pray daily for the wisdom to make the decisions that will keep the children safe and secure and support Lydia and Greta until they are established in households of their own."

"And do you never pray for yourself?"

"That would be selfish and you know it."

Hannah leaned on a long-handled hoe. "You haven't a selfish bone in your body," she said. "You are praying for guidance in your dealings with the children and your sisters. How is that any different than praying for guidance in your personal dealings with Jeremiah?"

Pleasant bit her lip as she got to her feet and deposited a small pile of pulled weeds into the now-empty water bucket. "I don't want to be hurt yet again," she admitted.

Hannah relieved her of the bucket and started back toward the shed where she stored her gardening tools. "Think of it this way, Pleasant. You agreed to marry Merle even when you knew his interest in you was to gain a mother for his children rather than his undying love for you. Am I right?"

Pleasant nodded. "He made that plain enough."

"And now Jeremiah is making it plain that he has come to love you—as a woman he wishes to share his life with."

Pleasant felt her heart swell with hope. "Did he say those things to Levi?"

"He did, but more to the point, I would guess that he has said those things to you."

Pleasant could not deny the truth of that for every night when he was about to leave, he held her with such tenderness as if she were fragile and might disappear, and every night he murmured, "I love you, Pleasant." And although she had yet to say those words back to him, he had not stopped telling her that he loved her.

"Trust your heart, Pleasant," Hannah advised. "As I did with Levi."

Tears of happiness and gratitude filled Pleasant's eyes and in the shadow of the garden shed, she grinned at her friend. "You really think that...?"

"I really do," Hannah assured her as she squeezed Pleasant's hand.

And in that moment, Pleasant decided that the picnic would be the perfect venue for her to find a time to truly open her heart to Jeremiah Troyer. *And if he breaks it?* an inner voice nagged.

"He wouldn't," Pleasant whispered under her breath, and as she followed Hannah back to the house where the other women were waiting, she had never felt more certain that this time—with this man—things would be different.

John Troyer had picked the perfect day for a celebratory picnic. After a cold winter—even by Florida standards—the day was perfect with temperatures in the mid-seventies, blue skies and not a hint of humidity. Church elders had chosen a spot along a branch of the meandering Phillippi Creek for the event and by mid-morning buggies filled with smiling adults and excited children had already started to arrive. By noon the area was packed with people of all ages, all similarly attired and all smiling broadly. Women, helped by their teenaged daughters and granddaughters laid out a spread of food while the men and older boys wandered down to the creek to try their luck at fishing or pounded stakes into the hard ground for a game of horseshoes. The younger children needed no organized activity to fill their time. The place was rife with the possibility of adventure and the children made their own games.

"We're pioneers," Will announced when Pleasant asked what they were playing. She could not help thinking that in many ways the people of Celery Fields were indeed pioneers. Every adult present had migrated here from somewhere else. Only the children could claim to be native Floridians—and not all of them.

"And just what do pioneers do?" she called back to her son.

"Explore," Henry shouted with glee and took off running toward the banks of the creek.

"Be careful," Pleasant said and had taken a step to follow them when she felt Jeremiah's hand on her shoulder.

"I'll go," he said. "Just save me a place next to you for the picnic." He winked at her and instead of glancing around nervously to see who might be looking, Pleasant simply smiled. The fact was that after today—

after she had finally told him she returned his feelings and was ready for the two of them to plan a future together—it wouldn't really matter what anyone else thought.

"Don't fall in the creek," she warned. "I believe somewhere along the way I heard you admit that you never learned to swim?"

He grinned and waved as he headed for the creek.

It was that kind of day, Pleasant decided. A day when everyone regardless of age felt a bit like a kid again. A day that invited friends to joke with one another. A perfect day for admitting to yourself and the world around you that you had fallen deeply in love and never in your entire life felt happier or more fulfilled. Pleasant just wished that her parents could be here to share in this moment of unadulterated joy.

She hummed to herself as she mixed up a salad from the bounty that several gardens had yielded. Nearby Hannah was squeezing fruit for the fresh lemonade, limeade and orangeade that they would all enjoy with their meal of cold fried chicken, beans simmering in pots over open fires and cold side dishes such as the salad she was making. For dessert there would be pies of all flavors and cakes that stood three layers high and cookies for the children to grab as they went back to their adventures.

She was just about to place the salad on the table when she looked toward the creek and her heart stopped. Jeremiah had just roughly snatched Henry into one arm and was raising a stick high over Will's head. Both boys were howling with fear. As he brought the stick down next to the boy, Pleasant dropped the salad and started to run.

Not again, she prayed as she ran, images of Merle's disciplining Rolf in the barnyard behind their house, a switch raised and lowered again and again striking the boy who refused to cry out.

"Stop that right now," she ordered when she was close enough to be heard.

Jeremiah looked at her and then slowly lowered Henry back to the ground. "You're all right," she heard him murmur even as he cupped the back of Will's head. "It's over."

"Boys, come away from there this instant," Pleasant ordered and when they ran to her without question and clutched at her skirt, she felt that the one thing she had hoped to be wrong about had been confirmed. Jeremiah had lost his temper and her boys had been the object of his fury. Without a word to Jeremiah, she turned and shepherded them away from the creek. "Bettina, go find Rolf. We're leaving."

She saw disappointment reflected in the girl's eyes but her daughter did not question her. Instead, she ran to a cluster of older boys and pulled Rolf away. Pleasant saw the two of them whispering as they cast glances first at her and then at the creek bank where Jeremiah was still standing, no stick in sight.

"Why do we hafta go?" Henry wailed.

"We're all right," Will told her. "We promise to stay away from the creek, Mama."

Was that what had set Jeremiah off? Had he called for the twins to come away from the creek and they had refused? It would certainly have been enough to spark Merle's temper. She shuddered and snapped the reins to urge the horse away from the gawking crowd of friends and neighbors. Once again, Pleasant Goodloe Obermeier was no doubt going to be the main topic of gossip for the next several days.

Once again she had made a fool of herself and all because of some man.

Jeremiah stood watching her drive away thinking about the way she had looked at him. He understood what she thought she had seen. From that distance she would never have even noticed the alligator that had started to slowly snake its way along the bank to where the boys were playing. Jeremiah had had only seconds to act. He'd grabbed the boy closest to him and then with God's blessing had found the thick tree branch within easy reach.

Quietly he had told Will not to move and then with a force he had not thought himself capable of, he had struck the alligator across its long flat nose. Instantly, the thing had slithered back into the water, leaving Will a trembling mass on the shore and both boys in tears. But before he could comfort the boys, Pleasant had ordered them away from him—as if he would harm a hair on their golden heads.

But her doubt had been there in the glare with which she met his confused look. Her accusation had been silently hurled in the way she had turned away and herded the children back to the gathering, then without stopping to say a word to anyone, had loaded all four children into her buggy and driven away. She had not waited for explanations—she had not even considered that there might be one. She had simply assumed that he—like her late husband and like his uncle—was a man who could not control his temper.

He had lost her. Who was he kidding? He had never had her trust, her love—not really.

By the time he made his way back to the picnic, the speculation was rampant about why Pleasant had left so abruptly.

"One of the twins must have taken ill," Hilda Yoder announced. "The boy was in tears and who knows what those children might have been eating. Some wild berry out there in the brush. It happens when children are allowed to go unattended."

No one else seemed to have witnessed the scene that had made Pleasant drop the bowl she was carrying, scattering salad all over the ground and take off running toward the creek. By the time others had looked around it seemed that the twins were clinging to her as she brought them back to the family buggy and sent Bettina to find Rolf so they could leave. But Hannah Harnisher glanced at Jeremiah and raised her eyebrows in an unspoken question. Blessedly she did not ask that question aloud and he hoped that others had forgotten that he was with the boys and might offer an explanation for Pleasant's sudden departure.

"Jeremiah, you were down there with the twins," his great-aunt said and immediately others turned to him, seeking answers.

Not wanting to scare the other mothers, Jeremiah decided against talking about the alligator. "I'm not sure what happened," he said and that was not a lie. Until he could talk to Pleasant, his interpretation of her actions was pure conjecture. "But I'm certain that the boys will be fine."

Seemingly satisfied with this, Mildred turned to her husband. "Well, John, everyone is famished. Shall we eat?"

The bishop offered grace and Pleasant and her children were forgotten as everyone gathered to fill plates and find a spot in the shade to enjoy the picnic with friends and neighbors.

Jeremiah found that he didn't have much of an appetite and the fact that he had invited everyone to stop at the ice cream shop on their way home for a cone of his newest flavor—key lime vanilla—was no more appealing than the mounds of food that filled the plate Hannah handed to him.

"Will you join us, Jeremiah?" she invited, indicating a spot where Caleb and Levi and the Harnisher twins were settling to enjoy their food.

"Thank you." He was grateful for her kindness and knew that in spite of her curiosity, she would not pry. He could eat in peace and then make the excuse of needing to get back to town before everyone else came back for the promised ice cream.

He forced down half of the food and set his plate aside. He seemed incapable of thinking about anything other than the fact that in spite of everything they had shared these past evenings, Pleasant had assumed the worst. And the more he thought about the unfairness of her action, the more irritated he became. By the time he felt that he could reasonably make his escape, he was so upset with her that if she had been anywhere near him he might have taken her by the shoulders and forced her to hear him out. And then as likely as not, he would have kissed her.

Caleb Harnisher rode back to town with him and Jeremiah had his doubts that Rolf would be available to help out as they had planned.

"Want me to go get Rolf, sir?" Caleb asked as they passed Pleasant's house.

"No. I expect he's got other things he needs to do. Looks like it's just the two of us."

"Yes, sir."

But when he pulled his buggy into the yard behind his living quarters he saw Rolf waiting for them. As if nothing unusual had happened, the boy stepped forward to unhitch the horse and lead it into the barn.

"Your mother sent you?" Jeremiah asked as he watched Rolf wash up.

"I came on my own."

"Then go home."

"No, sir. I have a job to do. I'm not a quitter."

Jeremiah studied the small quiet boy for a long minute. "No, you're definitely not that," he said softly, recalling a time when he had stood up to his uncle in spite of the older man's threat to beat him within an inch of his life if Jeremiah dared disobey him. "Is everything all right at home? The twins are all right?"

"Yes, sir."

"And your mother?"

Rolf met his eyes directly. "She was crying in her room. Bettina tried to go to her, but she wouldn't let her in. I don't know what happened, sir, but she's very sad and I was thinking maybe I could take her some ice cream. She has a special fondness for key lime pie so I was thinking…"

"Good idea. Why don't you boys go fill two of those small buckets and set them in the ice box to take to your families once we're done here? Just to be sure we don't run out."

"Thank you, sir." Rolf and Caleb ran off to do as he had suggested. Jeremiah walked slowly to the front of his shop and then turned to look at the large white house that dominated the far end of the street. He focused on an upstairs window and thought about Pleasant there crying. And he couldn't help wondering if her tears were the product of the fear and disappointment he had seen in her eyes at the picnic or the product of her own regret at having judged him.

He opened the front door of his shop and called out to the boys. "I've got an errand to run. Get those cones lined up and ready and if I'm not back when the first customers arrive you know what to do."

"Yes, sir," came the chorus of young male voices from the back room.

He was halfway to Pleasant's house when he stopped walking. What was he doing? What was he going to say that would change anything? Even if he explained about the alligator, that wasn't the point. The point was that she had made an assumption—one based on things he had told her about his past and his fears that the temper of his uncle had been visited on him. Furthermore, she had good reason of her own to assume that he might have become irritated with the twins, so irritated that he had lost his temper and raised his hand to them. In their talks, she had confirmed what he had suspected—

that her late husband had struck the children often—
especially Rolf. She had even admitted that Merle had
struck her when she tried to interfere. So what could he
possibly say that would ever rid her of those memories
and those fears?

And even if he did explain and she did accept his explanation, nothing could ever erase that look of doubt
that he had seen in her eyes. She would always wonder,
always be on her guard. He had no one to blame but
himself. After all, instead of trying to show her that
he was nothing like her late husband, he had done an
excellent job of making sure that she understood that
he, too, had a temper and he, too, came from a family
where that temper could lash out at others—even loved
ones. No, he had done everything he could to convince
her that he was not worthy of her love or trust.

He took one long look at her house and then turned
around and walked back to the ice cream shop.

Pleasant had been unable to stem the rushing waves
of tears that had consumed her almost as soon as she
reached home. Bettina had taken the twins to the
kitchen to wash their tear-stained faces and prepare
them something to eat while Rolf had announced his
intention to go to work. Pleasant had instinctively protested that decision but Rolf had stood firm, using her
own words to make his argument. "You always told us
that a promise is a promise and a job left undone is a
broken promise," he reminded her. His eyes had challenged her to argue the point, and she had waved him
away. Caleb would be there and soon everyone in town
would be at the ice cream shop. Rolf would be fine.

Realizing that the children were out of harm's way, Pleasant felt exhaustion overwhelm her. Slowly she climbed the stairs, went into her room and closed the door. The tears had come then in a gush as if only her will to make sure the twins were rescued and all four children were safe had kept them at bay. Tears escalated into choking sobs and she was helpless to keep herself from making the guttural sounds of her misery.

"Mama?" Bettina knocked softly on the bedroom door.

"I'll be there in a bit," she managed.

"Mama?" She was surprised to hear Rolf's voice. "If you don't want me to go I'll stay. Herr Troyer...."

The mere utterance of his name was enough to make Pleasant double over. "No, you're right," she said, forcing her voice to remain steady. "A promise is..." But the rest was lost in a fresh deluge of sobbing.

She heard both children retreat downstairs, whispering to one another worriedly as they went. She stood at the window and watched Rolf trudge up the street to the ice cream shop. She remained there, unable to move or to make any decision beyond the ones she had already made. Once again she had misread the signs. Once again she had given her heart to the wrong man.

She saw Jeremiah pull his buggy past the bakery and on into the backyard of the ice cream parlor. She waited—for what she could not have said—her sobs coming now in intermittent shudders that racked her entire body. After what seemed a very long time she saw Jeremiah start to walk up the street, his hat tipped back as he looked straight at her house, as he seemed to be looking straight through the upstairs window where she stood.

He walked with purpose and she felt a glimmer of hope. Perhaps there was some plausible explanation although she could not think what it might be. Perhaps he had realized the error of his ways and come to apologize. Perhaps...

Suddenly, he stopped in the middle of the deserted street. He stood there for a long moment, his fists clenched at his sides and then he turned around and walked back to his shop.

"No," she whispered, her fist jammed against her lips. "We can work this out." But she had thought the same of Merle and had finally had to admit defeat when her husband had turned on her.

She remained standing at the window until the street was lined on both sides with parked buggies and at the far end of the street a crowd had gathered around the ice cream shop. She was still standing there when the last of the buggies pulled away and still there when she saw Rolf walking home carrying a tin bucket that she knew would be filled with ice cream. She dabbed at the remnants of her crying jag with the hem of her apron and went downstairs to make supper for her family, more certain than she had ever been that God's plan for her life was to make safe and secure the lives of those blessed children.

Chapter Seventeen

"Where did you run off to yesterday?" Hannah asked the following day as the community gathered for the biweekly service.

"I...it was the twins."

"Yes, they had quite a scare. I couldn't believe it when Caleb told us last night what had happened."

Pleasant was confused. How could Caleb...?

"Rolf told him that according to the twins, the alligator was huge and headed right for Will. The boys were so blessed that Jeremiah was there and of course, it was only his quick thinking that spared them both." Hannah shuddered. "You have much to be thankful for today, Pleasant."

Alligator?

"Will you excuse me a moment, Hannah?" she asked and did not wait for permission as she hurried outside in search of any one of her children. She saw Rolf returning from the Yoders' barn where he had led their horse to the trough. "Rolf, walk with me a minute," she invited and put her hand around the boy's thin shoulder as she guided him a little ways from the house.

"Services will be starting," he reminded her.

"I know and we'll be there in time. But I need you to tell me what happened yesterday at the picnic with the twins and Herr Troyer."

His eyes widened. "You saw. Will and Henry had gone down to the creek bank and they were playing a game there and you sent Herr Troyer to fetch them and when he got there he saw this alligator coming up the bank. He grabbed Henry and a big stick and he hit that 'gator smack across the snout and that thing made a beeline right back into the creek." He spoke with increasing enthusiasm as the details unfolded. "Then you got there and well, you know the rest."

Jeremiah had not been disciplining the boys. He had saved them.

Pleasant closed her eyes tight against the memory of her horror and the way she had looked at him, how she had assumed the worst of him without even considering that there might be some other explanation for his actions.

"Mama? Everybody's inside," Rolf said, nodding toward the Yoder house where Pleasant could hear voices raised in the opening hymn.

"Yes. We should go," she said but her mind was definitely not on church. All she could think about was how she could ever possibly get Jeremiah to forgive her.

He was sitting in his usual place at the end of the second row of benches close to the door. Rolf squeezed in next to Caleb in the row ahead of the women while Pleasant took her place between Bettina and Lydia.

"Is everything all right?" Lydia whispered and Pleasant nodded.

But nothing would ever be all right again, she thought. For now she understood why Jeremiah had walked halfway to her house and then changed his mind and turned back. What was there to say? Even once he explained what really happened, there was no taking back the look of mistrust and doubt that he must have read in her eyes. How could she possibly convince him that she did trust him when in her heart of hearts she had to admit that for that instant she had not? She had believed the worst of him, believed him capable of striking her child.

Oh, Jeremiah, she thought as she stared at his proud straight back, *how can I ever make this up to you?* A day earlier she had been filled with excitement, planning to admit her love for him at last. On this day she still loved him—perhaps more than she had even imagined she could—but she understood beyond all doubt that in an instant she had ruined everything they might have shared.

The service that she wished would go on and on so that she could at least have some cause to be in the same room with him seemed to be over in the blink of an eye. Before she knew it everyone had scattered to attend to the after-services rituals of resetting the benches and preparing the meal they would all share. But instead of joining the other women in the kitchen, Pleasant followed Jeremiah out to the yard.

She was relieved to see him walk a little away from the other men and then realized that he was going home. Heedless of the looks her actions garnered from the other men or of the gossip that was sure to ensue once the men talked to their wives, she caught up to Jeremiah.

"I owe you an apology," she began and even to her ears her voice sounded tight and insincere. She understood that it was a case of nerves at not having taken time to plan what she might say to him, but when he glanced back at her and then kept walking without commenting on her presence, she knew that she was only making matters worse.

Yet she could not seem to stop herself. She was practically running to keep pace with his long and determined strides. "Please, Jeremiah, let me explain."

He stopped so abruptly that she almost ran into him and when she looked up at him, she was forced to take half a step back so that she could withstand the fury and accusation in his expression. He was looking at her now, boring into her with eyes that glinted with anger and hurt.

"Let you explain?" he repeated with a mirthless laugh. "Oh, that's a good one, Frau Obermeier. Would that be as in the way you gave me the opportunity to explain yesterday?"

"I…oh, Jeremiah, I…"

"Let's be clear about where we stand with one another, Frau Obermeier…."

"Stop calling me that," she hissed, her own temper rising to the bait he offered.

He kept on talking as if she hadn't spoken. "We have a business arrangement. I need you to supply the cones for my shop because I have foolishly built my reputation of the combination of those cones and my ice cream. Besides, I shook hands with your father on the matter and I will not go back on that."

"My father is no longer here. I run the bakery now," she reminded him.

"And yet because I trust that you are a woman of honor, I assume that you will hold to whatever agreements your father may have made while he was living."

"This is not about business and we both know it."

"That's where you're wrong, Pleasant."

She noted the use of her given name and took hope from the fact that his voice had softened. He was looking at her as he had those evenings when they had sat talking for hours, as he had when he had gently caressed her cheek before saying good-night.

"The only thing we have between us is business. Now, forgive me, but yesterday was a difficult day and I would like to take the rest of this Sabbath to consider whether or not I made a mistake in coming here altogether or whether my mistake was simply one of falling in love against my better judgment."

Pleasant was incapable of either calling out to him or going after him as he resumed his march back to town, leaving her standing in the middle of the lane that led back to the Yoders' house. On the previous day she had thought that she couldn't possibly have more tears to shed. As she watched Jeremiah walk away, she had to wonder if her tears would ever stop.

For the week following the church service, Jeremiah made sure that his days were filled with business that kept him away from Celery Fields. He not only needed to put as much distance as his current situation would allow between Pleasant and him, he also wanted to avoid the unasked questions in the eyes of his friends and especially his uncle and aunt.

But in spite of his best efforts, thoughts of Pleasant stalked him hour after hour. The nights were the worst. He had quickly gotten used to going to her house in the evenings after the town was quiet and her children were in bed. There, the two of them would sit together on her back porch, looking up at the starlit sky or listening to the rain. There, they had slowly told their stories—her childhood a happy one until her mother died suddenly and unexpectedly in the influenza epidemic of 1918, when she had just turned eighteen. His childhood similarly happy while his father was alive but cut even shorter when his father died. The loss of a parent had changed everything for each of them. Gunther had remarried within a year and his new wife had presented him with two beautiful daughters—Lydia and Greta. Pleasant's brother had married Hannah and moved to his own farm on the edge of the community. In Ohio, Jeremiah's mother had taken him and his siblings to live with his father's brother, where he had quickly and painfully learned that his tendency toward inquisitiveness and natural thirst for knowledge did not sit well at all with his uncle's old-style ways.

It had been these similar experiences that had drawn them closer and led to long conversations about the future she hoped for her children and his dreams of making his mark in Florida. From there it was a natural leap to talk of a future together—at least he had hinted at that. He realized now that she had remained reserved although the night before the picnic she had for once not dismissed such talk as the idealistic ramblings of a dreamer.

More than once she had chided him in a gentle teasing way about his tendency to act first and consider the full consequences afterward. She had illustrated her observation by reminding him of his decision to leave a perfectly stable situation in Ohio to pursue a profession about which he knew very little in a state he'd never even visited. And the night before the picnic he had kissed her before leaving her, noting with a smile that he had a reputation for being spontaneous to maintain. And he had foolishly believed in his own dreams—that they could share a life together. One that would include her adopted children and perhaps, with God's blessing, children of their own.

That's what he had been thinking the day of the picnic as he'd wandered down to the creek bank where the twins were playing. He had imagined teaching them things and watching them grow into fine young men— the kind of young man that Rolf was already becoming. And then he had seen the alligator. He had acted purely on instinct, his fear for the safety of one or both of those children blocking out everything else. There had been no time to consider his actions. No time to think that they could be misinterpreted. No time for anything but to strike out at the present danger. He had brought the tree branch down with such force that the 'gator had been momentarily stunned—long enough for him to grab the second boy and haul both clear of the threat. His breathing had come in heaves as if he had just run a long distance in the blazing sun.

And then he had looked up and seen her and in her expression he had read their fate. She believed the worst—without reason or cause, she had simply assumed. With the benefit of time he had told himself that given her experience with Merle, perhaps it was understandable. But he could not get past the fact that he was not Merle—not like Merle in any way from everything he knew about the man. How could she not see that?

Day after day he was aware of her early morning arrival at the bakery, the smell of bread baking, the spicy scent of molasses cookies that followed him as he left to work his shift and then make his deliveries. Night after night he replaced those scents with memories of the softness of her cheeks cupped in his hands and the feathery touch of a wisp of her hair against his face.

He loved her—in spite of everything, he loved her. And because he loved her he never again wanted to be the cause of that expression of abject fear and disillusionment that he had seen in her face the day of the picnic. Rolf had told him of her tears and that news had very nearly been his undoing. But what did he have to offer her that could possibly assure her that he was not like her late husband? What assurance could he give himself that over time he might not become the hardened and embittered man his uncle had become? No, it was best to leave her alone. In time, he hoped that they might settle back into the comfortable if slightly contentious friendship they had known when they first met. Neighbors and business associates—nothing more.

Having made his decision, he snapped the reins and urged the team of Belgians homeward—back to Celery Fields. Back to the loneliness of his rooms. Back to another night where sleep would not come without dreams of Pleasant.

* * *

The days passed in a vacuum of work and loneliness. Pleasant could not fathom how it could be possible that a man she had known for only a few months could have filled her life to such a level that without him she felt as dried up and useless as the fields behind her house. She tried to keep up a front for the sake of the children, but their sudden silences and tentative reactions whenever she entered a room spoke volumes.

She tried to cheer herself with the fact that business at the bakery was improving every week, Lydia was back to teaching and earning her stipend and even Greta had gotten a job in the Yoders' general store. On Mondays, she and the other women still took turns staging a frolic at one of the houses and for a few brief hours, she was able to focus on others and even enjoy a laugh now and again.

But running the bakery was solitary work and with Jeremiah's place right next door—even if he was absent most of the time—she had more than enough time to think about what might have been. She had developed the habit of arriving at the bakery even earlier hoping to catch sight of Jeremiah—perhaps exchange a greeting. Anything that might start to rebuild what she had destroyed with one look. She longed to see him sitting on the steps leading to the bakery, waiting for her, and chided herself for her foolishness in believing that would ever happen.

She trudged down the street in the dark of predawn and felt the weight of her unhappiness with every step. She might have been carrying the five gallon buckets of lard that she used in her baking so slumped were her shoulders and ponderous her steps. With a sigh, she navigated the three shallow steps leading to the bakery's back door and as she did every morning, glanced over to Jeremiah's kitchen window before going inside and propping the door open for the day.

There was a light in his window but no sign of him and she wondered as she always did if he ever stood drinking his coffee and looking over to see if she was there. *Probably not.*

She thought she caught a movement in the shadows by the barn and hesitated. Perhaps he, too, was getting an early start. "Jeremiah?" she called, taking a step toward the edge of the porch. But there was no answer and at the same time she saw a shadow pass by the light in Jeremiah's kitchen. With a heavy sigh, she went into the bakery kitchen and sat down at her father's desk.

She had arrived so early that it was too soon to start the baking. She had some accounts that needed her attention and decided to take care of those first. The first streaks of daylight were visible through the window but she lit the kerosene lamp and set it on the desk. She had just bent to pull the heavy ledger from the bottom drawer of the desk when she heard footsteps crossing the back porch.

"Hello?" she called and peered around the high back of the rolltop desk. The screen door squeaked open and then shut. "Jeremiah?" The word was no more than a prayer that he would be the one standing hesitantly in the doorway, but she already could see that the man who had entered her kitchen was shorter and heavier than Jeremiah was.

She stood up and reached for the lantern, lifting it

to the top of the desk so that it would throw more light. "May I help you?" she asked when what she wanted to say was, "Get out of here now!"

The man was dressed in mismatched old clothes, a battered fedora pulled low over his forehead. The stench of him reached her from across the room. "You alone?" he growled.

"I think you should leave," she said, forcing herself to her full height and clutching the edge of the desk as she tried to think of how best to protect herself. "There's some bread by the front door—take it if you're hungry and…"

The man gurgled a laugh that sounded as if he might become hysterical. "Hungry? You have no idea, lady. And I'll take the bread—when I'm ready."

He had begun to walk around the kitchen as if perfectly within his rights to do so. He picked up a large knife that Pleasant used for chopping dried fruit and nuts. Brandishing it, he started toward her. "Money, lady. Whatever you've got."

"I…"

He raised the knife and moved within inches of her. "Now!"

She considered her options and saw a chance to put some distance between them, perhaps make it to the door and cry out for help. "The cash box is there in that bottom drawer," she said, inching away.

He grabbed her wrist and twisted it painfully. "So, get it out," he sneered, his unshaven face inches from hers.

She took the box from the drawer and set it on the

writing surface of the desk. She opened it and waited for him to lower the knife so he could fill his pockets.

But to her horror, he merely glanced at the money and then closed the lid and looked at her with a smile that made her nauseous. "You're a pretty one, aren't you? And so clean and proper like all your kind." He ran the point of the knife under the edge of her prayer covering and Pleasant closed her eyes.

"Yeah, pray, little lady. For all the good it will do you." He moved against her so that she was blocked between him and the desk. She felt his rough hand cup her jaw, pinching it painfully to force a pucker to her lips.

She braced herself against the desk and felt the handle of the knife within reach. She closed her fingers around it and waited for his next move.

The sound of the bell jangling over the door in the front of the shop signaled someone's arrival. *Please don't let it be Rolf and the other children,* she prayed as she grasped the knife even more firmly.

"Keep quiet," the man demanded and then changed his mind. "Send them away."

"We're not open yet," she called, her voice shaking almost uncontrollably.

"Sorry," Jeremiah called. "I'll come back later then."

"No," she whispered but the bell jangled and the door closed and the man holding her captive grinned.

"Now where were we?" he muttered as he clutched her face once again and wrapped his other arm around her crushing her to him.

"I believe you were leaving," Jeremiah said, his voice not two inches away from the man's back.

Pleasant's entire body melted against the desk with relief as the vagrant spun around to face Jeremiah. But then she heard the man's sickening laugh.

"You're one of her kind—you won't fight. Bunch of cowards hiding behind religion." He spat out each word as he taunted Jeremiah by getting right in his face. "Come on, put 'em up. Best man wins the little lady."

A look crossed Jeremiah's face that was so terrible in its fury that Pleasant almost cried out to him. She saw that his fists were clenched tight at his sides. He moved half an inch closer to the man so that he was towering over him. "Leave now," he said and it was the quiet menace in his tone that made the words a threat.

"Or what?" The vagrant was standing his ground but he seemed less certain.

Realizing that she was free to move away from him, Pleasant grabbed the knife and ran to Jeremiah's side. He wrapped his arm around her and pulled her tight against him, holding on to her as if he would never let her go.

The vagrant grinned. "Oh, my apologies. This is your woman then?"

"That is none of your business," Jeremiah replied. "Right now you have a choice—leave and never come to this area again or stay and I will restrain you while she goes for the authorities."

"You and what army?"

Jeremiah released Pleasant so quickly that she staggered and by the time she had recovered her balance he had bodily lifted the vagrant, plopped him into her father's desk chair and wheeled the chair as close to the desk as he could. Now he was leaning against the back of the chair pressing it and the man into the edge of the desk.

"I can't breathe," the man protested.

"Then you have one last chance to make this right. Leave now and we'll consider the matter resolved, but if ever I see you around here again…"

"I'm just so hungry and there's no work and…" He was whining now.

"Get yourself cleaned up then and come back here tomorrow and I'll find you work," Jeremiah said. "The rest will be up to you."

The vagrant twisted his head around to see if Jeremiah could possibly be serious. "You don't mean that," he sneered.

"I do." He eased up slightly on the pressure he'd put on the chair. "Those of my faith stand by their word. How about you? Are you a man who can be trusted?" He signaled Pleasant to pass him the knife—a decision she questioned but when he raised his eyebrows as if to ask would she doubt him again, she handed him the knife.

When he set the vagrant free and offered him the knife, Pleasant could not restrain a gasp. The man held up both palms, refusing the gesture. Jeremiah then tossed the knife onto the worktable. The clatter of it was the only sound in the room.

The vagrant looked first at Jeremiah and then at Pleasant. "I apologize, ma'am. Don't know what got into me—just so hungry and tired." Wearily he walked toward the door, his back bent into the posture of a man twice his age.

"Wait," Pleasant called and hurried into the shop

then returned with three loaves of day-old bread. She put them into a flour sack bag and handed it to him. Then she took three dollars from the cash box and gave him that as well. "You can pay for a room and a bath and a proper meal," she suggested.

Tears ran down the man's weathered face and he became so emotional that all he could do was nod as he made his escape, leaving Pleasant and Jeremiah alone for the first time since that fateful day at the picnic.

"Thank you for coming," she said, focusing on the floor rather than him. "I don't know..." Suddenly the enormity of what had just happened—what might have happened had he not come to her rescue—struck Pleasant with a force that left her trembling.

"Pleasant, I'm right here," he said and when she looked up, he was holding his arms open to her and before he could change his mind, she ran to him and said the words she had been holding inside for all this time.

"I love you so, Jeremiah. Whatever becomes of us, I do love you—I think I have loved you from the day you first walked into this bakery."

"Good," he whispered, his lips tickling her ear, "because I love you and we will find a way, Pleasant. Whatever our pasts, together we can find our way to a future if you'll have me." He placed his forefinger under her chin and lifted her face to meet his. "You have my word on it," he told her.

"Will we marry?" she asked unable to believe what was happening.

He grinned. "Why, Pleasant Goodloe Obermeier, are you proposing to me?"

She blushed but stood her ground. "Will you have me?" she replied with a sassy tilt of her head.

All trace of teasing disappeared instantly from his expression. "All I want in this life is to spend the rest of my days loving you, Pleasant. We've been proud fools, the two of us and wasted precious time. I'll talk to my Uncle John right away—that is, if you'll say yes."

She smiled and stroked his cheek. "You'll look quite distinguished with a beard, Jeremiah," she said dreamily, reminding them both that married men of their faiths wore beards.

"Is that a yes?"

"What was the question again?"

"Will you marry me?" He enunciated each word, savoring each syllable.

"Yes," she whispered and wrapped her arms around his neck as she stood on tiptoe to kiss him. "Yes, a thousand times, yes."

He lifted her and twirled around the bakery kitchen with her until they heard the unmistakable clatter of the wagon that would be Rolf bringing the milk and eggs and Bettina taking the twins to Hilda's for the day.

"Shall we tell the children now?" she asked.

And like children themselves, they ran hand in hand out to the backyard so that when Rolf drove the wagon around the bakery, they were standing together to greet him and the other children.

Bettina's shrieks of sheer delight brought Moses Yoder and the Hadwells at a run to see what had happened and after that, news of the pending nuptials of Jeremiah Troyer and Pleasant Goodloe Obermeier spread like wildfire through the town.

"Well, high time," Hilda announced to Pleasant when she heard the news. "The two of you have been walking on thin ice—spending so much time together, and alone at that. People were beginning to talk."

Pleasant knew that the person leading that talk was Hilda herself but she was far too happy to allow anyone—especially Hilda—to dampen her spirits. "He'll be a good father to Merle's children," she told Hilda.

"You won't allow the children to forget their father," she stated firmly and it was not a question but more of a command.

"Of course not. They will keep his name—your family name."

"Because although I know my brother could be—difficult," Hilda continued as if Pleasant had not spoken, "he was their father and they need to remember that."

Pleasant could not help but notice that Hilda felt no need to make the same demands regarding the children's mother—a woman she had never cared for and one she was certain had tricked her brother into marriage. Pleasant had long ago learned that it did no good at all to remind Hilda how much Merle had loved his first wife, how he had grieved for her and how he had chosen Pleasant not out of love but out of the practical need for someone to raise his children.

"I will see that all four children continue to honor their parents' memory," she assured Hilda.

"And when you and Jeremiah have your own?" Hilda demanded.

Pleasant pressed her hand on her sister-in-law's forearm. "We will still be a family, Hilda. Just one that has grown as your family has grown over the years."

Hilda snorted. "My children are all of one parentage."

"And equally loved as will Merle's children be and any offspring that Jeremiah and I may be blessed to birth." She sighed, weary of Hilda's constant tendency to always see the negative. "Can you not be happy for me, Hilda? I love this man as you love Moses, and he loves me."

To her astonishment, Hilda's eyes softened to a girlish dreamy look. "He does at that," she said softly. "Everyone has been saying as much for weeks now. Hannah talks about the two of you as if you invented true love."

Pleasant laughed. "Oh, Hilda, I am so very happy."

"Well, then I am happy for you. You've had many hard times, Pleasant, and everyone admires the way you have moved forward in spite of everything you've had to face. It seems to me that it's about time you were given the opportunity to enjoy your life a bit." And having made this pronouncement Hilda spent the next several days presenting Pleasant with her ideas for exactly how, where and when the wedding should take place.

Chapter Eighteen

Jeremiah was not particularly happy about the idea of moving into the house that Pleasant had shared with her first husband. On the other hand, he could hardly expect her to bring the children and come live with him. One solution he had considered was suggesting that they move into Gunther's house, but that brought up the question of sharing the initial weeks of the marriage not only with four children but also with Pleasant's two half sisters.

He stopped at the Harnisher farm on his way back to town. Levi was a good listener and if asked would likely offer some suggestions for Jeremiah's dilemma.

"What would you think about starting fresh?" Levi asked.

"Leave Celery Fields?"

"No, but with a house that neither you nor Pleasant has occupied and one that would comfortably house the children."

"I'm listening," Jeremiah said.

"A man who used to work for me when I had the circus—Hans Winters—has decided to go back north permanently. He and my former secretary plan to marry and settle there in Wisconsin."

Jeremiah had met Hans once at Levi's farm. "So he wants to sell his place?" He nodded toward the house that sat a hundred yards down the road from Levi's house.

"He does. He'd make you a fair price. He's just that kind of a man."

Jeremiah looked out over the land that surrounded them and then down the long road that led into town. "I don't know. Pleasant has the bakery and I have my businesses and those are all in town. Living out here..."

"Peace and quiet," Levi said, "and Pleasant would be close to Hannah and her kids would have our kids as neighbors."

"You make a good case," Jeremiah admitted. "But then there's the house that Merle left her and the land..."

"Things are changing, Jeremiah. You might want to talk to the Palmer brothers. Word has it that they've been quietly buying up the land of those who have given up and gone back north. Merle's place might not be good farmland but it is prime real estate for an area that's growing."

Jeremiah thanked Levi for his suggestions and started back to town, but as he passed the house that Hans Winters owned, he slowed his team of horses to a walk. The house was smaller than the one that Pleasant occupied with the children now, but it was a charming house nonetheless. There was a screened front porch where two rocking chairs sat at an angle to one another. Jeremiah imagined sitting there with Pleasant in the evenings and on Sunday afternoons as together they watched the children playing or just enjoyed the sunset.

Almost without realizing what he was doing he turned the horses onto the road that led to the house and five minutes later he was knocking on the door. An hour after that he walked out of the house—a house he now owned or would own as soon as he delivered the down payment to Hans Winters. Levi's former butler followed him out to the porch and watched as Jeremiah climbed aboard his wagon.

"Remember, you can always change your mind," Hans told him.

"I won't change my mind," Jeremiah assured him, but he wasn't so sure about Pleasant. If there was one thing he understood it was that where he was spontaneous and some would even say impulsive, she was far more cautious. She thought about the smallest details of any decision she made—how it would affect the children, how it would impact Lydia and Greta now that Gunther had died, what it would mean for managing the business that her father had built. He thought about all of that as he allowed the horses to find their way back to town.

Pleasant was in the bakery when he got there. He could see through the open door that she was hardly alone. The children were there as were Hilda Yoder and Greta. It was not at all the right time to tell his future wife that he had bought her a house. A house that was two miles from town—and the bakery. A house that she had never seen except from the outside. A house that she might not think was at all suitable for their needs.

But he and Hans Winter had shaken hands and that had sealed the bargain between them.

Jeremiah sighed and climbed down from his wagon. Sooner or later he was going to have to tell her what he had done and perhaps the buffer of the children and the others was a blessing in disguise. He crossed the yard and mounted the steps to the bakery.

"Well, I don't trust them," Hilda announced as he entered the room.

"Don't trust who?" he asked.

"The Palmers," Hilda replied with a derisive snort. "They go around offering to buy people's houses as if there were no sentimental value at all."

"They made a very generous offer," Greta argued.

"And how would you know what is generous and what is insulting?" Hilda asked.

"Josef says that…"

Hilda dismissed the mention of the young carpenter with a wave of her hand. "The question before you, Pleasant, is what will you do?"

"About?" Jeremiah asked, trying hard to make sense of the conversation that had continued as if he were not there.

Pleasant glanced at him and then down at her hands. "Mr. Potter Palmer has offered to buy my—Merle's— house and land," she said softly.

"And what did you say?"

"I told him I would need to discuss it with you—and the children, of course. After all, that is their inheritance."

"Not to mention the only home those children have ever known," Hilda grumbled.

"Well, the children are here," Jeremiah said, nodding to Rolf who was sitting at Gunther's desk working on a column of figures, and Bettina who was grinding nuts at the far end of the worktable. He had passed the twins out in the yard playing a game of marbles. "Why don't you ask them what they think?"

Rolf and Bettina exchanged a look and stopped pretending to be otherwise occupied. Rolf chewed the stub of his pencil. "Where would we live then?" he asked, and Bettina nodded, abandoning her work to move closer to Pleasant.

"Well, we could live in the house where I grew up," Pleasant said slowly, trying to put the best possible face on the idea. "You know that house almost as well as you know our own and…"

"You mean live with our teacher in her house?" Rolf looked decidedly alarmed at this idea.

"I would be there and so would Jeremiah once we marry and…"

"Or," Jeremiah hastened to add, "we might just buy a new house—one where we could start fresh as a family."

"I like that idea," Bettina said. "What kind of a house? Could it be in the country?"

"You mean, close to where Caleb Harnisher lives?" Rolf asked and he grinned at his sister whose cheeks had taken on a most becoming rosy glow.

"No," she protested. "I just happen to like the country."

Jeremiah drew in his breath and took the plunge. Facing Pleasant instead of the children he started to describe the house. "What if there were a perfect house not a hundred yards from Hannah and Levi." He glanced at Bettina and added softly, "And Caleb."

"You're talking about the house where Hans lives?" Pleasant asked.

Jeremiah nodded. "I stopped by there today and well, I sort of bought the place."

Greta clapped her hands excitedly while Hilda scowled at him. "How does one 'sort of' buy something as momentous as a house, Jeremiah Troyer?"

But the only reaction he needed or wanted was Pleasant's and to his astonishment, she burst out laughing. "Oh, Jeremiah, you never cease to surprise me. You bought us a house?"

Jeremiah nodded and held his breath, hoping her laughter was not of the hysterical variety.

"That is so romantic," Greta whispered to Bettina as Rolf rolled his eyes.

"Hans Winters's house?" Pleasant asked.

Again, Jeremiah could manage only a nod.

"I love that house," she said softly. "I always have."

Hilda cleared her throat loudly. "Am I to understand, Pleasant, that you are going to sell Merle's legacy for his children to the highest bidder?"

Pleasant faced her sister-in-law. "That is precisely what I intend to do, Hilda, for what greater legacy could Merle have left his children than one that secures their future? With the money that Mr. Palmer has offered there will be more than enough for Rolf and each of the twins to one day own a business or property of their own—and Bettina…"

"I'm going to run the bakery," the girl announced.

Hilda's lips thinned for a long moment as she worked

through her feelings that somehow this might be disloyal to her late brother.

"Pleasant is right, Hilda," Jeremiah assured her. "Merle's house needs work and the land hasn't produced a viable crop in…"

"Oh, don't speak to me as if I can't possibly see God's hand in all of this, Jeremiah," Hilda huffed.

Pleasant placed a gentle hand on Hilda's shoulder. "I'm going to need your help, Hilda. Hans has lived there alone all this time and the place will surely need a woman's touch."

"No doubt." She turned to go then paused and looked up at Jeremiah. "You bought her a house?"

"I did."

"But how did you know—I mean, what if she…"

Jeremiah looked at Pleasant. "Sometimes, Hilda, you just have to put your doubts aside and know that whatever happens, the person you love will understand that you acted out of love—always out of love."

He was so blinded by the smile that Pleasant gave him that he was only vaguely aware that Hilda had scurried off or that Bettina and Rolf had run outside to tell the twins that they would be moving or that Greta had made some excuse about needing to attend to something in the front of the bakery. There was only Pleasant and him. He held out his arms and she came to him and in that moment he saw them standing here years from now, their arms around each other as they looked back over a life shared and forward toward the days still to come.

"I thought it was impossible for you to make me any happier than you already have," she said. "But…"

He chuckled and kissed her temple. "If I had known buying you a house would have this effect I would have bought you half a dozen houses."

"Not just any house," she protested. "This house— our house."

"Our family," he reminded her as he nodded toward the back door of the bakery where the four children stood watching them. He kept one arm around Pleasant and spread the other to welcome the children, and in moments the six of them were dancing in a circle of delight, their laughter and excitement the only music any of them needed.

It rained all week before the wedding and even that seemed to Pleasant to be a sign that God had blessed this union. The community desperately needed the rain and the steadiness of the downpour seemed to promise no letup until the earth had once again drunk its fill. She had decided to hold the ceremony at her father's house. After all, that was the place she had always thought of as "home" and it was tradition for weddings to take place in the home of the bride. She had always felt a little like a visitor in Merle's house, furnished as it was with all of the things his first wife had chosen—furnishings that Merle had forbade Pleasant from moving from their assigned position.

At her father's house surrounded by happy memories, she felt such a sense of peace and calm and Jeremiah had agreed that it was the perfect setting in which to be married. Lydia and Greta were delighted to have the house used for such a joyous occasion and even the children got caught up in the preparations. Pleasant had to keep reminding Bettina that this was a second wedding.

"Not for Jeremiah," Bettina reminded her. They had agreed that the children should start to call him by his given name within the family and continue to refer to him as Herr Troyer when others were around. "This is his first wedding and just because he's a man that doesn't mean we shouldn't take that into consideration."

Pleasant was so busy with the bakery and the sale of Merle's property to the Palmers and making herself a new dress for the wedding that she had little time to pay attention to the whispered conversations Bettina was constantly holding with either Rolf, Greta or Lydia—conversations that stopped abruptly the moment she entered the room.

But two days before the wedding was to take place she was surprised to see Hannah enter the bakery, her lovely face wreathed in a smile. "Come with me," she instructed.

"I can't...the bakery."

"Yes, you can," Mildred Troyer announced as she took up Pleasant's usual position behind the work-table and began cutting out cookies from the pastry that Pleasant had just finished rolling out. She used the open mouth of a glass jar, efficiently plopping it into the dough, giving it a twist and then repeating the process. "I can mind the bakery for a few hours. You go with Hannah. Go on, now."

"I don't understand," Pleasant said when they exited the bakery. Caleb was waiting out in front with Hannah's buggy.

"You will," Hannah said as she climbed into the

buggy and waited for Pleasant to join her. "Well, come on."

They headed for the Harnisher farm and then by-passed it and pulled into the lane leading to the house that Jeremiah had bought from Hans Winters. "What's going on?" Pleasant asked, her suspicions on high alert when she saw several buggies lined up outside the house and a welcoming party of friends, neighbors and customers lining the walkway to the front porch.

"Just wait," Caleb said, giving her what for him amounted to a radiant grin. He hopped down and then offered her his hand to assist her down from the buggy. Hannah hooked arms with her and practically pulled her up the walkway as everyone shouted, "Surprise!"

Bettina ran to her and took hold of her free hand. "Wait 'til you see, Mama. It's all so perfect."

"We'll start the tour here," Lydia announced, pointing to two bentwood rockers on the small front porch. "Hans said to tell you that he wished he could be here to give these to you and Jeremiah himself. He wanted them to be his wedding gift to you."

"Oh, how lovely," Pleasant crooned, running the flat of her hand over the smooth wood.

"There's more," Bettina said, tugging her through the front door.

Inside, Pleasant blinked several times with disbe-lief as she took in the polished wood floors, a fully furnished sitting room. "Everyone helped furnish this room," Hannah told her, "and look how perfectly the bits and pieces came together—as if they belonged here."

"I don't know what to say," Pleasant murmured,

glancing shyly at all the faces pressed in at the front door to watch as she discovered her surprise. "You are all just too kind."

"The dining room table and chairs are our gift," Greta told her. "Mine and Lydia's and the children's."

"It's so beautiful," Pleasant said, "but…"

"Josef Bontrager found the set discarded behind an abandoned house in Sarasota. He repaired it and we all sanded and refinished the pieces," Lydia explained.

Pleasant moved closer to the table with six chairs surrounding it and already set as if just waiting for a family to sit down. "These are Mama's dishes," she whispered as she picked up a plate and studied it.

"Papa had them boxed up and stored in the attic," Lydia told her, "along with several other things you've yet to discover." She nodded toward the hall that led to three small bedrooms.

The first two were already set up to welcome the children. The third at the end of the hall would be hers to share with Jeremiah. A double bed there had been made up with a quilt that she recognized as one made by her mother.

"And there's the kitchen," Bettina said when she saw the first tear trickle down Pleasant's cheek. "You'll love the kitchen, Mama," she promised.

And indeed she did for sitting at the kitchen table was her husband-to-be, sipping from a mug of steaming coffee and grinning up at her. "Welcome home," he said softly and when she started to cry in earnest, he stood up. "Now, now, anything you don't like can be changed or moved or gotten rid of."

"Don't you dare touch one dish or chair," she warned, sniffing back her tears. "It's perfect."

Around her everyone smiled with relief.

"Thank you," she said, finding her voice in spite of her tears. "Thank you so very much. Jeremiah and the children and I feel so truly blessed that we have all of you with us as we start our life together in this beautiful house."

"And as soon as we are married, you're all invited for ice cream and shoo-fly pie," Jeremiah added.

Everyone laughed at that and there was some good-natured ribbing about how Jeremiah was always thinking about business before the others got back into their buggies and went on about their day. Hannah was the last to leave, taking Lydia, Greta and Pleasant's children with her.

"I'll assume you can get Pleasant back to the bakery, Jeremiah," she said with a teasing laugh.

"I do know the way," he replied. "On the other hand, it might be fun to get lost at least for a little while."

Pleasant felt the heat of pleased embarrassment rise to her throat. "Stop that," she chided, but inside she was smiling at the realization that with God's blessing she and Jeremiah would have days and months and years to spend together in this place, surrounded by their children and the dear friends they had made.

"I thought maybe I could hang a swing there in that tree for the twins," Jeremiah said as they walked back to the house. He offered her the choice of rocking chairs on the porch and then sat in the other one next to her. He took her hand. "And speaking of children, do you think there's enough room?"

"Plenty. Rolf and the twins can be in that front room—it's a little larger and then Bettina can have the smaller room next to ours." She blushed as she realized they were talking about such intimate things as sharing a bedroom—a bed—and not yet married. "I mean…"

"I was thinking beyond right now," Jeremiah admitted as he leaned forward and took both her hands in his. "What about when we have children? Where will they be?"

"I…that is…" She was already overwhelmed with the blessing of spending the rest of her days with this wonderful man.

"You don't want more children?" he asked, frowning.

"More? I've never had…" The way he looked away and his mouth tightened and she realized that he must be thinking that once again she doubted him, remembering what he had told her about his uncle and his fears. She tightened her grip on his hands and leaned closer. "Of course, we're going to have children together, Jeremiah," she said as she brushed an errant strand of his hair away from his cheek. "And the matter of where they will sleep will resolve itself. You'll see."

He bowed his head and before raising it, he lifted her fingers to his lips and kissed them. "I love you, Pleasant," he murmured.

She leaned in and kissed his cheek. "And I love you, Jeremiah and that, with God's help, is all either of us will ever need to find our way through life's challenges."

They sat together for a long time then, rocking their chairs in unison and staring out at the tree where he would hang a swing for the twins—and the little ones to come. Words were not necessary—their fingers intertwined spoke volumes about their love for each other and their gratitude for the blessings they had been given.

* * * * *

Dear Reader,

This is the sequel to my novel *Hannah's Journey,* and both stories are set in my adopted city of Sarasota during the early part of the twentieth century. The characters are Amish and reside in the fictional community of Celery Fields, but they are based on the wonderful people it has been my pleasure to meet in the popular Amish/Mennonite community of Pinecraft just outside the city limits of Sarasota. My fascination with the lifestyle of these "plain" people has blossomed over the course of writing these two novels. They are good and simple people who place a great deal of emphasis on the importance of family and community—a lesson we might all take to heart in these difficult times.

I offer deep appreciation to the Sarasota County History Center and its wonderful research library as well as to those in the Amish community who have been kind enough to answer my questions and tell me of their ways. And as always I thank you, dear reader, for taking time to read my story and for letting me know your thoughts about it. To do so please visit my website (www.booksbyanna.com) or write to me at P.O. Box 161, Thiensville WI 53092. Writing can be a solitary profession and your letters and emails definitely brighten my days!

All best wishes,

Anna Schmidt

Questions for Discussion

1. Consider the variety of "parenting" scenarios in this story. Pleasant for her adopted children; Jeremiah's experience with his uncle; Pleasant's relationship with her father. How are they different?

2. How does Pleasant's relationship with Jeremiah change over the course of the book?

3. What experiences does Jeremiah share with Pleasant's eldest son, Rolf, in terms of how Rolf related to his father and Jeremiah related to his uncle?

4. What are some of the most difficult challenges that Pleasant is facing throughout the book and how does she handle them?

5. In what ways have you faced difficult times? What did you find helped you weather them?

6. How does Pleasant change over the course of the story?

7. In what ways is this a story about trust?

8. In what ways is it a story about family blessings?

9. In what ways is God's hand visible to the reader (but sometimes not to the characters) over the course of this story?

10. Projecting ten years into the future after the book ends where do you think each of the characters will be?

INSPIRATIONAL

Inspirational romances to warm your heart & soul.

Love Inspired.

HISTORICAL

TITLES AVAILABLE NEXT MONTH

Available November 8, 2011

SNOWFLAKE BRIDE
Buttons and Bobbins
Jillian Hart

THE RANCHER'S COURTSHIP
Brides of Simpson Creek
Laurie Kingery

AN HONORABLE GENTLEMAN
Regina Scott

THE DOCTOR'S MISSION|
Debbie Kaufman

REQUEST YOUR FREE BOOKS!

2 FREE INSPIRATIONAL NOVELS

PLUS 2
FREE
MYSTERY GIFTS

Love Inspired

HISTORICAL
INSPIRATIONAL HISTORICAL ROMANCE

YES! Please send me 2 FREE Love Inspired® Historical novels and my 2 FREE mystery gifts (gifts are worth about $10). After receiving them, if I don't wish to receive any more books, I can return the shipping statement marked "cancel". If I don't cancel, I will receive 4 brand-new novels every month and be billed just $4.49 per book in the U.S. or $4.99 per book in Canada. That's a saving of at least 22% off the cover price. It's quite a bargain! Shipping and handling is just 50¢ per book in the U.S. and 75¢ per book in Canada.* I understand that accepting the 2 free books and gifts places me under no obligation to buy anything. I can always return a shipment and cancel at any time. Even if I never buy another book, the two free books and gifts are mine to keep forever.

102/302 IDN FEHF

Name	(PLEASE PRINT)

Address	Apt. #

City	State/Prov.	Zip/Postal Code

Signature (if under 18, a parent or guardian must sign)

Mail to the Reader Service:
IN U.S.A.: P.O. Box 1867, Buffalo, NY 14240-1867
IN CANADA: P.O. Box 609, Fort Erie, Ontario L2A 5X3
Not valid for current subscribers to Love Inspired Historical books.

Want to try two free books from another series?
Call 1-800-873-8635 or visit www.ReaderService.com.

* Terms and prices subject to change without notice. Prices do not include applicable taxes. Sales tax applicable in N.Y. Canadian residents will be charged applicable taxes. Offer not valid in Quebec. This offer is limited to one order per household. All orders subject to credit approval. Credit or debit balances in a customer's account(s) may be offset by any other outstanding balance owed by or to the customer. Please allow 4 to 6 weeks for delivery. Offer available while quantities last.

Your Privacy—The Reader Service is committed to protecting your privacy. Our Privacy Policy is available online at www.ReaderService.com or upon request from the Reader Service.

We make a portion of our mailing list available to reputable third parties that offer products we believe may interest you. If you prefer that we not exchange your name with third parties, or if you wish to clarify or modify your communication preferences, please visit us at www.ReaderService.com/consumerschoice or write to us at Reader Service Preference Service, P.O. Box 9062, Buffalo, NY 14269. Include your complete name and address.

LIH11B